KILLING
THE
VIBE

*A stubborn detective risks making
the wrong moves*

LINDA HAGAN

THE
BOOK
FOLKS

Published by The Book Folks

London, 2022

© Linda Hagan

ISBN 978-1-913516-46-8

www.thebookfolks.com

Killing The Vibe is the fourth novel in a series of standalone murder mysteries set in Belfast and beyond.

Chapter 1

It was a dark night. The darkest of nights. He felt a darkness in his very soul such as he hadn't known for many years. It was so dark that the Belfast street lighting barely made any difference at all, offering only weak pools of illumination which served to emphasise the blanket of blackness all around. And it was so quiet. The only sounds – traffic far in the distance, a dog's howl, a tin can blown by the wind along the empty street – sliced through the silence for a second only for it to return, more smothering than before.

The figure looked left and right before stepping into the roadway even though there had been no passing cars for the long minutes of waiting. He walked slowly, a faint squeak accompanying his steps as he trod carefully, not wanting to risk his precious load. He reached the rusty railings with their peeling paint and stopped. He waited again now, listening once more, looking all around, his senses on high alert.

Nothing. No one. It seemed as if he was alone in the world. All he could hear now was his own breathing, shallow and ragged, disturbingly loud to his ears in the silence. He was aware of a bead of sweat sitting on his forehead and rubbed it away before it could fall. With difficulty, but also with what amounted almost to reverence, he lifted his heavy cargo and with an effort heaved it over the fence, struggling with its weight and awkward shape, almost falling backwards until he had to grab hold of the metal railing to save himself. He vaulted after it with an agility that would have reminded any watcher of an Olympic gymnast. Only there was no watcher. No one to see him. No one to hear his laboured breathing as he hauled his bulky burden down the slippery riverbank until it rested only inches from the lapping water's edge. Then he prodded it forward with his foot and watched, as it slipped almost silently into the river with a grace reminiscent of the launch of some great liner from the slips not far downstream. No splash. Only the sound of scurrying feet and startled squeaks as rats disturbed by the unwelcome visitor to their domain skittered through the long grass back to their nests.

The first drops of rain began to fall as if the sky was gently weeping. The figure looked down then and even in the low light, he could see the eyes, staring back at him. Accusing. Glassy eyes. Dead eyes.

Chapter 2

Rose was feeling twinges in both her knees and this morning she couldn't pretend she wasn't well on her way to her three score years and ten. She could have travelled by bus, but she liked the exercise. It was good for her and at sixty-five she wasn't going to start going to the gym.

It wasn't raining today. Last night's rain had washed the streets, but a brightening sky offered hope for better weather this morning. She enjoyed seeing people all around as they hurried to their offices or headed into the city centre for a day's shopping. And she liked to feel useful... still. That was why she volunteered at the charity shop. After a lifetime as a nurse, first in the Mater Hospital and then in the local community, her family and friends had all been surprised that she wanted to spend three mornings a week trawling through others' cast-offs and dealing with people trying to bargain her down from the already rock-bottom prices. And all for no pay. But it gave her a structure to the week and a bit of a social life. She didn't drink, she didn't play bingo. Her daughters and their families lived in Dublin and London so she only saw them the occasional weekend or at Christmas and Easter, and her son was in New York so this got her out of the house and gave her a sense of purpose. The church and the charity shop were her world now.

She approached the front of the shop on the corner of a row set back from the road and noticed, with some annoyance, that the shutters were still down. She had managed to get here on time. Why couldn't Veronica, who only had to drive down the main road in her fancy sports car – a present from the latest man in her life. She'd probably had trouble getting parked. That was always her excuse anyway.

The elderly woman's eye was caught by a bulky black plastic bag left propped against the building. It was good that someone had wanted to donate something to them but a pity they had chosen to discard it in the street. She remembered the time when a bag left carelessly like this would have caused panic with police and bomb squad arriving sirens blaring, the road closed, shops and offices evacuated and everyone on edge waiting for the explosion. Now it just made the place look untidy and pedestrians walked by unconcerned, the bad old days forgotten or, in the case of the younger generation, never really understood. At least it wasn't bin collection day today when their donation might have been picked up and whisked away.

As Rose arrived at the graffiti-covered metal shutters, Veronica approached from the opposite direction, hurrying round the corner, almost at a run, her high heels click-clicking on the pavement. She managed to look harassed, but Rose knew she wouldn't really be bothered at keeping her waiting or that the shop wasn't open for business on time.

'Good morning, Rose. Bit of a late night last night.'

She was rather breathless. The younger woman patted a non-existent wayward piece of platinum blonde hair back into place and smiled only half apologetically. Theoretically Veronica was the boss. She worked five days a week and was designated 'manager' although Rose didn't think she was paid very much for her labours. But then she didn't work very hard. It was Rose and the other lady volunteers who sorted and ironed and catalogued all their donations, who stocked the shelves and interacted with the customers, mostly students from the house-shares nearby or some of the Roma and Eastern European women who were in increasing evidence in this part of the city.

Veronica spoke with that polite Belfast accent Rose recognised from recordings she had heard of local comedian James Young. His 'Cherryvalley Lady' was all fur coat and no knickers as she had remembered the older women laughing when she was a girl listening to their conversations. Veronica could be a bit like that. She thought very highly of herself but Rose thought she probably wasn't any better than she should be. Her tales of nights on the town and boyfriends didn't impress her. Rose was Belfast born and bred and proud of it. She didn't believe in putting on any airs and graces.

'What's this?' the younger woman asked, indicating the bag and touching it lightly with the toe of her shoe as if it might bite.

As if she didn't know, Rose thought.

'Someone's left us a wee donation. Don't you worry about it, love. You get the shutters open. I'll deal with it.' Rose knew Veronica wouldn't want to dirty her hands or risk chipping her expensive acrylic nail job handling anything before it had already been sorted.

Rose reached out and began to pick the bag up. It was heavier than she'd anticipated and it split open when she tried to lift it, scattering some of its contents over the street. That was when the screaming started.

Chapter 3

Well, that's all for this morning's show. Thank you for joining me once again, folks, and making this the number one music and chat show on the airwaves across this wee island of ours. Keep listening. Love ya all.

The upbeat voice held a slight transatlantic twang, a hint of somewhere more exotic than Belfast with its mural-adorned peace walls and tattered flags flying from lamp posts and telegraph poles. It was a voice which brought a daily dose of chatter and music to help listeners on their way to work in the mornings.

The man pushed the off button with a flourish and sat back in his revolving chair, letting out a self-satisfied sigh. The 'On Air' light went out and the engineer gave a thumbs up sign through the studio glass.

'Great show, Dave.'

'As usual,' came the reply, all traces of America gone now from his voice. He expected instant agreement, which he got.

'As usual, of course.' It didn't pay to contradict Dave Osmond and it always paid to feed his ego. Andrew Milligan had found that out soon enough after he'd taken over as sound engineer on the show, *The Sound of Morning with Dave Osmond*. Osmond was a public favourite, a local celebrity and Andrew enjoyed working with him most of the time. It was good experience and he saw it as a springboard to better things. He had his eye on a job at Radio 2. Osmond just needed his ego stroked from time to time and he didn't take criticism well but Andrew was sure he would have to deal with even bigger egos if he ever made the move to national radio.

'Hey, Dave, there's a guy on the line, says he really needs to speak to you. He says it's something you'll want to hear.' Kirsty Miller, Dave's long-time PA and sometime girlfriend, put her head around the door of the studio and gave him the message. She and the deejay were an unlikely pairing. Osmond, brash and self-opinionated, didn't seem like the sort of man to appeal to the thoughtful, better-educated woman. And he was ten years her senior. Perhaps she simply liked older men but Milligan had conjectured that she, like him, saw Osmond as a stepping stone. Kirsty was ambitious too. She had already sat in for Osmond a few times when he'd been overindulgent the night before and couldn't make the show.

'Tell him the show's over for today. He should phone back tomorrow. I'm outta here.'

It had been a good show in the end but interviewing an up-and-coming actress from Birmingham who had family roots in County Tyrone had been a bit of a struggle. He hoped her acting skills were more successful than her PR efforts. Now he was tired and hungry. He'd been up since 4am to get ready for the show and he wanted an early lunch and then to meet his friend, Jonah, for a round of golf.

'I already did.' She smiled sweetly at him. 'He said you'd definitely want to hear what he has to say.'

It was on the tip of Osmond's tongue to tell her to get rid of him quick when the girl added, 'He said to "Tell him, Hopewell."' Both Kirsty and the sound engineer saw the colour drain from the presenter's face. He looked as if he had been punched in the stomach. He had been halfway out of his chair, preparing to leave the studio. Now he fell back down into it, expelling the air from the seat cushion with a rude noise which at any other time would have brought a smile to Andrew Milligan's face but he knew better than to laugh this time.

'Are you alright, Dave?' Kirsty asked, genuinely worried that he had been taken ill.

Dave Osmond's voice when he spoke was strained. 'Put the call through. Then the two of you, get out.'

Seeing the expression on Dave's face, they both knew better than to argue with him.

Chapter 4

Daniel Anderson sat at the dining room table with an untouched plate of toast and an overlooked cup of tea gradually getting colder in front of him. The sound of his neighbour's Pekingese yapping at the postman didn't draw his attention. He was focused only on the opened letter which he held in his trembling hands.

'Do you want any more tea, love?' Eva Anderson, his wife of nearly eleven years, walked into the room carrying a teapot. One glance at her husband's face and she hastily set it down and walked quickly across to him, taking his arm and looking him full in the face.

'What is it? What's wrong, Dan?'

She wondered if he was feeling ill. She was always telling him he worked too hard and she feared he would have a heart attack as her own father had done, leaving her mother with three small children to bring up.

Anderson seemed almost not to hear her at first. He didn't respond immediately and when he did his words and his movements were almost in slow motion or like a man floundering under water. He stood up still clutching the piece of paper in his hand and ignoring her hold on him, pulled away out of her grasp and walked to the window. He looked out over their tidy lawn, the quiet street, the neighbours' houses so well-kept and his two-year-old Jaguar, his pride and joy, standing gleaming in their driveway but when he spoke to Eva it didn't sound like her husband's voice at all. He sounded frightened.

'What would you do if we had to move?'

'Move?'

What was he talking about? They had never discussed moving. This had been their home for over ten years ever since they had got married. Their first home together. Their only home. And it was a home, not just a house. They had renovated it and got it exactly as they wanted it. It was convenient for her work in a local solicitor's office and only a quick drive to his work too. They were settled. At least she had thought they were.

'Where would we move to, Dan?'

'We could go to Australia.'

'Australia!'

Her voice rose in surprise. Was he serious? The other side of the world? Starting over when their careers were well established here? Had he gone mad? Was this some kind of nervous breakdown? She knew men had midlife crises and she knew his job could be stressful. He had maybe had another run-in with one of his colleagues. She knew one or two of them were difficult to work with. Maybe he was joking? She didn't really think so. He didn't have that kind of a sense of humour.

Suddenly he swung round. He faced her. He smiled weakly, trying to reassure her.

'Just a bit of wishful thinking, pet. Of course, we can't move.'

He crumpled the paper he was holding into a ball and stuffed it deep into his trouser pocket, lifted his jacket from the back of his chair and gave her a quick peck on the cheek on his way past.

'Big day today. Just pre-performance nerves. You know how it always gets to me. We're having our first dress rehearsal and then I have an audition this evening. I'll probably not be back until late. Don't wait up for me.'

Eva moved to the window and watched as Dan walked to the car, climbed in and backed carefully out of the drive and into the street. She waved back as he waved goodbye and headed to the school on the outskirts of Belfast where he was Head of the Music Department, but she couldn't forget the worried look on his face.

What was in that letter? She lifted the envelope which he had discarded on the table. His name and address were printed on the front, except it was addressed to Danny Anderson. She hadn't heard him called Danny for years. She had never called him Danny. There was no return address and the postmark was blurred. Impossible to read. Whoever had written to him must have known him a long time ago. She wondered what they could want with him now. Whatever it was, he had been... she thought for a minute... scared.

Chapter 5

It was the middle of the night and Kevin Donnelly was in a deep sleep. He was snoring loudly. The insistent ringing of his mobile on the bedside table woke him. The girl in the bed beside him stirred and raised a sleepy head from the pillow.

'Go back to sleep, honey.' He couldn't remember her name, but he remembered picking her up at the hotel bar. After that it was all a blur.

He reached out and picked up the phone but, before speaking, slipped out from between the silk sheets and walked naked across the floor of the Imperial Suite. The curtains were open. They had not taken time with niceties like closing them, tearing at each other's clothes in a frenzy of passion as soon as the hall door had closed behind them. They had barely made it to the bed. So now light streamed in from Louisiana Street and illuminated his way to the living area, where he knew he would not be overheard. His head was thumping. What was it now? Someone needing reassurance; needing their hand held? Some last-minute panic over the deal he had made earlier that evening?

'Do you have any idea what time of night it is?' he began but a voice broke into his words. Even in his sleepy condition, Kevin recognised the effect of an electronic voice distorter. His senses sharpened. He knew a few of the people he dealt with were dangerous but he didn't think he had crossed any of them recently. Who could it be?

'Hopewell. Remember, Kev?'

No one called him Kev. Not anymore. And not here. Kevin Donnelly, bright upcoming star among lobbyists, beloved by so many – especially women – on the Hill, with his head of thick dark wavy hair, his soulful brown eyes and cultivated Irish brogue, took an involuntary step backwards as if an unseen hand had pushed him hard. He found himself leaning against the wall. His eyes were wide open and he was fully awake now.

'You need to get back to Belfast, Kev. Pronto.'

'Who is this? What do you want?' he managed to ask, his mind searching for an answer to his own questions. Who could it be? Why did they want him back in Belfast? And why now, after all this time?

Kevin's brows were knit in confusion. His heart was racing. He glanced at the Rolex on his wrist, a symbol of his success. The little boy from inner city Belfast had made good. His mind wasn't at its sharpest at 3am after a night's heavy drinking with some Texan businessmen who had needed finessing to be encouraged to put their money where it was needed to support a bill coming up next week in the House, followed by a few lines of coke with the girl in the bed, whose name he still couldn't remember.

'Meet me at the old place on the thirtieth at ten. Don't be late and don't try anything clever. Remember, you might have got all the girls but you were always the daft one.' There was a weird laugh and he, or maybe she, Kevin couldn't be sure, rang off before he could respond. Who the hell was it? Who was raking all this up now, after all these years?

The thirtieth. Less than two weeks to sort out his business affairs here in Houston, get back to Washington and settle everything there too and then fly home to Belfast. At least his mother would be pleased to see him even if no one else was. With shaking hands, he searched his favourite airline's website and made the booking. First class of course. If he was going to his doom, he might as well travel in comfort.

Chapter 6

Detective Chief Inspector Gawn Girvin couldn't help being just a little nervous. It was nearly two months since she had last walked these corridors and a lot had happened in the meantime. When she left she never expected to be back. Now here she was, but carrying a secret with her – she was married. The silver drip ring designed by a young Belfast jeweller which she had chosen as her wedding ring was hanging on a chain around her neck hidden under her shirt.

Her other secret was the baby she had thought she was expecting. When she had been so seriously injured in

Afghanistan the doctors had told her it was unlikely she would be able to conceive and at that time it hadn't mattered to her. She didn't want to have a child. She hadn't even wanted to have a man in her life. When she had thought she was pregnant, her lover, Sebastian, had immediately proposed. Then, when it had become clear she was not, she could see how disappointed he was. They were still trying to have a baby, but she feared she might never be able to give him the child he so obviously wanted.

No one here knew about their marriage or their plans to have a family. Not even Maxwell. And she wanted to keep it that way. She was determined her personal life wouldn't interfere with her work.

She paused briefly outside the door of the Serious Crimes Unit. She could hear loud laughter coming from within. It sounded so familiar, she couldn't help smiling. It was like coming home. She visualised one of the team, probably one of her young DCs, Jamie Grant or Jack Dee, the two jokers of the group, saying something funny. Dee was probably teasing the younger detective about his love life. It was a constant source of humour and he took it all in good spirits. She took a deep breath, counted to three and pushed the door.

'Good morning, ma'am.' A cheery voice greeted her. It was Erin McKeown, the recently promoted sergeant, who had paused in her walk across the room carrying a stack of box files and looked across and smiled at her in welcome.

'Good morning, Erin, or should I say, "Sergeant McKeown"? Good morning, everyone.' Gawn's gaze took in the whole room. It really was like coming home. Even the smell, that mixture of Tayto cheese and onion crisps, the go-to snack of choice for everyone on the team, and male testosterone coupled with a strong whiff of mint which she knew DC Billy Logan sucked on to hide his drinking, was so familiar. Everything looked the same and yet utterly changed. She doubted anything was different. The murder board was empty now of course, the photographs from her last case long packed away. It was Gawn herself who was different but she hoped no one could see that.

'Good to have you back, boss.' Inspector Paul Maxwell had spotted her through the doorway of his office and walked out to greet her. She noted his use of 'boss' and realised he was signalling to her and all the others that she was in charge again. A smile was spread across his face. He looked relaxed and confident, so different to the nervous young sergeant who had been so keen to do well when he had first joined Serious Crimes. Now he was smiling, a genuine smile, she was sure. That had been one of her concerns. How would Maxwell feel about her coming back? He was an inspector, a good one. He had been running this team, reporting directly to the superintendent while she was away. Now she was back and would be supervising him. Decisions he had made yesterday would now be her decisions to make. It could be a tricky situation. She didn't want it to be. She respected his work and they had always worked well together. But if she was back – and she was – then she was really back. She would be the boss. It couldn't be any other way and that might be a problem. She just hoped it wouldn't be.

Chapter 7

Rose had gathered the contents of the black bin bag together and carried them inside off the pavement. She dumped them in the storeroom at the back of the shop. Veronica, after her dramatic reaction, had managed to pull herself together long enough to roll up the shutters but was now slumped in a chair behind the counter seemingly incapable of moving when Rose appeared back through the curtain. She noticed Veronica sitting, just staring into space. She had hastily pushed a piece of paper into her pocket when she spotted Rose appearing. She still looked pale and frightened, Rose thought, and she was wringing her hands. The woman remembered, from being taken along to her daughter's starring role in her school's production of *Macbeth*, many years ago, the way Aoife had wrung her hands in anguish in the sleepwalking scene. The look on Veronica's face and the repetitive movement of her hands reminded Rose of that now. What was going on? It had only been a few bits and pieces scattered over the street. Nothing had fallen on Veronica or her precious designer shoes so Rose didn't know why she had screamed or why she was still so upset.

Rose had dumped the contents of the bin bag on the floor in the back room ready for sorting. She needed to get started. Customers would soon start appearing. Monday morning was one of their busiest times. Ignoring Veronica, leaving her to gather herself together, she donned an apron to protect her skirt and began to pull items out of the bag. First out was a doll. Lifting it, she was struck by the marks at the wrists where the stiff plastic had been sliced open and red paint smeared all over the arms as if the doll had been bleeding. It looked gruesome like one of those horror movies she had never allowed her children to watch when they were growing up. But it was hardly something to evoke such a dramatic reaction from a grown woman. It was probably just some kid's idea of a silly joke which a parent had decided to discard. As if they'd be able to sell anything like this!

'Rose, I think I'm going to have to go home. I'm not feeling well.' Veronica's voice sounded shaky. Rose walked back into the shop and saw she did look ill. She couldn't help feeling a little sorry for her. Veronica could be a bit of a pain in the arse but she wasn't a bad sort most of the time.

'That's alright, love. You go on. I'll hold the fort till Mabel and Tracey arrive at lunchtime.' She wanted to put her arm around the younger woman's shoulder and give her a comforting hug but she held back. She didn't think Veronica would welcome the physical contact.

Veronica didn't need any further encouragement to leave. She grabbed her bag which she had slung carelessly into a corner and without a backward look or a word of goodbye, hurried out of the shop. Rose watched her scurry away and almost run up the street. She thought Veronica looked like someone escaping, but from what? Rose realised then she was still clutching the doll in her hand. She turned it over and, pulling the little cotton dress aside, read the label just below the neck. Made in China. It was just a cheap plastic doll. Nothing special. Not one of those porcelain figures which purported to be Victorian and cost the earth and whose facial expressions she often found a bit spooky. That was when she noticed the piece of paper which must have fallen from Veronica's coat pocket as she had rushed out. Rose picked it up. It might be something important. She would keep it safe. But she couldn't resist the temptation to read it. It was probably a receipt from some expensive restaurant where Veronica had met her fancy man last night but, when she unfolded it and looked, she realised it wasn't. One word, written in thick red ink, stood out in the centre of the page – Hopewell. Underneath were some numbers and a crude drawing of a figure with a smiley face. Somewhere in the back of Rose's memory something stirred. That name, Hopewell. She had heard it somewhere before but where and when?

Chapter 8

Maxwell had brought Gawn up to speed on all their outstanding cases. He seemed to have everything under control and then he filled her in on all the office politics and the latest news. The two new ACCs had already taken up their posts. One was an internal appointment, John Beattie. The other was an outsider, Sandra Wilkinson. Her Geordie accent was already being mimicked, with greater and lesser degrees of success, by some of the junior ranks, Maxwell told her, and some of the more senior too, Gawn suspected. She was an unknown quantity. They knew she was married but there was some speculation that she might have split with her husband for there was no talk of family joining her. She was the new Head of Crime Operations, their boss.

'Have you met her yet, Paul?' Gawn queried wondering if her own marital status would soon become the centre of speculation among her colleagues too.

'I was introduced to her briefly once but that's all. You know me, boss. I try to keep under the radar as much as possible.'

He grinned and Gawn realised just how much she had missed their chats. He had just finished his recital and they were about to have a cup of coffee when the phone rang on her desk.

'Girvin.'

'Chief Inspector.' He didn't need to announce himself. Gawn recognised the brusque tones of Superintendent McDowell without introduction.

'I was trying to reach Maxwell. Is he with you?'

'Yes, sir.' No words of welcome, she noticed. No 'good to see you back'. Probably he wasn't. She had given him more than a few headaches in the past. He had probably enjoyed working with Maxwell who would have been more cooperative and compliant.

'Put him on.' No 'pleases' either. Just like old times. She smiled wryly and passed the phone to Maxwell then watched as he nodded and responded with an occasional 'yes, sir' and 'of course, sir' and his eyebrows rose as he listened to the senior officer. He put the phone down.

'There's a body, a suspicious death.'

'And McDowell wasn't going to tell me?' Gawn could feel her temper starting to rise. What was he playing at?

'He said he wanted to give you time to find your feet and get up to speed with everything. He thought I could take the lead until you were over all the other cases.'

'We've just spent two hours going over all the current cases, getting me up to speed. What did he think I've been doing all morning? Sitting on my backside, drinking coffee and chatting about the latest daytime TV programmes I've watched?'

She was angry. Not with Maxwell. It wasn't his fault and she thought he might find himself uncomfortably sandwiched between the two of them more often over the next few weeks until she had convinced McDowell to back off and let her get on with her job.

'Where?'

'In the Lagan near Ormeau Bridge.'

'Right.' She was already on her feet and picking up her jacket before Maxwell had even started to move. 'I'll drive.'

Just like old times, he thought to himself and smiled.

Chapter 9

She climbed out of the car and then stood as if frozen in time. Maxwell walked off, keen to get into action. Gawn's approach was different. She wanted to take in the whole scene. She didn't allow her eyes to focus on the activity on the riverbank below her. Instead Gawn scanned from left to right. The greenery of Ormeau Park framed the river in the distance. Her gaze moved over the Ormeau Bridge, one of the main commuter routes carrying travellers from the ever-spreading new developments on the outskirts of the city as its voracious appetite for building land took in more and more green sites. What had once been farmland was now packed with new housing developments with names like Four Winds and Brooke Hall Heights, reflecting their elevated position. The road and bridge were busy. Traffic edged forward having been halted by a red light at the junction with the Annadale embankment. A bus sailed past down the bus lane, its passengers enjoying getting one over on the slower cars and basking on the moral high ground of doing their bit to save the environment by not taking their vehicles into the city centre.

Her eyes moved onto the public library on the corner which would have been long closed before the body would have gone into the river. The supermarket just directly opposite her, its car park full now, would have been blanketed in darkness last night. She saw a block of older apartments. They would need to be canvassed. Then the narrower, less-travelled Kings Bridge over the river which formed part of the one-way system and in the distance Governors Bridge.

Gawn swivelled on her heels to assess the area directly behind her. To her left, parkland, the beginnings of the Botanic Gardens and the rear of the university PE centre. Not too many would be strolling or running in this area late at night. She smiled ruefully as she remembered running here before the start of the case which she would for ever regard with mixed emotions. The Perfume Killer, as the newspapers had dubbed him, had come close to killing her too but he had also brought Sebastian York into her life.

Her eyes moved on to yet more apartments behind her. More door-knocking for the team. They would need to call in some additional help if this turned out to be more than some sad suicide. And then the gable ends of some of the narrow streets which gave rise to the popular name for this area, the Holylands, – Palestine, Jerusalem, Damascus, Cairo. They edged the university and were mostly populated by students, houses of multiple occupancy famous or perhaps more accurately infamous for the noisy parties and street disturbances which brought the occupants into conflict with the PSNI. They were probably the best chance of finding any witnesses. This seemed like one of those cases where there would be a lot of old-fashioned footslogging to try to get answers. But she knew the police were not much liked in this area. There had been too many run-ins; too many confrontations as young men and women spilled out onto the streets from house parties to continue their revelling on top of parked cars. Non-student residents blamed the PSNI for not doing enough to protect their peace and safety. Her team would have to brace themselves for some hostility as they went about their door-to-door inquiries.

Chapter 10

'Well, hello there, Chief Inspector. Good to see you back.'

The voice was warm and friendly with still a trace of Boston in its flat vowels. It was Jenny Norris, the interim pathologist and Gawn's friend. Her eyes twinkled as she removed her mask to reveal a welcoming smile to accompany her words.

'Thank you. What do you have for me?'

Norris knew her friend well enough by now not to be offended by the terse response and demand for answers. She knew Gawn didn't mix business and pleasure. They could catch up over a glass of wine later. For now, it was straight to business.

'Male. Late fifties, maybe early sixties.'

'Suicide?'

'No. You'll see for yourself. Though, by the going over someone was giving him, he may have felt like committing suicide.' Norris was moving past her as she spoke. 'If you're thinking of going down there, take care. It's bloody slippery. I nearly went on my backside a couple of times and it wouldn't be a good look for the chief inspector on her first day back. Phone me. We need to catch up.'

'I will.' Gawn nodded. She realised she needed to let her friend know she and Seb had married. Jenny Norris would be disappointed not to have been at the wedding but only close family had been there.

The pathologist, rustling in her white protective suit, walked on past her and Gawn heard her bidding Maxwell farewell as she headed back to her car.

'I've had a quick look-see at our victim, boss.'

She guessed this was Maxwell's way of saying he had ventured down the bank to see the body in situ before it was moved and saved her the indignity of a possible fall and, who knew, a dip in the Lagan?

As she watched, white-suited figures emerged from the crime scene tent struggling with a body bag. They were joined by two others slipping and sliding down the slope to help them and, between the four, they managed to get the body up to the road. They struggled to get it over the waist-high railings with some semblance of dignity and then placed it on a gurney. Gawn positioned herself blocking their way.

'I'll take a look.'

One of the figures partially unzipped the body bag and Gawn saw the battered face of a late middle-aged man. Blood had congealed at the sides of his mouth. His eyes were puffy but what attracted her attention most of all was just a glimpse of slashes on his chest which she could see starting below his throat and, she suspected, extending down his body.

'Thank you.'

She had seen enough to know this was not a straightforward suicide, if there even was such a thing. Their victim had been, the word 'tortured' came to mind, either as a punishment or perhaps to extract information. Those were her immediate suppositions but she was determined not to rush to any conclusions. She remembered being called to a dead Dutch businessman on a flight to Belfast and how that had turned out. There was a long way to go in this case. She had no idea at that moment just how long.

Chapter 11

'Do we have an identity for our victim?'

The ferocity of the beating the man had received and the type of injuries inflicted led Gawn to believe he must have had some criminal connections. She was hopeful her sergeant would already have an identification for them and an address where they could start their inquiries. Gawn had spotted McKeown typing on her tablet and knew she would be carrying out all kinds of searches. She walked over to her and posed her question. The younger woman looked up. She had bad news.

'He's not on any of our databases, ma'am.'

'No criminal record?'

'I checked his fingerprints. No matches.'

Before she could add any further comment Maxwell joined them. He stood staring down at his shoes.

'Kerri's going to flippin' kill me. These were just new.'

Gawn's eyes dropped to Maxwell's feet where his formerly well-polished black brogues were now covered in thick mud and wet patches were marking the leather, promising to leave a white stain when they dried.

'Do I need to go down?' It wasn't that she was afraid of losing her dignity falling, she was just scared of falling, full stop. Seb was so keen to be a father and they had been trying so hard. So, if she was pregnant, and she knew it was a very big 'if', she didn't want to do anything risky.

'Not really, ma'am. The CSIs have the immediate area taped off now but the whole place is like a quagmire from last night's rain. You'd only add to it all. They won't thank you for making their job more difficult. They're going over every inch. You know what Mark's like. He'll be cataloguing every blade of grass.' He laughed.

She hadn't spotted Mark Ferguson, one of their best SCMs. He must already have started work inside the crime scene tent by the time she arrived. She had worked with Ferguson before. She admired his work and knew he would miss nothing. When she accepted Maxwell's comment and made no move to head down to the riverside, he was rather surprised. He knew she always liked to check everything for herself; to get a feel for the crime and the victim. He wondered if she was still feeling the effects of her car accident in Amsterdam when she had been run off the road. Maybe her knee was still playing her up. Or maybe she just wanted to let him know she wasn't going to try to do everything herself but would let him get on with things.

DC Jack Dee strode purposefully across to them.

'I think I might have found us a witness.'

'Who?' Gawn and Maxwell asked simultaneously. Dee looked from one to the other. Then he half turned and looked over his shoulder nodding towards a group of what looked like homeless men huddled together at the street corner.

'The one at the end says he might have seen something.'

The man was dressed in a long dark overcoat which had definitely seen better days. His greying hair straggled down over his collar and was tied back in a loose ponytail. His beard was equally unkempt. Even from a distance, they could imagine the man's body odour. He was holding tightly to the handle of a child's buggy, minus child. Instead it contained a large black plastic bin bag. They could see a grubby looking sleeping bag sticking out of it and Gawn and Maxwell both had the same thought that it probably held all his worldly possessions.

'Who is he, Jack?' Maxwell asked.

'He says his name is Walter Plinge.' Dee smiled to show his disbelief and Maxwell had to stifle a laugh.

'He's having you on, man. I've never heard of anyone called Plinge before. He's probably looking for a free breakfast courtesy of the PSNI.'

'I know, sir, but he says he might have seen a van and someone dragging something heavy out of the back and pushing it over the railing. Then he heard a splash.'

'*Might?* What time was this supposed to be, Jack?' Gawn's voice was thick with cynicism.

'Around 3am, ma'am.'

'And what exactly was he doing, wandering around at that time of night?' Maxwell queried, not convinced they had a genuine witness.

'He's a bit vague about that. I gather they'd been doing a bit of heavy drinking all evening. He doesn't know himself how they ended up here.'

'Take him to the nearest café. Get him some breakfast, preferably with a cup of strong black coffee to sober him up, and then take his statement for what it'll be worth. See if he can give you any kind of description of the person he claims he saw.'

'Right, ma'am.'

Gawn turned to see McKeown walking across from where she had been talking to DC Jo Hill.

'Erin,' she called to the sergeant who was just about to brief a group of uniformed officers readying themselves to start on door-to-door inquiries. 'Can you get Jo or someone to start going through any traffic cameras for a van in this area last night? Maybe about 3am but tell her to leave a good margin on either side. The witness Jack has turned up says he saw one. How reliable he is, well, we'll see.'

'Right, ma'am.'

'Now what about whoever found the body?' She turned her full gaze on Maxwell.

'Over there.' He pointed to four young women dressed in T-shirts and shorts sitting on the ramp of an ambulance. Each was swathed in a foil blanket. Gawn shivered. That had been her once.

'Who are they?'

'Rowers. From the university. They were out for a morning practice session from the Boat Club. They're only young. Late teens probably. They're all very shaken.'

Gawn had to smile to herself. She knew Maxwell had an eye for a pretty girl and a soft spot for any damsel in distress. They would probably respond better to him.

'I'll leave them to you, Paul. I'll see you back in the office.'

Chapter 12

'Good shot!'

Jonah Lunn complimented his playing partner. It was good to get out of the office and enjoy some fresh air and he could put it all down to expenses and background research. He was Northern editor of a leading Irish newspaper and his playing partner was one of the most easily-recognised voices on the local airwaves. He and Dave Osmond were not close friends, but they got together to play golf once every couple of months. Sometimes Osmond had been able to give him some useful tips that he'd followed up and developed into headline stories and in return he had introduced the radio presenter to some of the local politicians and power players who could help his career. It was a mutually beneficial arrangement. Their rounds of golf and drinks afterwards in the clubhouse were pleasant but today

Osmond seemed out of sorts. He was not quite his normal ebullient self.

'You win again. How many times is it you've beaten me now?' Lunn asked in mock annoyance. He didn't take their games seriously and wasn't really keeping score but he knew Osmond enjoyed winning and he would enjoy crowing over his victory even more.

'I'm three up, old man.' Osmond patted him on the back in mock sympathy and smiled widely, more like his usual self.

'Then I'm buying.' Lunn feigned disappointment but it was all down to expenses. It wasn't costing him anything and, who knows, maybe Osmond would have something for him that he could turn into a worthwhile story. He knew the broadcaster got invited to all sorts of parties and events and was accepted in the company of people who wouldn't necessarily want to have anything to do with a journalist or answer any questions. Osmond had tipped him off last year about a well-known celebrity's dealings with a gangster from the Dublin underworld. That had led to an exposé in the newspaper and given him the basis for his book, *The Criminal Underbelly* which was riding high in the Irish bestsellers list at the minute. He owed him.

'I'm afraid I haven't time for any après-golf today, old man. You'll have to hit the 19th without me.'

Lunn was surprised. He didn't think Osmond played for the good of his health or his love of the game. He had always believed golf was a useful means for Osmond to network so he was surprised that the man was turning down the opportunity for a few drinks and to meet whoever was in the clubhouse today.

'A hot date to get ready for?'

Osmond tapped the side of his nose. 'Just my wee secret.'

Lunn prided himself on being able to read people. He suspected there was no woman involved in Osmond's plans for the rest of the day, unless he was cheating on

Kirsty and using Lunn as his cover. He knew they'd been dating for nearly six months, which was a long time for any of Osmond's relationships to last. Maybe he was simply moving on and hadn't decided to tell his young PA yet in case it didn't work out. Lunn had noticed how she fawned over him and was sure it would feed Osmond's ego to have someone like that he could call on whenever he felt like it. If it wasn't that, just a liaison, he wasn't sure what it could be but his investigative whiskers were twitching as his wife would have teased him. He wondered if there could be a story here for him. Osmond was a well-known figure. If he was up to something it could be newsworthy. Lunn filed the thought away, for now.

Chapter 13

Safely ensconced in one of the two well-used faux leather armchairs in her office, with Maxwell in the other and her habitual mug of steaming coffee in her hand, Gawn was thinking out loud.

'We need an identification, Paul. Quickly. If we know who our victim is – or rather – who he was, then we'll have a better chance of finding out where he was attacked and why, and hopefully that'll lead us to the who.'

She thought of Walter Plinge's story of seeing a van in the vicinity.

'We need to find out where this happened. Was there nothing found at the scene to identify him?'

'Nothing. They've searched the riverbank between the two bridges in case whoever did this threw his clothes or his wallet away but they found nothing.'

'And nothing helpful from the door-to-door inquiries?'

'Nothing yet, boss.'

'What about Special Branch?'

She didn't think it had the feel of a paramilitary punishment but she had asked him to check with Special Branch in case they recognised the victim.

'No. They don't know him.'

'Who the hell is he? And why was he tortured? If he turns out to be rich or related to someone rich, then it might be a kidnapping gone wrong,' Gawn suggested but not with any confidence.

'Do you think so? If you were trying to extort money for his safe return you wouldn't want to damage the goods.'

Gawn thought of the famous Getty kidnapping but said nothing.

'No. I see your point. So why else would he be tortured?'

'Maybe he had information someone wanted.'

'Like what?'

'Details of money shipments or access to somewhere,' Maxwell suggested. 'A bank, maybe. Or maybe they were holding him and it just got a bit rougher than they intended. They mightn't have meant to kill him. Or' – his face brightened as he had an idea – 'you don't think it was some kind of kinky sex game gone wrong, do you?'

Gawn pulled a face. She could do without another case involving sexual deviants and exploitation like her last one.

'Oh, I hope not, Paul. But you're right, of course. As of this minute we can't be sure about anything and certainly not about a motive.' She bit her lip in frustration. This part of an investigation, before it really got going, before they knew what they were dealing with and the chase could begin properly, was one of the most annoying parts of any case for Gawn.

Maxwell took a sip of his tea and looked across at his boss. There was something different about her. He couldn't quite say what it was. She hadn't changed her hairstyle again or anything but she seemed… what? He couldn't put it into words. Anyhow, it was good to have her back. He'd enjoyed most of the things about leading the team. He had heard her complain in the past about the paperwork and now he knew what she meant. He hadn't faced taking the lead in a major murder investigation while she was away and he was glad he didn't have to. If the press got hold of the story of a tortured victim they would play it up. He was glad it wouldn't be him feeling the heat from the newspapers and the super.

A knock on the door was followed by Jack Dee's head popping into view.

'You might want to hear this, ma'am.' He walked away even as he was still speaking so that they didn't hear his muttered, 'Or not,' under his breath. The two detectives had no choice but to follow him.

Three of the team were standing around Logan's desk listening to the latest local news bulletin.

> *Our main story this afternoon is the discovery of a mutilated body in the River Lagan near Governors Bridge at Stranmillis. From the scene, our reporter Donna Nixon brings us the latest. What's happening there now, Donna?*

Gawn knew of this reporter although they had never actually met. She was petite, curvaceous and looked like a cross between Marilyn Monroe and Lady Gaga but anyone dismissing her as a 'dumb blonde' would have been totally wrong. She might be young, and only started reporting on local radio recently, but from her work on the local paper Gawn knew she had a good nose for a story and she was ambitious – a dangerous mix for the police trying to keep anything under wraps in an investigation.

> *Police are still working here at the scene on the riverbank between Ormeau Bridge and Kings Bridge. A forensics tent is in place to cover the scene of the crime but the body was removed some time ago. Police haven't issued a statement yet and the victim hasn't*

been named but from talking to the young women who found the body in the water it seems the man was badly mutilated. One of the witnesses described the body as being like something from a horror movie, like some kind of ritualistic black magic rite or something.

'She can't say that,' Maxwell complained loudly.

'She just has, and no doubt that's what they and the papers will run with. We'll have "Black Magic Murder" across the front page in the morning. The sensational sells.' Gawn spoke bitterly. This sort of news coverage wouldn't help. They'd get all kinds of loonies coming forward with so-called information and theories.

Thank you, Donna. We'll come back to you later in the programme if there's any update.

The chirpy voice on the radio moved on to a story about sewage problems in Saintfield.

'How did she get onto our witnesses so quickly? Didn't we bring them in for questioning?' Gawn was livid.

'The paramedics thought they needed to be checked out, ma'am. They went off in the ambulance to hospital.' Dee offered the information, but it was Maxwell who looked sheepish. He had completely forgotten that she had left it up to him to question the girls. He had been waiting for them to be brought to headquarters and then had been distracted with other things.

'And no one went with them?'

'We were a bit short-handed because we'd started the door-to-door inquiries and the search of the riverbank so one of the PCs went with them,' Dee admitted.

'You know sometimes people don't want to talk to us. It's easier for the press. They can splash a bit of cash and get answers,' Maxwell suggested, glad that it seemed she hadn't remembered he was the one who was supposed to interview the girls.

'We haven't even found anyone to splash a bit of cash at, if we had any. Anyhow Donna and her ilk don't need evidence and facts, speculation's good enough for them. And where are the girls and the constable now? How did Donna Nixon get talking to them?'

Dee shook his head.

'Find out. Now.'

She hadn't raised her voice. She didn't need to but she spoke through clenched teeth, her anger controlled but evident to all. Dee scurried off in response to her order. Logan switched off the radio and the others slunk back to their own desks.

'Brilliant start to the case. We don't even know who our victim is. At this rate I should talk to Donna Nixon. She could probably tell us. By the way when were you going to interview the girls, Inspector?'

So, she hadn't forgotten. Of course, she hadn't. She had just chosen not to make a big deal of it in front of the others.

'We'll both speak to the girls, Paul.'

'Yes, ma'am.'

'As soon as possible.'

'Yes, ma'am.'

He wasn't going to argue with her. He thought he had gotten off lightly. A year ago she would have had his head on a platter for letting the press get to their witnesses before they had questioned them. She was mellowing.

Her glance fell on the murder board where a single photograph of their victim took centre stage in the empty white space. Above it was a question mark. They had nothing. No identification. No crime scene. No witnesses. No suspects. No motive. Nothing.

Chapter 14

They had brought the girls in and separated them. Gawn wanted them spoken to individually although secretly she wondered if there was much point to that now. They would have had ample time to talk over everything while they had waited together at A&E. Now she and Maxwell were standing, watching on a monitor, as one of the girls sat looking around her in the interview room. She looked quite relaxed, not nervous about what was about to happen. She had obviously been home and changed her clothes. Gawn remembered seeing the four shocked young women sitting at the back of the ambulance on the embankment all dressed in shorts and singlets. Now this girl was wearing ripped jeans and a pink hoodie.

'Let's go. Keep your fingers crossed, Paul, that she can actually tell us something useful.'

The girl's head came up and her eyes followed them as they walked into the room, Maxwell in the rear. She smiled but got no smile in return from either. They sat down. It was Gawn who spoke first.

'Good afternoon, Miss Greeves. I'm DCI Girvin and this is DI Maxwell.' At least the PC had got names and addresses before letting them leave the hospital. It was not his fault and Gawn had not called him in to rant at him as she might have done a year ago. He had only been out of the training college three months; no one had specifically told him to bring them to HQ, just to accompany them safely to the hospital. When they had phoned their families who had then turned up at City Hospital A&E, he had thought it was alright to let them go home. He didn't know what else he was supposed to do. His sergeant had given him a bit of a chewing when he got back to the station but he was relieved not to be called to Serious Crimes to answer to the DCI. He had already heard of her reputation.

'Hi!' Susan Greeves greeted them like old friends. She smiled at them both but her gaze lingered a little longer on Maxwell. He didn't seem to notice. Gawn did and realised the girl would respond better to him. She nudged her inspector lightly on the foot under the table to indicate he should start the questioning.

'Miss Greeves.'

'Call me Susie. Everybody does.'

'Susie, can you tell us exactly what happened this morning, how you came to find the body?' He smiled at her encouragingly and waited for her to start talking.

'Well, it was just an ordinary morning, Inspector. We row three times a week, you see. We're in training.'

'That's you and' – he looked down at his notes – 'Stacey McGrath, Ruth Bennett and Fionnuala O'Rourke?'

'Yes. Stacey, Ruth and I row together all the time but Finn only comes sometimes. She prefers pairs. But her rowing partner is away this term on a placement in Italy and our usual number four has a big exam this week so Finn was out with us today.'

'Right. So, you set out from the Boat Club at what time precisely?'

'Gosh. Precisely!' She paused and pulled a face before answering. 'Well, we'd arranged to meet at seven, to give us time before classes, but Stacey was a wee bit late. She'd been at a party last night so it was probably nearer half past by the time we were actually all organised and out on the water.'

Gawn felt she better say something if only to remind the girl she was there. Susie hadn't taken her eyes off Maxwell.

'You headed downstream first?'

'Yes. It was a nice morning. There was nobody else on the water. It was just ordinary. Normal.'

'You didn't notice anyone on the riverbank?' Maxwell asked.

'You kind of get into a rhythm and you're concentrating on getting the stroke clean and on your breathing. It wasn't a pleasure trip. We weren't sightseeing, you know. We're aiming to make it onto the university team, maybe even the Olympics one day. Well, I am anyway.'

Gawn didn't appreciate the girl's tone of voice. 'We get it, Susie. You take your rowing seriously, but do you think if someone had been moving about on the riverbank you would have noticed?' Gawn asked, annoyed that the girl was taking such a superior attitude. She seemed more interested in her rowing than a man's death.

Susie Greeves didn't answer right away. She scrunched up her nose thoughtfully and then said, 'I don't honestly know. I don't remember seeing anyone.'

Maxwell could sense Gawn's growing annoyance and stepped in.

'So, what happened on the way back then that was different, that made you notice the body?'

The girl sat back into her chair, more relaxed it seemed or perhaps glad that it was Maxwell asking the questions again and not Gawn.

'Well, it had been a good morning. We'd clocked up a good time. We were pleased with ourselves. We were looking forward to getting back to the clubhouse and we'd planned to have breakfast together at the Union before classes. So I suppose you could say we weren't focused on rowing just as much. We had a bit of time to look around us. In fact we were keeping a lookout for Stacey's boyfriend, Mike. He'd said he might join us for breakfast so we were watching out for him and we were nearer the park side this time so we would see him if he was standing about waiting for us.'

'And instead you saw a body. Did something attract you to it?'

'You mean apart from the fact it was a dead body floating in the water?' the girl responded sarcastically, scrunching up her nose again as if she could smell the decomposing body now.

'Inspector Maxwell means was the body moving or was there something colourful which attracted your eye?' Gawn was losing patience. She'd forgotten over the past few weeks sitting at home thinking about everything but work, how infuriating interviewing witnesses, even cooperative ones, could be.

'I think it might have come loose from the weeds at the side and sort of rolled over so the man's face was visible. And it was so pale and the blood...' She shivered and didn't finish her thought.

'Take your time, Susie,' Maxwell encouraged her.

'His face was so white it really stood out from everything and we saw his eyes staring.'

'What did you do then?' Gawn asked.

'We moved over a bit closer to the bank. Finn's studying medicine but you didn't need to be a doctor to see the man was dead so we decided not to touch him. I had my mobile with me. We always carry one in case something happens so we phoned your lot and then just waited until someone turned up.'

'Nobody touched him but you were able to see marks on his body. Is that correct?'

'I told you we moved over a bit closer. He was naked. Well, he had his pants on,' she giggled but it was a nervous giggle at the thought of the man they had seen, 'but we could see his chest and it was all marked and cut and there was blood on it and his face was all bashed about. It was horrible. Who was he?'

Gawn ignored the girl's question, instead asking, 'You'd never seen him before? Not around the river, maybe on the riverbank?' She'd had a sudden thought that their victim might have hung around the area watching the girls in their short shorts.

'Maybe. Sometimes there are some men that hang around but we just ignore them. I don't remember seeing him before.'

'You spoke to a reporter about what you'd seen.'

Before Gawn had time to finish what she was going to say, Susie interrupted, 'Oh, you mean Donna. She's my cousin. My mum was with my auntie Beverley when I phoned to tell her what had happened so of course they told Donna.'

Of course they did, Gawn thought to herself. She had never quite got used to how parochial this place could be, even after being back in Belfast for almost two years. Everyone knew somebody, was related to somebody, could introduce you to somebody. London, it was certainly not, where you could live for years without knowing your neighbours, as she had done. Here someone always knew your business and that made her think about how long she could keep any pregnancy a secret. If anyone spotted her at a hospital appointment it would be all over the force the same afternoon.

'Thank you, Susie. Unless there's anything else you want to tell us?'

'You mean like my phone number, Inspector?' Susie smiled impishly.

Maxwell blushed.

'About the body.'

'No. That's all.'

'By the way, did Stacey's boyfriend turn up to meet her?' asked Gawn.

'No. He slept in so he missed all the excitement.' Susie Greeves smiled at them.

'Thank you again, Miss Greeves. You'll be called to give evidence about finding the body at the inquest and at any court case but someone'll be in touch about that.'

The girl smiled at the inspector's words as if she would be happy if it was him who was in touch.

The constable who had been waiting silently in a corner of the room escorted the girl out in response to a nod of Gawn's head.

'God, what are young girls like these days?' Maxwell was almost shocked but secretly rather flattered.

'Well, at least it shows you've still got it, Paul,' Gawn teased him. 'And seeing you're on a roll, Casanova, I'll let you interview the other three yourself. I doubt you'll get anything more from them.'

Chapter 15

Paul hadn't managed to find out anything more from the other three girls, as Gawn had feared, so it was an increasingly disgruntled DCI who had gone home to her husband of just two weeks.

As soon as she opened the door, the aroma of something delicious cooking in the oven met her nostrils.

'Something smells good.'

'Boeuf bourguignon.'

Seb left the casserole he had just lifted out of the oven and moved across to enclose her in a hug. He kissed her and then, taking her gently by the shoulders, moved her back. He hooked a stray wisp of hair behind her ear.

'First day back. How'd it go? You look tired, darling. Are you sure it wasn't all too much for you?' He turned her around and started to massage her shoulders, feeling the knots of tension under his fingers. He was still hoping he could convince her to come with him to America now, not wait for another few months until she would be due leave. Then they could continue to try for a baby.

'Frustrated more like it.'

'Oh well, I can help with that,' he beamed like a little boy in a sweet shop as he turned her around to face him again.

'Not that sort of frustration!' She smiled back at him and hit him playfully on the arm. 'Maybe later.'

Seb's eyes twinkled. 'I'll hold you to that.'

'You're incorrigible, Sebastian York.'

'Sebastian Girvin-York. Remember?'

'How could I forget? No, it's my new case. A body found in the Lagan.'

'I heard about that on the radio. It's your case, is it?'

She could hear something in his voice. Was he worried or annoyed that she had a new murder case to take on already?

'Yes. We've made absolutely no progress on it all day. We haven't even been able to identify our victim yet.'

'Maybe Donna Nixon can help.' He knew she would have been annoyed that the press had got on to the story so quickly. 'She seemed to know a lot about it. It sounded a bit gruesome.' He screwed up his face to show what he thought of it.

'Murder's always gruesome, Seb. There's no nice way to kill someone. Not like in your books. Some ways are more bloody and messy than others but taking another human life is never easy. At least it shouldn't be.' She couldn't help her mind going back to her time in Afghanistan, but Seb didn't know all about that. She had never shared it with him and hoped she would never have to.

'Is she right? Is it some black magic thing, do you think?' he asked and then added, 'Sorry. I shouldn't ask, should I? It's police business.'

'I want to keep my life with you and my work life as far apart as I can. It's not that I don't trust you, Seb. I just think it wouldn't help either of us. I want our home to be a safe place, off limits to all the horrors in the world.'

Seb pulled her back into him and hugged her tight.

'And I'll do my very best to *make it so*, as Jean-Luc Picard would say.'

They talked no more about the case after this exchange. She obviously didn't want to and he didn't want to spoil even one minute of the time they had left together before he would be flying off to his dream job, screenwriting in Hollywood. Instead, they shared the meal he had prepared. It was delicious. Seb had opened a bottle of wine but Gawn just drank some sparkling water. She had decided to give up alcohol hoping that might help her conceive. She had no good reason to believe that. It was just she thought she should do everything she could to give Seb the child he so obviously wanted.

They watched a documentary together snuggled up on the sofa about some Americans hunting for Nazi treasure. Seb, being an historian who had specialised in the Second World War era when he was teaching at the university, was interested in the story of how paintings and statues had been spirited away from occupied France and were now believed to be in homes all over the world. Gawn was more interested in the former American Special Forces officer who was helping in the search. She recognised him. She had served alongside him but she didn't tell Seb that. That was her secret. One of many.

Eventually they had gone to bed. Seb was a considerate lover. They had made love slowly, gently, just enjoying lying in each other's arms, both aware that in only a few days he would be leaving for Los Angeles. Neither of them wanted to think too much about that. Afterwards they had both lain awake, Seb worrying about his wife and the child they might have created together and wondering how he was going to leave her now; Gawn wondering who on earth their man in the Lagan could be.

Chapter 16

The Regional Forensic Mortuary's anonymous-looking solid red-brick bulk stood blankly on its site within the grounds of the Royal Victoria Hospital. Thousands of patients and visitors passed it every day without realising what it was or giving a thought to its occupants. Suiting up and walking into the investigation suite with Maxwell by her side felt like a throwback to Gawn.

'Good morning.' Dr Jenny Norris' chirpy greeting sounded incongruous in the sterile surroundings. It was hardly good if you or one of your relatives had business here.

Thank you for joining me once again, folks, and making this the number one music and chat show in this wee country of ours. Keep listening. I've loved your company. Let's do it again tomorrow. Love ya all.

Norris switched off the radio. It was her habit to listen to music while she worked. Everyone was used to it now except the chief pathologist who was on a sabbatical and didn't know anything about it. Gawn speculated it would be interesting to be there when he found out and then decided no, it wouldn't. She wouldn't want to see her friend being reprimanded although she suspected Jenny could give as good as she got if it came to a slanging match.

'Do you actually like that show, Jenny? Don't tell me you're a fan of Dave Osmond.' Maxwell suspected Osmond appealed more to a female demographic. He had expected the pathologist to be more discerning. He found the man too smug and full of himself.

'I like the type of music he plays and some of his guests are interesting. I take it you're not a fan, Paul.'

'Can we get started please?' Gawn had no time for chit-chat in the middle of a case and she frowned on the sort of informality the pathologist and the inspector seemed to have developed while she was away. Paul Maxwell had been part of her team for nearly two years and Jenny Norris was now her friend but she still preferred the formality of surnames and titles when working and no casual chatter. She was aware too of DC Grant stationed in the corner of the lab taking notes.

'I hope you'll find something to help us, Dr Norris.'

They needed to make some kind of breakthrough. It just wasn't good enough that they hadn't been able to identify their victim. He wasn't on any missing persons' registers. No one had come forward seeking a missing relative. They had still not managed to find anything to identify him after a thorough search at the riverside. If something didn't turn up soon, they were going to have to put out an appeal on TV and in the papers and hope someone would know who he was. Maxwell had even suggested they could put an appeal on the PSNI Facebook page. Gawn knew that their Communications team used the media platform but she had no social media presence herself and didn't want their case becoming a source of sharing for casual browsers' entertainment. Seb had joked about asking Donna Nixon to tell them the man's name but it was no joke to Gawn that they didn't even know whose killing they were investigating. It made them look inefficient.

'Sorry.' The pathologist looked abashed. She had enjoyed the gentle banter and more relaxed relationship she had established with Maxwell while Gawn had been on sick leave. But she was glad to have her friend back. She had missed their chats over a bottle of wine. Although she'd been back in Northern Ireland for some time and had lots of casual acquaintances, Jenny Norris had made few close friends and valued her friendship with the chief inspector, even though she realised Gawn was a woman with secrets and a past which she seldom discussed.

'OK. Our victim was dressed in his underpants. There are no external signs of sexual assault although I will take a closer look and I've sent the garment to forensics for testing for semen or any DNA traces. Apart from that there's nothing remarkable about them. M&S, like at least fifty percent of the male population,' she laughed. 'Probably yours too, Paul.'

The doctor couldn't resist the dig at the inspector's expense and enjoyed his embarrassed reaction but the look which passed across her friend's face as she glanced at DC Grant quickly pulled her back to business.

'I would estimate he's mid to late sixties. He has his own teeth so we'll do an X-ray and take a dental impression which might help with identification for you. The teeth are in good condition by the way. He's had work done relatively recently so he was probably registered with a dentist here. We've X-rayed the body already and as you can see' – she pointed to an X-ray illuminated on a screen in the corner – 'he's sustained an injury to his leg at some time. He has pins and a rod in the leg and a plate in his ankle. We should be able to use the identifiers on them to trace who he is and get you a name. I'll get onto that once I've opened him up and retrieved the metalwork.'

Grant was standing by a table in the corner taking notes. He would observe the whole PM and report back but Gawn had wanted to be there for the start to see if Norris was able to turn up anything useful straightaway and specially if she could give them a definitive time and cause of death.

The pathologist's voice with its faint American accent began again, 'I would say he's been a reasonably healthy man, certainly well-nourished. No signs of neglect or malnutrition. A bit overweight for his height, but not obese. There are obviously lots of indications of external injuries, one or two of which would undoubtedly have caused some minor internal damage but I don't think enough to cause death. Maybe I'll be proved wrong when I get him open. Most of the cuts are reasonably superficial and I would surmise whoever did this started off very tentatively. See,' – she moved aside and the two detectives moved a little closer to see where she was indicating – 'these cuts barely mark the skin at all.'

'I see what you mean,' Gawn said.

'Our victim has a nasal fracture caused by a blow. There's extensive bruising to the face. The fact that there's little in the way of defensive injuries to the hands and arms suggests he was incapacitated in some way. Possibly drugged or drunk. The contents of his stomach should tell us and of course I'll run tox screens. He was certainly tied up at some point.' She held up one pale lifeless arm to show marks of some kind of restraint on the wrist.

'Any idea what caused the cuts?' Gawn asked.

'My best guess at the minute? A box cutter or Stanley knife. Help me turn him, Ken.' The doctor addressed her assistant. 'That's weird.'

The two police officers took a step nearer the body again to see what had surprised her. The man's back had a series of thick red numbers across it.

'Is that blood?' Maxwell asked.

'I don't think so. Blood would have washed off in the river. It looks more like paint or maybe a thick permanent marker. I'll test it of course. But what do you think it means? And the figure with a smiley face below the numbers is a bit freaky too. What do you think it's meant to be?'

Maxwell took a step closer still. 'It's a bit like an angel, I think.'

'Must be the angel of death then,' Dr Norris joked.

'Don't even whisper that. The press is already pushing this as some sort of ritualistic satanic killing. If they hear word of a freaky angel on his back that'll only add to their hysteria.'

Gawn looked and sounded serious. She took her phone from her pocket. She knew Grant would be photographing each piece of evidence and cataloguing it as the autopsy progressed but she wanted to get a picture of the victim's back now. The numbers 29, 3 and 11 were smudged but legible. She photographed the figure too. Was it meant to be an angel? She wasn't sure.

'Any idea what the numbers mean, Chief Inspector?' Norris asked.

'Not enough digits for a phone number. Maybe a bank card pin?'

'Are they not usually four digits?' asked Maxwell.

'Yes. I think you're right. Maybe it's some other kind of passcode. Everything these days seems to need one,' Gawn replied.

'Well, I'll leave it up to you two to sort your puzzle out while I have a look inside our friend here.' Norris took a scalpel from the tray beside her and deftly began a Y-incision starting on the shoulder from below the victim's right ear.

'Thank you, doctor. It would be good to get the report–'

'As soon as possible. I know.' Norris finished her friend's sentence, nodded and then smiled. 'Welcome back, Chief Inspector!'

Chapter 17

The team was all gathered. The room was crowded and stuffy. There was a hubbub of chatter until the door of Maxwell's office opened and Gawn, followed by the inspector, walked over to stand in front of the murder board. A serious-looking DCI glanced round at the predominantly empty board behind her. She saw someone had written up the sequence of numbers found on the victim's back. Probably Grant, she thought. And a blown-up photo of the drawing of the figure found on the victim's back took central position on the board now alongside a picture of his corpse.

'Both the numbers and that drawing mean something special to our killer. They must hold some significance for him, or her, I suppose I should say. It was important enough to them to take the time to leave that message.' She tapped the board. 'We need to find out what the numbers mean. Any brain waves?' she asked of no one in particular.

'Pin number, ma'am, maybe for online banking or something?' suggested Dee.

'Double check with the banks. And see if they use five-digit pin numbers for their safety deposit boxes, Jack.'

'Part of a phone number?' came a voice from the back of the room.

'Could be. Not the first half because there's no area code that begins with a 29 but it could maybe be the second half of a number,' Maxwell suggested.

'Is 29 not the country code for Austria?' a voice queried.

'No. That's 43,' McKeown responded. Neither Gawn nor Maxwell had said anything, just exchanged a look. They both hoped this had nothing to do with Austria or any other European country. They'd had enough of dealing with Europeans causing death and havoc on their patch.

'But why would someone want to write part of a phone number on a dead man's back?' Grant asked.

'Good question.'

'Unless they'd written the rest of it on a body we haven't found yet,' came Logan's raspy voice. Gawn knew – for Maxwell had informed her – that he had split from his latest lady friend and had taken up smoking again. Hence the cough and husky voice and the pessimistic outlook on life. She was sorry to hear the news for the woman had been a good influence on the veteran policeman.

'Don't even joke about that, Billy. Let's keep the body count to one in this case. If someone is out there picking people off to send some kind of crazy message, let's get them quickly before anyone else turns up dead. Anyway, I don't think it is a phone number. Look at the way the numbers are divided off with a space between the first two and the third and another space before the last two.'

'Could it be a date?' Maxwell suggested. He had been thinking about it. 'Could 29 March 2011 mean something to the killer or even be significant for the victim? Did something special happen on that day?'

'It could have. But what? Until we have a suspect we can't even begin to think of events from that date. The date his girlfriend dumped him?' Gawn hazarded a facetious suggestion.

'The day he got married,' chirped up Dee. Gawn noticed a look pass between him and Hill and wondered if there was anything going on between them even though Hill was married.

'How about the day his first child was born?' It was Maxwell who had suggested this. He was a real family man and that would certainly be an important date in his mind. Just as the date her daughter, Max, had been born was to her.

Gawn decided to bring an end to the speculation and random guessing. It wasn't getting them anywhere. But before she had a chance to speak, Erin McKeown asked, 'What about the angel, ma'am?'

'If that's what it is. But whatever it is, it must mean something to our killer. Maybe he sees himself as some kind of angel of mercy or retribution or–' Gawn began but Maxwell interrupted her.

'Dr Norris seemed to suggest the cuts on the body may not have been the cause of death.'

'So, what do you think, Inspector?'

'Just that whoever drew the numbers and the figure may not have intended to kill our victim. It might not be the start of some freaky killing spree. There might have been something else behind it.'

'Well, let's hope they didn't intend to kill – best-case scenario – but let's not take it for granted.' She wanted to instil some sense of urgency into the team but before she could continue, her mobile phone vibrated in her pocket. A glance at the screen showed her the call was from Jenny Norris. Hopeful of some news to help them, Gawn walked back into Maxwell's office and left him talking to the rest of the team.

'Jenny.'

'Gawn. I have news I thought you'd want to hear right away.'

'Yes?'

'We've identified your victim and his cause of death. Which do you want first?'

Thinking of what Maxwell had just been suggesting, Gawn said, 'Cause of death, please.'

'Heart attack.' Gawn let out a loud sigh. That was how her case had started when a Dutch businessman had been found dead on a plane at Belfast City Airport and it had ended tragically for her team. 'He didn't drown. There was no water in his lungs. He was dead before he ever reached the river but, like I thought, and said to you, none of his slash injuries were sufficiently deep or severe enough to do serious internal damage. He wasn't going to bleed to death. None of his major organs were damaged. He had a massive heart attack. I could speculate and say it was because of what was happening to him – he was scared to death but that's not a medical opinion, of course. I suppose a good barrister would argue murder was not the intent.'

'No *mens rea*. Yes, I get it. How about some useful news? Who is he? You said you'd identified him.'

'Yes. His name is Marcus Roberts. We got the name from the hospital records linked to the metal plate in his ankle. He was operated on in Manchester Royal Infirmary.'

'Manchester.' Gawn was surprised. 'I wonder what he was doing here if he's from Manchester?' she thought aloud, wondering if he had been a tourist and how that would send the press and her bosses into a tizzy fearing pressure from the local hospitality sector.

'The operation was done over ten years ago so he could have been living anywhere. That's down to you. I've done my bit.'

'What about his stomach contents? Does that give us anything?'

'He'd been drinking heavily. Whisky and Guinness.' She half laughed. 'Not much in the way of food. His last meal was an Ulster fry of sorts – sausage, egg, some bread. Not gourmet stuff.'

'So, he had his breakfast at home and then what happened to him? I don't expect you to answer that. That's our job to find out,' she added hastily.

'He would have been pretty incapable with all that booze in his system, easy to subdue. I don't have the tox screen results yet but I did a very careful check and there were no syringe marks on his body so if he had drugs in him they would have been taken orally.'

'Thanks again, Jenny.'

'I'm still waiting for that drink and catch-up.'

'Soon. I promise. I'll be in touch.'

At last, some progress. They knew their victim's name but nothing else about him. She strode purposefully back out into the general office.

'Right. Progress at last. Dr Norris has got a name for us and a cause of death. Our victim is Marcus Roberts. Roberts is quite a common name but Marcus, less so, and we know he had some connection with Manchester. Let's find out where he lived, where he worked, any family we might need to notify. Seeing the way he ended up, he may well have had some dealings with the police even though his prints didn't show up in our system. Maybe the guys in Manchester know him. Check that first. Erin, can you sort out who does what, please?'

'On it, ma'am.'

'Paul, I want to have a word with Donna Nixon.' She started walking away from him. He followed but waited until they were out in the corridor before speaking.

'Do you think that's wise?'

Her stare showed him she wasn't pleased about being challenged but then her look softened.

'You obviously don't.' She needed to give him his place. This time last week, he would have been taking the lead, making the decisions, giving the orders. She didn't want to trample all over him.

'It's just you know what journalists are like, Gawn. They twist everything. She's already made us look stupid once. I don't think she really knows anything but if we go to her that will encourage her to stick her nose in even more and she's already got her angle – black magic.'

'It's a calculated risk to talk to her. Our witnesses may have said something more to her than they did to us. She's related to one of the girls and she got to question them much closer to the time of them finding the body.'

For one second, Maxwell thought she was going to mention that he'd let that happen and was the reason the journalist had got talking to their witnesses before they could, but she didn't.

'Maybe they told her something they forgot to tell us. She's a clever journalist. She'll not have missed anything important,' Gawn added.

'I know sometimes people don't want to talk to us but the girls didn't seem like that. It's just easier for journalists to get their facts. People like to get their names in the paper.'

'Donna Nixon and her sort don't need facts, Paul. Speculation's good enough for them. I want to give her enough to stop her developing this black magic angle and starting some kind of media witch hunt or public hysteria.'

She didn't tell him she had something she needed to find out from the journalist. She had made up her mind. He realised. He hoped the decision wouldn't rebound on her.

Chapter 18

Gawn knew she couldn't just arrive at the newspaper offices and demand to speak to Donna Nixon. Anyway, if she was any sort of investigative reporter – which she was – she wouldn't be spending her time sitting behind a desk. She'd be out and about nosing into whatever she had on her radar and Gawn was sure that would be their victim. She would have to approach the woman carefully; be more subtle in her dealings. She phoned and invited the journalist to meet her for a quick lunchtime drink on the recently-opened roof terrace at a new Belfast hotel. She gave nothing away but knew that just suggesting having a drink together would be enough to get the woman hooked. Her curiosity would be piqued. And she was right. Donna took the bait.

Gawn parked in a multistorey car park near the Anglican Church whose building reflected something of Belfast's own mottled and turbulent past. The grey nineteenth-century version standing here now offered a more inclusive Christianity and Gawn had even attended an Irish-language carol service in the building. She glanced across at Belfast's own leaning tower, the Albert Clock, and checked she was in good time.

She arrived before the journalist. That had always been her intention. She had said 1pm but made sure to be there by 12.45. She selected a table with a stunning view over the rooftops of the surrounding buildings across to the SSE Arena. The sophisticated ambience was a little spoiled by the noise of vehicles moving along Victoria Street down below her, wending their way towards the motorways, and by just the faintest whiff of car fumes. But selecting this seat was not just for the scenery. It gave her a commanding view of everything and everyone in the bar. Being early also gave her the opportunity to speak to a waiter and order some apple juice in a wine glass so she could pass it off as wine. She didn't want Donna Nixon getting any ideas about her. She could imagine the woman might surmise she had some sort of drink problem if she ordered apple juice. She didn't want to end up as a target for Nixon's investigations.

Just two minutes after one, the journalist arrived. Gawn was impressed. She had been prepared to be kept waiting. Donna Nixon was wearing a practical puffy full-length waterproof coat over a classic, simple plain navy-blue dress. Her shoes, Gawn noticed – she always did – were stylish and the heels, she judged, were at least three inches. It was a slightly incongruous pairing but no doubt she could be called to breaking news anywhere, in any kind of weather conditions and she had to be prepared to look business-like no matter where she was sent, be it to interview a local government minister outside Stormont or a farmer in a field in Broughshane. Gawn wondered if she kept a pair of wellington boots in her car for such occasions. She knew she did.

The woman looked around, taking a moment to identify the policewoman. Then she walked over. She was not smiling, Gawn noticed. No doubt she didn't want to encourage the idea that this was a social meeting. This was business. For both of them.

'Chief Inspector.'

'Ms Nixon. Thank you for accepting my invitation. What can I get you? I'm on the wine but I only ordered a glass, not a bottle. I'm driving,' Gawn explained and smiled, trying to be suitably but not overly friendly.

'Wine's fine for me too. Red, please.' The woman slipped off her coat to reveal a white blazer underneath.

The waiter approached them and took the order.

'You'll be wondering why I asked you to meet me.'

'I assumed you wanted something from me.' A bold statement, its tone verging on aggressive. Donna didn't take her eyes off Gawn's face. She waited for a reaction.

'I thought we might be able to help each other.' Gawn took a sip of her apple juice. It was so sweet she had trouble not pulling a face.

'And how do you think I might be able to help you, Chief Inspector?'

Now Gawn needed to be careful. If she straight out suggested Donna tone down her idea that there was a black magic element to the killing, she ran the risk of the woman twisting her words and making it seem like the police were trying to cover up some satanic connection. Donna Nixon wrote for a local newspaper as well as freelancing for the radio station. The sensational sells and gets you noticed. The British papers would want a share of a story like that. It could be important for the woman's career.

'I was hoping you would share anything which your cousin and her friends told you about finding the body.'

'Surely you've questioned them!'

'Yes, of course we have.' Gawn tried to keep any tetchiness out of her voice. 'But you had the chance to talk to them when it was all much fresher in their minds. They didn't go near the body or touch anything so I just wondered how much they had actually seen.'

'They saw the blood and the cuts on the man's body. That was more than enough. They were freaking out when I spoke to them.'

'When exactly was that?'

'I drove my aunt to the hospital and spoke to Susie in A&E.'

While the PC was standing outside. Gawn could feel her blood pressure rising. Maxwell should have made sure someone more senior, or at least more experienced, had gone with them. No one should have been able to question them before him. It was a rookie mistake and she wasn't thinking of the young PC.

'When you say "freaking out" what exactly do you mean?'

'They'd been watching some horror slasher movie on Sunday night and they had convinced themselves it was something like that. You know what young people are like.' She said it as if she were much older and experienced when Gawn knew that the journalist was only twenty-four and had only been in her part-time radio reporting job for a few months. Not exactly the older experienced woman of the world she was trying to portray. She was no cynical Fleet Street hack like some of those Gawn had come across in her days at the Met.

'So that's where you got the idea of a black magic connection.'

Gawn noticed an expression cross the journalist's face.

'That wasn't me. Susie came up with it all by herself. Is the murder connected to black magic? Have we got a ritual killing with some madman on the loose?' Her voice couldn't conceal her excitement at the prospect. Gawn knew the woman was seeing headlines floating before her eyes and maybe a job on TV.

'No. We do not. Certainly not. Nothing like that.' Gawn was aware she was being a little too definite and worried her words would have the opposite effect to her intention.

'Really? If it's not that, then what is it?'

'We're in the very early stages of our investigation.'

'You mean you haven't made any progress yet.'

'Forensics is a slow business. It takes time.'

Gawn thought to herself that they didn't even know where the attack had taken place yet so Forensics couldn't even get started. Only very limited trace evidence of any kind was likely to have survived at the scene by the river, if any, she was sure.

'So how do you think I could help and, more importantly, what's in it for me?' Nixon finished with a cynical laugh.

Before Gawn could say anything, the waiter approached obviously keen for them to order some more drinks. Gawn smiled and held up her palm to him.

'Thank you. We're fine.'

She didn't want to prolong the meeting and she was eager to see if she could enlist the journalist's help.

'You'll be following up on this case anyway. Sometimes people will talk to you when they won't talk to us. We could exchange information.'

'You'd be prepared to pass information to me?' Nixon sounded incredulous. She'd had a few titbits thrown to her by cops – usually, no, invariably, men – and she knew enough about this policewoman's reputation to be totally surprised at her suggestion. She was known as someone who avoided the press and here she was offering to feed her information. Nixon was suspicious but she was prepared to play along, at least for now.

'I'd be prepared to give you first access to information we would be making public anyway. Give you a head start on your colleagues.'

Gawn could tell the woman was calculating whether she could trust her or not and whether it would be worth her while to agree to the arrangement. She filled the waiting time until the journalist came to a decision by taking another sip of the sickly apple juice. She didn't want to appear too eager.

Eventually Donna Nixon spoke.

'So, I'd let you know if I heard anything to help your investigation and you'd give me a heads up if there was a break in the case or you were going to make an arrest?'

Gawn had never made such an arrangement with any journalist before. But then she'd never had a case where there was the potential for widespread hysteria if people started believing there were Satanists roaming the streets selecting victims at random. She wouldn't have admitted it to anyone else, not even Maxwell, but she secretly wondered if there could be a ritualistic element to the death; if they really did have some maniac who thought he had a direct line to the devil telling him to slaughter random victims.

'Yes.'

'And what can you give me now?'

'We believe the killing was an accident.' She went on quickly as she saw a look of disbelief pass across the woman's face. 'I mean we don't think the man was meant to die. That wasn't the intention. The wounds the girls saw weren't the cause of death. He had a heart attack.'

'A heart attack? But doesn't that suggest that he was involved in some sort of ritual or something then? Something went wrong. Wouldn't that explain it?'

'We haven't established exactly why he was attacked but we don't believe there was any ritualistic element and we're following other lines of enquiry.' Gawn knew she was pushing the truth but she needed to convince the other woman. 'It would be scaremongering to suggest that black magic or anything like that was involved.'

She realised from Donna Nixon's comments that she knew nothing about the numbers and drawing on the man's back. If she had, Gawn was sure there was no way she would have held it back. It was just too sensational a detail and would have supported her claims of rituals and black magic. The girls had obviously been telling the truth that they hadn't touched the body. Thank God for small mercies then. If this meeting did nothing else, at least it had confirmed for her what the journalist didn't know and Gawn was determined to keep it that way.

'So, you want me to play that link down?'

'You have no link. No facts to support any link. We certainly have none.'

'I need something else instead then, that I can use in my next report.'

'I can give you the victim's name. We'll be issuing a statement at four but if I give it to you now you'll make the earlier news.'

She saw the light in the journalist's eyes and knew she had her.

Chapter 19

Veronica Fisher had spent a sleepless night. She had cancelled a hot date with a rich businessman who had been wining and dining her for weeks and who had been expecting to seal the deal with her last night. He had not been best pleased to be stood up at short notice but she didn't care. It was coming up to the anniversary next week. Every year she remembered although she tried not to. Now, it was obvious, someone else remembered too. Someone had sent the doll. It was meant for her, not just a chance donation to the shop. She couldn't have gone out on the town as if nothing had happened. She needed to think. Or not think. If she allowed herself to think too much, she started to shake.

After three gins, although it was still early, as she sat in an armchair in her modest two-bedroom terraced house on the outskirts of South Belfast, she began to convince herself she had just overreacted. The doll was just a fluke. It didn't mean anything and the note – she suddenly remembered the note – she had glanced at it briefly and then pushed it out of sight into her pocket so Rose wouldn't see it. She walked into the bedroom where she had flung her coat carelessly onto a chair when she had finally made it home. She lifted it and put her hand into the left pocket. Nothing. Then the right. Nothing. She went back to the left pocket again and pushed her hand down hard into the silk lining feeling for a tear where the note might have slid through. Nothing. Then the right pocket. There was a tear. The note must have fallen out. But where? In the street? In the shop? Would Rose find it?

She tried to convince herself it would mean nothing to the other woman.

She hadn't seen Rose today. She wasn't due into the shop again until tomorrow and Veronica hadn't gone near the charity shop today. She couldn't face it. She would wait and see if Rose mentioned anything to her about finding a note. If she didn't, then Veronica determined she wouldn't say anything about it. With luck it would have been brushed up at the end of the day and put into the bin and no one would ever see it again.

She had made herself a sandwich and was sitting down to listen to the local news on the radio. The first feature was about a mutilated body which had been found in the Lagan the previous day. This was the first Veronica had heard of it. She had been too zonked out last night to worry about the news. The victim had now been identified and the reporter was explaining that his name was Marcus Roberts. Veronica froze, the sandwich halfway to her mouth, and made no attempt to stop it when the plate, holding the other half of the bread and cheese and tomato, slid gracefully off her knee and smashed onto the tiled floor.

Chapter 20

Dan Anderson was driving home from another catastrophe of a rehearsal with the school band. How he hated it all. Everything that could go wrong, had gone wrong. This is not how he thought his life would turn out and he knew who was to blame. They only had one more week left before everything had to be perfect and it was all far from that now. Last night's rehearsal had been the worst ever and his audition for a residency in a local hotel restaurant afterwards hadn't gone well either. He didn't expect to ever hear from them again.

He hadn't gone straight home afterwards. He couldn't face Eva and having to explain to her, make excuses, tell lies. She had been asleep whenever he had slipped into bed beside her and he had made sure not to wake her. This morning he had told her he had an early staff meeting and would get breakfast in the school canteen, then left before she had time to ask him any questions. He had then spent an hour sitting over a cup of coffee in a local café. Just thinking.

Now he was sure she would be waiting for him. He shouldn't have reacted like that when the letter arrived yesterday. It was just that it brought it all back and he hadn't allowed himself to think about it for so long. Next week would be the anniversary. Fifteen years. A lot had happened in that time. He had thought it was all in the past. Now someone wanted to dig it all up. No one could possibly gain from raking up what had happened.

The car radio had been playing softly in the background but now he turned up the volume as the jingle for the news headlines came on. He hadn't heard the news since the weekend. The main headline was about a body found in the Lagan. The newsreader said the victim had been identified as a Marcus Roberts. Dan swerved violently, nearly taking to the footpath to avoid an oncoming truck. He had veered over onto the wrong side of the road in his shock at hearing Roberts' name. The truck driver had blared his horn and Dan could see his mouth moving, no doubt producing a few expletives aimed at him. As soon as he could he pulled onto the side of the road. A wave of nausea swept over him. He looked down at his hands on the steering wheel. They were shaking. It wasn't just because of his near miss, he knew.

Chapter 21

Dave Osmond was sitting, glass of malt in one hand and his arm around a pretty blonde, probably half his age, in the dimly lit bar of a Belfast hotel. She was guzzling another cocktail at seventeen pounds a time, he thought ruefully to himself. He wished she would slow down. He didn't want her to be paralytic when he propositioned her. That would spoil the fun. The hotel was a good place to pull, even during the week, always full of pretty young things wanting to be seen out on the town, hoping to meet a handsome new boyfriend or maybe a new sugar daddy. He made a face as he realised he would be falling into that category all too soon. He hoped she was going to be worth it later.

The girl finished the dregs of her drink and leaned in closer to whisper coyly in his ear, allowing her tongue to brush suggestively against his earlobe. He placed his hand on her thigh as she leant across him. Her heavy perfume almost made him cough. 'I'm going to visit the little girls' room. You could order me another drinkee while I'm away.' She smiled and pouted, her eyes making all kinds of promises.

'Same again?'

'Yes, please.' She giggled. Another one of these and he'd be onto a sure thing. Not that that was a problem. Most weekends he had his choice. He was *the* Dave Osmond after all. Girls wanted to be around him to have some of his local fame rub off on them, to get him to introduce them to his friends who could maybe get them recording contracts or modelling jobs.

Osmond stood up to make his way to the bar when his phone rang in his pocket. He took it out and looked at the screen but didn't immediately recognise the number calling. He didn't give out his number, too many loonies out there who would phone you at all times of the day or night and he didn't think Kirsty would have given his number to anyone. She knew to screen his calls. He had her well-trained, he thought, in all sorts of ways. And smiled to himself. If blondie didn't come through, he could always head over to Kirsty's.

'Hello?' He didn't say anything else, didn't identify himself.

'Dave?' It was a woman's voice.

He recognised it and yet he didn't. He knew he'd heard the voice before but he couldn't place where or when. Was it some girl he'd given his number to after a drunken one-night stand? That would have been careless of him.

'Dave. It's Veronica. Veronica Fisher.' She sounded breathless, as if she'd been running. He thought that was unlikely. The last time he had seen her, maybe three years ago, she'd been perched on a high stool propping up the bar at a launch party for some new local fashion magazine. He couldn't picture her as a runner.

'Ronny, how are you? Lovely to hear from you.' He tried to inject some warmth into his voice. What the hell did she want? Why had she turned up in his life now? They'd got together a few times when they were younger, just a bit of fun, nothing serious. They were just out of their teens. He liked his women a bit younger now. She was the same age as him.

'Have you heard the news tonight?' Her voice was breathy. Not her trying to sound sexy, he was sure. She sounded scared. Immediately he realised what it must be about. He thought of the phone call he'd received yesterday morning, the man's distorted robotic voice, his meagre words. He'd really only needed to say one word and then give his instructions.

'No. What's happened?'

'The body in the river, the one they found yesterday morning in the Lagan, it was Marcus Roberts. The police have just named him.'

'Roberts? Old Creepy Roberts?'

He hadn't heard anything about a body found in the river. After his round of golf with Jonah Lunn he'd been busy the rest of the day on calls with his agent and preparing for his show. He'd gone to bed at 8pm ready for his 4am alarm call to get to the studio. During the week he seldom stayed out late knowing lack of sleep would take its toll on his famous chirpy persona. He could hide it if he was looking a bit rough, hadn't shaved, had bags under his eyes but if he was off form it sounded in his voice and his listeners knew. He usually saved his socialising for the weekends. Tonight was an exception. He'd wanted a distraction after yesterday's phone call; not to be sitting at home by himself mulling it all over.

'Topped himself, did he, the stupid old bugger?'

Even as he responded he recognised the ugliness of his words and wasn't surprised to hear Veronica's sharp intake of breath.

'No. He was murdered, they think. The girl on the radio said that yesterday a witness had said it was some kind of satanic ritual or something. But now they think it isn't. But he'd been tortured, Dave.' She said it as if she expected Dave Osmond to realise its significance.

'My God. Poor old guy. I wonder what he'd got himself mixed up in. He always was a bit of a weirdo, wasn't he?'

'Dave, I got a note.' He knew what she was going to say before she said another word. 'It was from someone who knows about Hopewell.'

He took a moment to speak. Should he tell her about his telephone call or play it cool? By the sound of her voice she was already freaking out. Better not give her anything more to worry about.

'What do you mean? They know. They know what? And who are *they*?'

'Well, they must know about us.'

'Did it say that?'

'No. All I saw was Hopewell before I had to hide it in my pocket. Now I've just got a call from a weird voice telling me to meet at the old den. Dave, I'm scared.'

That's what he'd been told as well. What the hell was somebody playing at? Were they trying to pick them off one by one? And do what to them? Torture them too?

'It's probably Danny wanting to have a reunion with you. He knows you're way out of his class, Ronny. You'd never agree to meet up with him.' Last time he had heard Danny was settled down, married with a mortgage and a boring teaching job. Osmond tried to laugh off Veronica's concerns. 'He probably realises you wouldn't be interested in meeting up with him to talk over old times. I'm sure you've better things to do with your time than play "remember the good old days" with him. I know I have.'

'Do you really think that's what it is?'

'What else could it be, Ronny? Nobody else knows what happened, what we did. Anybody who knew anything about it is long dead.' It must be either Danny or Kevin but the last time he had heard Kevin was in the States and had been involved in another failed business which had sailed very close to the wind. Word had it he had had to leave Miami or New Orleans or some place with the cops or the FBI not too far off his tail according to gossip anyway. So that meant it must be Danny.

'Look, I'll get in touch with Danny and see what he has to say for himself. If it's his idea of a joke, I'll let him know you didn't think it was very funny. You just chill, princess.' No one had called her that since… well, since then.

'But he wouldn't have sent the doll?'

'What doll?'

'There was a doll with the note. It had red all over its arms like, like…' She couldn't finish the sentence.

'Hi there. I'm back.' The girl looked disappointed that Dave hadn't managed to get her another drink yet.

'Where's my drinkee?' she whined.

'Never mind your fuckin' drink.' He pushed her aside and walked quickly across to the door still talking into his phone.

Chapter 22

'At bloody last.' Maxwell's reaction to the news that they had finally managed to trace where Roberts had lived took the words out of Gawn's mouth. It wasn't that the case was stalling. It had never got going at all.

'Get a forensics team over there. See if Mark can go himself.' Gawn regarded Mark Ferguson as the best crime scene manager she had ever worked with. 'What more have we found out about our victim?'

It was Sergeant McKeown who replied. 'He was sixty-two, ma'am. Retired. Never married. No close family that we've been able to trace. We know his parents are both dead and an older brother too. He seemed to be living off a pension he got after being injured in a factory accident in Manchester and recently he was just doing odds and ends, some general handyman work at a couple of clubs and pubs around the Golden Mile area. He seems to have spent quite a bit of time during the day around the church down the road helping out. One of his neighbours said he was a quiet wee man. Just nodded and passed the time of day.'

'And definitely no criminal record?' Maxwell asked.

'No.'

'Then I think I'll take a wee trip to church.' Gawn nodded to the inspector.

'Bit of divine help, ma'am?' Logan suggested with a smirk.

'I wouldn't say no to help from any quarter at the minute, Billy, but I think if Roberts spent his free time at the church, the priest there may be able to give us some idea of what he could have been involved in that would have got him killed. At the very least, if he knew the man well, he should be able to identify the body for us as there don't seem to be any close family members to do it and we can get that formality out of the way.'

* * *

It was only a fifteen-minute drive into the city centre. Gawn knew there would be nowhere to park around City Hall. Double yellow lines and the ubiquitous bus lanes had seen to that. So she was delighted when she arrived at the front of the church and found it had its own car park and the gate was open so she was able to drive in, ignoring the 'Private Parking Only' sign and stopping almost at the front door. One side of the heavy studded wooden doors was open and as she walked up the steps a little woman bustled out.

'Good morning. I haven't seen you here before. Can I help you at all?' She offered her friendly greeting and a smile.

'Good morning. I wonder, is the priest inside at the minute?'

'Father Stephen is just finishing off in the office. He'll be glad of the interruption. He hates working on the parish accounts.'

'Thank you.' She nodded and walked past the woman into the church.

She was immediately struck by the brightness and the peacefulness of the interior of the building, a tangible sense of enveloping warmth that was not just the result of good central heating. There was an almost overwhelming calmness and tranquillity which seemed to draw her in.

Light was streaming through the stained-glass windows and bouncing off the white walls and the wide steps leading up to a white marble altar. It was almost dazzling. Her eyes were drawn to a magnificent painting hanging above the altar and then to the fan vaulted ceiling, like an inverted iced cake hanging over her head. All the noise of the busy city just metres beyond these walls was closed out. Here there was only silence. The noise of a door closing drew her attention away from the beauty all around and she saw a tall man entering from a side door. She saw his clerical collar and realised this must be the priest. He was younger than she had anticipated.

'Excuse me. I'm DCI Gawn Girvin. Could you spare a few minutes to answer some questions, Father?' She held up her ID but the man barely glanced at it. Instead there was a wariness in his look as he scanned her face.

'What can I do for you, Chief Inspector?'

'I believe you have a parishioner, Marcus Roberts, who volunteers around the church.'

'Marcus? Yes. What's he done or maybe I should ask what do you *think* he's done?'

Gawn was taken aback by the priest's slightly hostile attitude.

'I take it you haven't heard the news?'

'I'm usually too busy during the day to be watching TV or listening to the radio. Why? What was on the news?'

'I'm sorry to have to tell you but Mr Roberts is dead. His body was found in the Lagan near Ormeau bridge on Monday morning.'

Father Stephen reached out a hand to the back of a nearby pew to steady himself. 'Give him eternal rest, O Lord, and may your light shine on him forever. In the name of the Father, Son and Holy Spirit, amen.' And he made the sign of the cross. Gawn merely watched. She wondered if she should have joined in the amen but decided against it.

'You obviously knew him.'

Father Stephen had been visibly upset by the news. Gawn was surprised. He was a priest. He must meet with death on a regular basis and Roberts hadn't been a young man so she guessed it was the suddenness of the death that was particularly upsetting to him, unless he knew something about the man, something that Roberts had told him perhaps. Gawn hoped she wasn't going to come up against the seal of the confessional. That had happened to her once in London when, because they couldn't get information they needed from a priest, a young woman had been seriously injured. They'd managed to get there in time to save her life but not soon enough to prevent an attack. Gawn was not a fan of anything that protected the guilty.

'Yes. He was here most days. In fact I was wondering this morning where he was. I expected him here today. He was supposed to help set up for a meeting later this afternoon.' He seemed to consider where they were and then spoke again. 'Would you like to come through to the parochial house? It's just next door. We could talk there without being disturbed.' Gawn had been aware, as the priest must have been too, that two elderly women had entered the church behind them. One had seated herself near the back but the other was close to them praying in front of a statue to the side of the altar.

'Yes. Thank you.'

Father Stephen led the way out of the church, across the car park past her car and into a solid red-brick detached house within the precincts of the church grounds and guarded by the same high railings. She thought it seemed like a very big house for just one man. And it would be on prime building land, right in the centre of the city. Any developer would be eager to cram an apartment block into the space.

The priest didn't offer any conversation as he strode along and that gave her time to study him in profile. He was young. Just as she had heard it said that policemen seemed to be getting younger as you got older, so she was finding more and more people seemed to be getting younger-looking. She estimated he was in his early thirties. His fair hair was cut neatly just sitting on the top of his jacket collar. He was wearing a pair of sombre black trousers but he had on a bright mustard-coloured cardigan which brightened his more formal black shirt and suited his olive complexion. He led her into a cosy sitting room replete with family photographs, a guitar sitting propped against the wall in the corner of the room and lots of books. The books made her immediately think of Seb.

'Have a seat, Chief Inspector.' She sat down on a comfortable armchair to one side of an unlit fireplace and he took a seat on the sofa against the wall opposite. Before she had a chance to ask anything, he looked straight at her and spoke. 'Chief Inspector, I must apologise for my behaviour earlier. I was less than gracious in my response to you.'

'I'm used to much worse than someone being ungracious, sir.'

'I'm sure you are.' A thin smile formed on his lips. He appeared embarrassed by how he had reacted. 'But even so, I shouldn't have taken the attitude I did. It's just that some of my people have been having their difficulties with the police. We have young folks being stopped and harassed at every turn just because they're young and for where they live, and older folk in the parish who aren't getting support from the anti-social behaviour in the area, the drug addicts who hang around. They feel threatened and the police don't seem to be doing anything about it.'

'So, we're damned if we do and damned if we don't.'

'A difficult situation, I appreciate. But still. I shouldn't have been so sharp with you. It probably didn't help that you caught me when I'd just spent an hour struggling with the parish accounts – my least favourite duty. I did not enter the priesthood to be an accountant.' His smile widened and she found herself thinking how it lit up his face. 'Now, Marcus. How can I help? I knew he was troubled but I didn't expect him to take his own life.'

So that was why the priest had been so shocked at her news. He thought Roberts had committed suicide.

'Mr Roberts didn't take his own life. His body was placed in the river.'

'He was murdered?' It was clear the priest had not been expecting to hear that.

'A suspicious death which we're investigating.'

'I see.'

'What can you tell me about him, Father?'

'Not really that much. I've only been here six months. I'm just getting to know everybody. He turned up here about three months ago. He started attending mass regularly for a few weeks and then one day he offered to help around the church. Money's tight and I'm glad for any help I can get and it's always good to get people engaged in the parish, to create a sense of community where we can all help each other in the name of Christ.'

'Did he talk about his past? Did he say where he came from?'

'At first, he said very little about himself at all but gradually he did open up a bit and talked a little about his upbringing, here in Belfast and then about working in Manchester, I think it was. He had a limp where he'd been hurt at work. He didn't tell me exactly how but from bits and pieces of what he said I took it he was able to make a claim and have money to live on.'

That fitted well with the injuries and information Jenny Norris had found. 'He didn't have a job?'

'Not that I know of.'

'Did you know any of his friends?'

'No. I can't help you there I'm afraid. I never saw him with anyone in particular. Oh, except Rose.'

'Rose?'

'She's one of my most faithful parishioners, salt of the earth. She would help anybody. She took Marcus under her wing. She does that with people.'

'Could you give me Rose's name and address?' Gawn hoped Roberts had been more forthcoming with the woman.

'I'm surprised you didn't bump into her this morning. She was here just now doing a bit of tidying.' Gawn remembered the friendly little woman who had greeted her at the door.

'Rose O'Hare. She lives just round the corner. Number 22.'

'There's one other thing, Father. Would you be willing to identify the body for us? We haven't been able to find any family members, I'm afraid.'

'Of course. I'd welcome the opportunity to pray for him, offer the comfort of his faith. It's the least I can do. What about yourself, Chief Inspector? Are you a woman of faith?'

She was taken aback by the question. She hadn't been expecting it and took a moment to consider before answering. 'I believe in good and evil. I've seen them both. I know they exist. I'm not so sure about believing in your God.'

'That's a pity because He believes in you.' He said nothing more but stood up and extended his hand. Gawn took it and was impressed with his firm handshake.

'Thank you for your help. I'll get my sergeant to ring and arrange a time for you to identify the body.'

Gawn was halfway to the door when the priest spoke again.

'Oh, there is one thing.'

'Yes?'

'A man came here looking for Marcus.'

'When was this?'

'About two weeks ago. It was one of the days when I wasn't expecting him here to help and I told the stranger he'd have to come back the next day.'

'Did he ask for Roberts' address?'

'He did but I didn't give it to him. I couldn't give it to him. I never knew exactly where he lived, just that it was somewhere up towards Stranmillis. But I wouldn't have given it to him anyway.'

'Did he say why he was looking for him?'

'No. I'm afraid not.'

'And did he come back the next day?'

'I don't know. Marcus never mentioned it and I don't think I ever told him about it.'

'What did this man look like, Father?'

Father Stephen paused and looked upwards as he tried to remember.

'He was young.'

'When you say "young" what do you mean?' Gawn had been caught out by that before. She remembered once early in her career having a witness describe a mugger as young only to find when he was caught that he was a man of nearly fifty but to his victim, a woman in her early eighties, he'd been 'young'. She didn't think the priest would make that mistake but she wanted to try to get as accurate a description as possible.

'Maybe twenty, maybe twenty-five. Definitely not more.'

'And what did he look like?' She waited. This could be important. Someone looking for Roberts could suggest he was hiding out; that he had crossed someone somehow. And whoever it was may have caught up with him. He was definitely a person of interest.

'Maybe about 5'9" or 10". Under six feet anyway cos I'm that and he wasn't quite as tall as me. Dirty fair hair. Designer stubble. He was wearing glasses but I noticed he had vivid blue eyes, really unusual.'

'And he was from Northern Ireland?'

'No. He spoke with an English accent. Liverpool, I think.'

'Thank you again, Father. That's really helpful.'

So, they had someone to begin looking for. As Gawn made her way out to her car she looked around the street and saw security cameras on several of the nearby government buildings and on the church. When McKeown contacted the priest to arrange for him to identify the body, she could ask for the security footage too. Maybe they would be able to spot the mystery man looking for Roberts and get an identity for him.

Chapter 23

Gawn decided she might as well talk to Rose O'Hare while she was in the area. It would save another journey. Leaving her car where it was parked at the church, she walked along the busy street and rounded the corner. This was a part of Belfast she didn't know well. She could see that the area had been redeveloped because where she had expected the rows of Victorian back-to-back houses which would once have been home to the working classes of industrial Belfast, she now saw neat, modern red-brick terrace dwellings with railings to divide them from the roadway and provide somewhere for a few plants; in at least one case she could see a place for a pram to sit out allowing a baby to get some fresh air and sunshine.

Number 22 was the second house in the row. Its frontage was concreted over and a row of planters provided splashes of colour. The front door was lying open and Gawn could hear country and western music coming from inside as she opened the gate and walked up the short pathway. She knocked and waited. The same woman she had met outside the church came up the hall wiping her hands on a tea towel. A streak of flour on the front of her apron revealed she was in the middle of baking. As she came nearer, her eyes showed recognition.

'Oh, it's you. From the church.' The woman smiled.

'Yes, Mrs O'Hare. I'm DCI Girvin.' She held up her warrant card. 'I'd like to talk to you for a minute.'

Gawn didn't know what to expect. Thinking of what the priest had told her, she guessed she might be viewed with suspicion or even animosity.

'Me?' The smile had gone and the woman's eyebrows had risen until they disappeared under her fringe. She was shocked. 'What do the police want with me?'

'It's nothing to worry about. I just wanted to talk to you about Marcus Roberts. Father Stephen told me you were friendly with him.'

'Marcus? You'd better come in then.' Rose guided Gawn past her into the hallway and looked left and right out into the street before closing the door behind her. 'Is Marcus in some sort of trouble? I didn't see him this morning. He usually helps out on a Wednesday – for the bingo tonight.'

'Maybe you should sit down, Mrs O'Hare.' Obviously the woman hadn't heard the news either so she would have to break it to her that her friend was dead. But, she didn't have to. Rose knew right away as soon as Gawn had said about sitting down that it wasn't good news.

'He's dead, isn't he?' She took a handkerchief from her apron pocket and blew her nose noisily before she asked, 'Was it his heart or did the drink get him? I was always warning him about the drinking.'

'Was Mr Roberts a heavy drinker?'

'Not particularly but he did like his wee drink. He used to hang about with some of the men from the hostel up the road. I saw him a couple of times sitting with them in the garden at St George's.'

Gawn knew where she meant – a space beside the church in High Street which was set out with plants and garden seats where some of the homeless of Belfast spent their days and sometimes their nights too. They could be found clutching their brown-paper-bagged bottles of whatever alcoholic drink they could afford that day.

'When was the last time you saw Mr Roberts?'

'Some time last week. Thursday, I think.'

So he could have been held prisoner and tortured since Friday. Three days of terror. Gawn shivered involuntarily at the thought.

'Did Mr Roberts ever talk to you about himself?'

'He was quite a private man. I suppose you would say he was a loner. He didn't seem to have any family left or any friends. He mentioned his mother to me a few times. He'd been very close to her. She only died recently. She was in a nursing home with dementia and he'd moved back from England to be closer to her when she took a turn for the worse.'

He'd only returned recently, then. It might mean that whatever trouble he could have been in, whoever was looking for him was from England and it had nothing to do with Northern Ireland. That would make it more tricky. Gawn would have to check if they had got anything useful from their counterparts in Manchester. She thought of those numbers on his back. Could they be a date? Had something happened in 2011 when Roberts was living in Manchester? That would need to be checked too, she thought.

'Thank you, Mrs O'Hare.' The woman had given her plenty to think about.

Chapter 24

'So that's all I managed to find out. Not a lot.' Gawn let out a sigh.

She and Maxwell were in his office. She had told him of her visit to the church and the follow-up interview with Rose O'Hare. He had updated her on what the CSIs had found at Roberts' house so far.

'It's definitely the scene of the attack. Mark says there's blood and vomit all over the place.'

'I wonder if any of it belongs to our perp?'

'It's possible especially if he was a bit hesitant with the knife or whatever he used. He might have been nervous and sicked his guts up. Anyway I've got them doing house-to-house in Roberts' street and Erin and Jo are going over any CCTV footage we've managed to get from the area. There's quite a lot on the main Ormeau Road between banks and pubs. If he and his attacker met up in town and walked up the road, they should show up somewhere together. If they got a taxi or a bus, then we're snookered. And, if his attacker just arrived at his front door, we'll have to depend on witnesses and so far everyone we've talked to saw nothing and heard nothing, it seems – well, nothing they're telling us anyway.'

'Do we have any idea when he was last seen for sure? He could have been held for days, maybe since Thursday or Friday. We need to get a timeline.'

'Agreed.'

* * *

It was Jo Hill who first spotted Roberts. She had gone back to Saturday and begun trawling through footage.

There were no cameras close to the victim's house and there were several ways he could have chosen to leave it. She struck lucky. Eventually she had identified him leaving the embankment around 10am and heading into the city centre down the main Ormeau Road. He had walked, easily identified by his limp, and she followed his progress, picking him up on security cameras outside an office block and then on the council CCTV cameras near the Fire Station as he headed along Ormeau Avenue. The city centre had been busy. It was a Saturday after all. Erin McKeown had offered to help and between them they had spotted him again on Great Victoria Street talking to a girl sitting on a rug with her dog outside the Grand Opera House.

'There. See. He's met someone else he knows. A man.' Hill sounded excited. The new man had his back to the camera so they couldn't see his face but it was obvious from the way the two were interacting that they knew each other. They had walked off together towards the Crown and the women watched as they walked inside the famous bar.

Maxwell had moved in behind them unnoticed while they were watching.

'Do you have footage from inside the Crown?'

'Not at the minute, sir.'

'See if you can get it.'

She got it but it didn't help them much. The bar was busy. Its fame as a film location meant it was a tourist magnet. Every cruise ship tour included a drink at the Crown; local guidebooks extolled its virtues as a working example of a Victorian Gin Palace. They watched as Roberts made his way up to the bar and brought back a tray of drinks to the booth he was sharing with the stranger. The women watched as the two men sat drinking. From the timestamp they saw that they had spent at least two hours there and Roberts had been back and forth to the bar several times replenishing their drinks. By his last trip, he seemed slightly unsteady on his feet and as the two men left the bar the stranger had his arm linked through Roberts' helping him.

Chapter 25

Eva Anderson was frantic. Dan hadn't come home last night. He had been in a funny mood when he had got home on Tuesday night. Yesterday he'd left for school before she was even up. She'd meant to wait up to speak to him, to have it out with him whatever was troubling him, whatever had been in that letter he'd got, but she'd fallen asleep. When the alarm went off at 7am she rolled over and reached across only to feel the cold empty space on his side of the bed and knew immediately he'd never been home at all.

She couldn't decide what to do. Once or twice over the years he had gone on a bender. He didn't normally drink much at all. They liked to save their money and then have a holiday somewhere exotic and expensive like the Bahamas. That was where they were planning to go this year. But just sometimes, if he'd been playing at a nightclub or a private event and had got started drinking with some of his old musician buddies, he'd stayed out all night. Then he'd slink home the next day feeling sorry for himself with a hangover and a very contrite attitude. So, she'd waited.

Lunchtime came and went. She wondered if she should phone the school. If he had gone straight there he would be angry if she showed him up in front of his colleagues by ringing and checking up on him like some errant schoolboy. By teatime she could stick it no longer. She knew one of the other teachers in the Music Department and decided to phone her. With shaking hands she dialled the number.

'You have reached the voicemail of...' She shut the call off. She wasn't going to start leaving some message, trying to explain she didn't know where her fifty-year-old husband was. She couldn't think of anything else to do so when the clock reached 6pm and she hadn't seen Dan for over thirty-six hours, she grabbed her coat from the peg in the hall and her bag from the chair beside the front door and drove off to the nearest police station.

Chapter 26

They had already found Anderson's car earlier in the day in the car park at Shaw's Bridge on the outskirts of South Belfast by the time his wife was reporting him missing. Police from Lisburn Road Station had identified the registered owner and were about to call at the Anderson home. At almost the same time, Eva Anderson was standing in front of the desk sergeant at Holywood Police Station on the verge of tears. The sergeant who had taken her missing person's report had told her that her husband would turn up. That is what he had assured her anyway, although secretly he thought the woman was a bit neurotic, overreacting after her husband had only been missing a little over a day. They'd probably had a row and he'd stomped off in a fury or something, although she'd sworn nothing like that had happened.

Shaw's Bridge, where his car had been found, was a popular spot for dog walkers and hikers and it was two of those dog walkers, an elderly couple, who had noticed the Jaguar sitting, door lying open with Anderson's jacket complete with wallet in full view on the front passenger seat. They had immediately phoned the police and the report had come through to Sergeant Matt Moore. Newly promoted and keen to impress his superiors he had wasted no time in heading over to the car park at the Giant's Ring.

There were half a dozen cars parked but the couple who had phoned their find in, had stood guard over the Jaguar.

'You didn't touch anything?' the policeman queried.

'Certainly not, officer,' the woman replied, righteous indignation sounding in her voice. 'We watch *Midsomer Murders*, you know. We know you're not supposed to contaminate the evidence.' Moore took their details and then let them go. They had seen nothing. From the damp look of the carpet, the young policeman reckoned the car had been sitting there all day with the door lying open to the elements when it had rained in the afternoon. He touched nothing but instead alerted CID and waited for the detectives and CSIs to arrive. It was at the very least a missing persons case and, who knows, it could be a kidnapping or even a murder. You didn't abandon your jacket, mobile phone and wallet without a good reason even if it was a crazy reason. He could feel his pulse quickening.

Chapter 27

After hours of watching, with their eyes beginning to sting from concentrating on the sometimes fuzzy images, McKeown and Hill had a timeline. At a briefing they took the group through it. McKeown began.

'Our victim left home at 10am on Saturday morning and walked into Belfast City Centre straight down the Ormeau Road into Ormeau Avenue. He stopped a couple of times to chat to people on Dublin Road and again on Great Victoria Street. They looked as if they could be rough sleepers or maybe from one of the hostels in the area. Whether he was trying to score drugs or not we don't know. We couldn't see anything change hands. A couple of our men are out now canvassing the area to see if they can turn up anyone who admits knowing him or having spoken to him that day.'

Hill moved across and pointed to a photo on the whiteboard.

'It's not great quality but it's the best we found. Roberts met this man, we've called him Mr Mystery because we could never get a clearer image of him.'

The photo was of a figure dressed in a long black overcoat. He was wearing a baseball cap which disguised the colour and style of his hair or if he even had any. A long scarf was also wrapped around his neck and the lower half of his face and hung down over his shoulder.

'Is there anything significant about the scarf? Is that a badge on it? Could it be a school scarf?' Gawn asked, peering closely at the grainy image.

'We never thought of that. We'll check. The two of them talked for a while in the street. It all seemed very amicable.'

'They definitely seemed to know each other?' Maxwell double-checked.

'Oh yes, sir. Then they went to the Crown together.'

Everyone knew where she meant. The liquor saloon had a world-wide reputation. Its situation on Great Victoria Street almost directly opposite the almost equally iconic Europa Hotel, once dubbed the most bombed hotel in Europe, ensured it constant popularity and Saturday had been no exception. The area in front of the bar was packed and each little booth or stall was filled. Hill indicated a picture of the two men in one of the famous dark wood and stained-glass booths sitting over pints of what was obviously Guinness, the creamy heads expertly poured.

Their mystery man had his back to the camera at all times. He had never removed his cap either so they still didn't even know the colour of his hair.

'It's almost as if he knew where the camera was and was avoiding being seen. This may all have been planned. He could have chosen their seat and their route so he could avoid being identified,' Gawn suggested.

'That seems very premeditated,' Maxwell commented. 'Then what, Erin?'

'They walked up Great Victoria Street and then Botanic Avenue. Roberts was staggering quite a bit by that time. I don't know if the mystery man could hold his drink better or whether he'd been going at it more slowly but he seemed fine and he was supporting Roberts as they walked. They stopped at an off-licence on Botanic but, even though he was the worse for wear, it was our victim who went inside. Mr Mystery stayed outside with his back to the camera on the hotel opposite where we got this footage. Jamie got a copy of their receipt. They bought twelve cans of Guinness and two bottles of Bushmills.'

'They were either planning some serious drinking or going to a party,' Logan suggested with a smirk.

'Check with Inspector Ferguson whether any alcohol was found at the house or just empties. And make sure all the cans and bottles are tested. We know from the PM report that the tox screens didn't show up any drugs, at least not any of the usual ones that Dr Norris would test for. Your mystery man could still have slipped something into his drink, something unusual but it's unlikely.' Gawn issued her orders, although she knew all bottles found would already have been fingerprinted and no doubt were already at the lab being tested. Mark Ferguson was thorough.

Hill indicated a picture of the back of the dark figure standing gazing into the window of the off-licence. It had obviously been taken from some distance away and was not of great quality. A picture from inside, on the shop's security camera, provided a clear image of Roberts but didn't capture the mystery man outside looking in.

'Send that over to Tech Support. They may be able to clean it up a bit and maybe get a reflection of your mystery man in the window.'

'Right, ma'am.'

'When it comes back, take a copy of all of the photos down to Father Stephen and see if this could be the man who came to the church looking for Roberts. And arrange for an artist to work with the priest and see if he can give us some kind of image of his visitor. He talked to him face to face. He should be able to give us some idea of what he looked like. And see if he'll give us any security footage he has from that day.'

'Where did they go then?' Maxwell asked.

'As far as we can tell, they went back to Roberts' house. It's possible they went somewhere else, called into a friend's house or somewhere, or went to a party in one of the houses in the area, but as far as we have any trace the last time we have them on camera they were heading back in the direction of Roberts' house.'

'And that would have put them back at the house at what time?'

'Maybe around 4pm if they kept the same pace.'

'And Roberts was obviously going with this mystery man voluntarily. He wasn't under duress, just a bit drunk so what happened between then and the early hours of Monday morning when he went into the water? What changed? There was enough time for him to be incapacitated and then tortured.'

'But for what, ma'am?'

'That's the $64,000 question, isn't it, Billy? He wasn't rich. He wasn't working anywhere that a criminal gang might have wanted information about to carry out a robbery or something. He hadn't had a falling-out with anyone we're aware of. He doesn't seem to have had any paramilitary connections. What did he know that someone else wanted to know so badly that they would do this to him? Could it be something to do with his time in Manchester?'

Her sergeant spoke up in response to the question. 'I've been on to Manchester again, ma'am. They confirmed Roberts had no police record. He wasn't on their radar at all. The local community police had never had occasion to speak to him. Squeaky clean, as far as they're concerned. And 29 March 2011 doesn't ring any bells with them either. If something happened on that date, it wasn't a police matter.'

'So, it was probably something here he was involved in,' Gawn mused. But was it something from 2011 or were they getting side-tracked by a date, that mightn't even be a date at all?

While she had been speaking, Mark Ferguson had slipped into the back of the room.

'Have you got anything for us, Mark? We could do with some help here.'

'Lots of trace evidence, ma'am. We lifted lots of fingerprints and lots of blood and there'll be DNA for sure but whether it's only our victim's or our perp got careless, I don't know yet. He'd done a bit of tidying up but it still looked like the whole place had been tossed. He was looking for something. We found a partial shoe print in some mud in the backyard where someone must have been standing outside. It doesn't match Roberts' so it might have been our perp. He was a size 10 and this is a 12. It's being run through the National Footwear Reference Collection. And I thought you would want to see this.'

He walked forward proffering a photocopy of a piece of paper, the corner ripped off a larger piece. 'The original is being tested for prints and anything else we can lift from it.'

Gawn took it and Maxwell looked over her shoulder as she turned the piece of paper over in her hand.

'It's the corner of a newspaper page. You can see "graph". We double checked the print to make sure it matches. It's the *Belfast Telegraph*. There's part of a date as well and the corner of a photograph on one side and a bit of a report of some kind of an accident on the other. Either Roberts or his attacker or, I suppose, someone else must have cut it out of the paper for some reason. You can see two sides have been neatly cut but then it looks like they or someone struggled over it. You can see it's been ripped and we think that's blood on it. We're checking out whose but I would bet it's Roberts'.'

'An accident or a photograph was important to either Roberts or our perp,' Gawn said.

'Or maybe it could have been something further down the page,' Maxwell suggested.

'We need to see the full pages. Jamie, get down to the Newspaper Library and find them.'

Jamie Grant was about to complain. It was nearly 5pm. He was sure the library would close at six, if not earlier and it would take him time to drive there. Then he only had a partial date – '15 Ma'. Was it March or May and which year? It could take hours if he was very lucky; days if he wasn't. And he had a hot date. But he knew there was no point in complaining or suggesting going first thing in the morning. The boss wouldn't be satisfied until they had made some progress. It might be worth missing his big night out if he was the one to provide it.

Chapter 28

Gawn had just finished talking over progress on the case – or lack of it – with Maxwell and McKeown when her mobile rang. She was surprised to see Seb's name on the screen. It was almost 6pm. Maybe he was getting anxious. She hadn't said what time she would be home and he knew when she got involved in a case she worked all the hours she could but he would also know this was their last night together and she would want to be home with him. So maybe he was afraid something had happened to her or maybe he wanted her to bring something home that he needed for a special farewell meal. She waited until her two colleagues had left her office before answering. She still hadn't said anything about being married and although she suspected Maxwell would realise she and Seb were together she didn't want her domestic arrangements becoming a source of office gossip.

'Hi, honey.'

He never called her 'honey'. 'Darling' or 'babe'. But never 'honey'. Was something wrong?

'What's wrong?'

'Does there have to be something wrong because I phone you at work?'

'Yes. Especially when I'm practically already on my way home. Has something happened? Are the children alright?' She immediately thought of Murphy and Charlie, Seb's nephew and niece. He had phoned her once before at work when Murphy had been abducted.

'Everybody's fine.' She was relieved but she could still detect something in his voice which made her suspicious.

'Then what is it?'

It was one of the downsides of being married to a detective. She always seemed to know when he was lying or at least not telling her the whole story. There was the slightest pause before he said, 'I have a favour to ask.' Then he waited.

'A favour?'

'Not for me. For my friend, Jonah.' Gawn had never officially met Jonah Lunn but she knew the name well. He was Seb's best friend but also a newspaper editor. All she could think was he wanted an inside track on her body in the river case and was prepared to use his friendship with Seb to get it.

'You know I can't discuss a case with anyone and certainly not with a reporter.' She immediately thought of her little arrangement with Donna Nixon and felt just a very slight pang of conscience.

'It's not about your case. He has a friend who needs some advice.'

'And suddenly I'm Dear Abby?' She realised how sarcastic her words sounded. 'Sorry. We're not making as much progress as I would like with this case and I'm a bit crabbit as Billy would say. But I don't know what advice I could give your friend's friend. If it's a police matter he should go to his local station and report whatever it is.'

'Look, Gawn, I don't know what it's about. I only know Jonah asked me as a favour and I owe him. Please, Gawn.' She knew Seb was a sucker for anyone in distress. She above anyone should know that.

'I suppose I could talk to him. I could maybe fit him in sometime tomorrow when I get back from the airport.'

'How about tonight?'

'Tonight?'

'I kinda told Jonah we'd meet him and his friend at Albert Mooney's at seven o'clock. I'll buy you dinner.'

She was tired. It had been a long day and after all her experiences at Albert Mooney's it was one of her least favourite places in the world. She would forever associate it with her stalker. So, although it was a lovely restaurant and she'd enjoyed many pleasant meals there in the past, including her first ever dinner with Seb, she wasn't keen to go back.

'Please, darling.'

She didn't want a row. Nor to disappoint him. They only had tonight together. She hesitated. A few minutes wouldn't hurt. Much.

'OK. But just a quick drink. I'll listen to Jonah and his friend and then we head home.'

'Absolutely. Great. I'll meet you there.' He sounded pleased and relieved. She couldn't deny him the chance to help his friend although she really couldn't think what sort of problem Jonah's friend might have that she could help with. But she would listen and then pass him on to someone else. Ten minutes, fifteen at the most.

* * *

Just before 7pm she walked out of the tiny car park behind the library and as soon as she turned the corner, saw Seb standing outside waiting for her. He was lounging against one of the standing tables for smokers.

'I'm not late, am I?' She had a thing about being on time.

'No. I just wanted to be sure I was here. I didn't want you having to meet Jonah and his mystery friend by yourself.' Another mystery man in my life, she thought, just what I don't need. He kissed her on the cheek and took her arm to walk with her.

He opened the door for her, and they could see the place was already busy. The buzz of conversation and the heat of bodies packed into the smallish space hit them. Gawn hoped the two men they were meeting wouldn't be sitting on the raised area at the front of the bar. The armchairs there were lovely and comfortable, but they were also very exposed to people in the bar and anyone passing on the street. She guessed if Jonah's friend had some kind of issue, he wouldn't want to be too exposed either. And she was right. Seb led her towards a far corner, an area half hidden by a glass partition forming a little snug and as they approached two men stood up. One she recognised. She'd come across Jonah Lunn at police press briefings when he'd always managed to pose the odd awkward question or two. But the other man, she didn't think she'd ever seen before. However it was the stranger who spoke first, holding out his hand first to Seb and then to her and greeting them in a confident voice, as if he was the one doing the favour meeting them.

'Dr York. Chief Inspector. Thank you so much for agreeing to listen to my wee problem – well, my friend's wee problem really.' He smiled but she could see worry behind his eyes. She semi-recognised his voice now and when he said 'my wee problem' she immediately thought of 'our wee country', part of Dave Osmond's sign-off line each day. His voice was deep and rich and just made for radio, she thought. A toned-down Dave Osmond. Little trace of any American accent tonight. He didn't introduce himself. He obviously expected her to recognise him.

'I really don't think there's anything I'll be able to do to help *your friend* but I'll listen.'

'That's all I'm asking.'

She knew, of course, that wasn't true. She knew his type. He wanted to offload whatever his friend's problem – or more likely his own problem – was onto her so he'd be able to walk away feeling good about himself without any publicity and without any comeback on him.

'I hear congratulations are in order,' Jonah said and looked from Gawn to Seb. So Seb had told his friend they were married. She only hoped he hadn't mentioned they were trying for a baby. It was the kind of thing he would do.

'Thank you. Maybe my husband,' – it was the first time she had referred to him as her husband to anyone and it sounded strange to her and yet nice too – 'could get me a drink and your friend can tell me what his friend's problem is.'

Chapter 29

'So this friend…'

'Well, I'd call her more of an acquaintance really, rather than a friend. I mean I haven't even seen her for over three years until she phoned me out of the blue.'

Osmond had begun a recital of his story. Gawn could tell right away he had prepared it, probably practised it so he could ensure to tell her only what he wanted her to know and didn't let slip anything he wanted kept secret. You didn't rush to find a DCI for some woman you've not seen for three years and barely knew unless there was something more than simple humanitarian concern. She didn't see Osmond as much of a humanitarian. Perhaps she was being harsh in her judgement but he was taking up her precious time with Seb as far as she was concerned.

'She obviously told you something that raised your suspicions or your concerns.'

Gawn took the glass of orange juice that Seb held out to her. 'Thank you, darling.' To stave off any comments, she explained, 'Just on the soft stuff tonight. I can't risk getting stopped and breathalysed, can I? I imagine your paper would have something to say about that, Jonah.' She nodded across the newspaperman who had the good grace to look slightly embarrassed.

'She told me she'd received a threatening note.' Then he seemed to remember something and added, 'And a doll.' He noticed Gawn's puzzled reaction and hurried on. 'She volunteers at a charity shop. A doll and a note were left outside. She said the doll was gruesome, mutilated. It scared her.'

'How did she know it was for her? It might have just been someone donating something. Not anything meant for her.' Seb asked the question, drawn into the story by his writer's instinct. He could see the basis for a good plot.

'She didn't say exactly but she obviously felt it was directed to her. Anyway, when she spoke to me she was up to high doh. I tried to convince her that it was just one of our friends from the old days. Maybe he was trying to spook her out. He always had a weird sense of humour or maybe he was just trying to get in touch again. Whatever it was, I suggested I would contact him, find out if it was him and tell him to back off.'

'And did you?' Gawn was being sucked into his mystery almost against her will.

'I phoned his house and spoke to his wife. That was when I started to get a bit freaked out too.' Osmond looked at the trio of listeners and seemed to be enjoying having their full attention. 'She told me her husband's missing and she was going to report it to the police.'

'Did you tell her about your friend?'

'No. I thought maybe he had sent the note and he might have got in touch with her again and they might be together. I didn't want to get anybody into trouble.'

'Had they been an item before?'

Seb and Lunn sat back, both now just spectators as Gawn questioned the radio presenter.

'We were a group, a gang of young people. We paired off from time to time. I don't think they were ever… you know. And he was a bit older than any of the rest of us. But it was nothing serious for any of us and I don't think Danny and Ronny had kept in touch. My friend's called Veronica but we all call her Ronny, Ronny Fisher. Danny is Daniel Anderson. As I said he was a bit older than the rest of us. He was one of the tutors.' He saw her expression and explained, 'We were all members of a musical group. That's how we all knew each other. Danny tutored the woodwind players.'

'We?'

'There were about thirty of us in all in the band but our wee group was Ronny and Kellie and Kevin and me and then Danny sort of tagged along. He didn't seem to get on so well with the other tutors. He preferred to hang around with us. The Five Amigos we called ourselves.'

'Mr Osmond–'

'Dave, please,' he interrupted her.

He smiled, the smile that had won him many a pretty girl's heart and invariably got him what he wanted. Not with Gawn. He was not her type at all. 'Ronny's not answering her phone so I went round to her house last night. I knocked but I couldn't get a reply so I tried looking through the window. I was expecting to get arrested as a Peeping Tom or something.' He laughed half-heartedly. 'The place looked as if a bomb had hit it.'

'Dave,' she tried to speak as authoritatively as possible. She wanted to get home. 'Mrs Anderson, was it?' He nodded. 'Mrs Anderson will probably have already reported her husband missing and they'll be following up on that. I suggest you speak to the station nearest your friend Ronny's house and share your concerns about her with them. They'll try to check on her but, as you said yourself, she may just have gone off with Danny or with somebody else. There was no indication of foul play, was there?' She waited for his response.

'No.'

'And there's no other reason you know of that suggests Ronny might be under threat or in any danger, other than the doll and the note? And you don't know what was in the note that upset her so much?'

There was a millisecond of hesitation before Osmond spoke, 'No.'

The other two men would have noticed nothing but to Gawn's practised eye, it indicated he was holding something back. But what and why, she had no idea and to be honest she didn't really care. She was tired, hungry and just wanted to spend time with her husband; these were their last few hours together before he flew off and she wouldn't be with him for another three months.

Chapter 30

And so, it had come – that moment they had both been dreading ever since the decision had been made that he would go to California without her and she would follow later for a holiday. She had been sure about it at the time. She knew she wouldn't be happy just sitting around in the sun while Seb was busy working. It would be different if she were pregnant and waiting for their baby to be born. Maybe.

But now the moment had come for him to leave, she wasn't so sure about it. In all her years of deployments she had never had a loved one to see her off, to hug her and tell her they would miss her. While colleagues all around were kissing their partners and children and parents and tears had flowed, she had busied herself with making sure everything was in order. That was when her Ice Queen reputation had begun.

'It'll be OK.' Seb sounded as if he was trying to convince himself as much as her. 'I'll be busy working. I promise I won't be getting into any mischief. And you'll be busy with work too. We'll video call. Every night if you want. The weeks will fly by, you'll see.' His voice trailed off. They both knew it was going to be difficult.

The departure board, which they were standing in front of, refreshed and they could see that his United Airlines flight was now on it and destined to leave on time. He would need to go through to 'Departures' soon.

'There's no point hanging around here once I go through, darling. It'll be at least two hours before we take off with immigration pre-clearance and everything. You can head back up to Belfast and get back to your man in the Lagan.' He managed a smile. They had been holding hands but now he put his arms around her and pulled her tightly into him. She clung on to him. She could feel tears prickling at her eyes. She had promised herself she wouldn't cry. He would be worried enough about her without having to worry about her having some kind of meltdown again. She didn't trust herself to speak.

'I won't call you tonight. We might be delayed in Newark and I guess I'll probably be zonked anyway. I'll text and let you know I've arrived safely and then we can talk tomorrow night. 10pm sharp.'

She nodded. He took her by the shoulders and moved her back so he could look at her face.

'It'll be OK,' he repeated but she could see a tear slide from the corner of his eye and she reached up and wiped it away gently with her thumb.

She knew it would be OK. Of course, it would be. She had lived alone and coped by herself all her adult life until she had met him. Then he kissed her. They were in the middle of the concourse in Dublin airport, people all around them and she wouldn't have cared if the whole Top Brass of the PSNI had been standing there watching them with the Police Band playing in the background and the PSNI Ladies Choir harmonising some schmaltzy song. The kiss went on for a long time – just not long enough for either of them – and then he gently moved her back again and smiled, that lop-sided grin that always made her heart flip. She remembered how gentle he had been when they were making love last night. He had told her he wanted to commit to memory every inch of her body, touching, stroking, kissing her until she could contain her desire for him no longer and pulled him over on top of her.

'Goodbye, my darling. Take care of yourself and no bloody heroics, Gawn – right?'

'I promise.'

And then he was gone. He had turned sharply and walked away and he didn't look back, didn't stop as he passed through the doorway to wave. He didn't want to see her crying and he didn't want her to see his tears too.

'Oh gee, sorry, ma'am.' A tanned American in a smart cream linen jacket and with startlingly white teeth which he flashed in a smile of apology, had hit his wheeled suitcase off her leg as he had made his way past her. She watched his back as he strode purposefully towards the exit.

Gawn made her way out to the car park and began the journey back to Belfast. The M1 was a good road. With luck she should be in the office before the 10am briefing she had arranged, which Maxwell would lead.

She noticed the exit sign for a service area and decided she could take the time to have a cup of coffee and gather herself together. She pulled in, parked and headed straight for the ladies. She splashed some cold water onto her face but when she looked up at herself in the mirror over the washbasins, there were still signs of her tears. Her eyes were red and puffy where she had cried when she got back to her car, but she was sure by the time she was driving into Police HQ in Belfast, it would be fine.

Back out in the airy plaza, noisy and buzzing with travellers, she joined a queue at the little coffee area. She ordered a cappuccino and treated herself to a croissant too and then found a seat. This time she merely sat, lost in thought. She was surprised how little she was upset. What did that say about her and her relationship with Sebastian? She would miss him. Of course, she would. She would miss his physical presence around the apartment, his raucous singing of rugby songs in the shower, the lovely meals he cooked for them but she wouldn't miss his clothes lying discarded over the bedroom floor or his chaotic timekeeping. Yes, she would miss the sex, but more she would miss that special sense of being loved when her head rested on his shoulder and he held her tight and told her he wanted to share the rest of his life with her. To know someone cared whether she was dead or alive, that someone wanted to share every part of her life and put up with all her faults had changed her. She thought it made her a better person; she feared it might make her a poorer police officer.

Suddenly she noticed that the American from the airport was sitting across from her at the far side of the café. So, he had stopped for coffee too. What she didn't notice in her distracted state was another man who had not taken his eyes off the American. He was watching him closely.

She finished the last mouthful of her cappuccino and gathered the crumbs of the croissant into a neat pile in the centre of her plate. She didn't notice then that the watcher's eyes had moved from the American and were now following her as she walked out the door. Nor did she know about the scrap of paper on which he had been doodling. He gathered it up and put it in the bin on his way out the door after her. On it was written Gawn Girvin 29 3 11 in thick red marker pen.

Chapter 31

The serenity of the interior of the church enclosed her as soon as she stepped inside. Just as she remembered from her first visit. After driving back from Dublin Airport and checking in with Maxwell to hear how the briefing had gone, she had spent the rest of the morning at the High Court for a consultation with the barrister who was prosecuting the case against a former policeman facing charges relating to the murder of a witness in one of her previous cases. She had been drawn to visit the church again before heading back to the office. She wasn't sure exactly why. She just knew she had felt a warmth and sense of peace the previous time she had been here and thought just taking a few moments to sit and reflect would be good. She smiled to herself as she remembered the exchange with Logan when he had asked her if she was looking for some divine help and she'd said she'd take help from wherever she could get it. Maybe not only about the case. There were other things on her mind too.

She had chosen a pew off to the side near a statue where she was aware of the shadows cast by the flickering lights and the smell of burning wax. She cleared her mind – or tried to – and just sat breathing deeply. After only a few minutes she stood. She couldn't allow herself too much time. That was a personal indulgence. She had work to do. She was about to turn and leave when she found herself drawn to the statue. She lifted one of the candles, reached into her pocket for some change and threw it into a collecting box. The noise of the coins hitting the tin box echoed through the space, cutting into the stillness, the sound rippling outwards like a pebble thrown into a pool of water. She lit the candle and placed it in a holder. *This is for Seb. Keep him safe for me, please. And for our…* But she couldn't finish the thought. She wasn't sure what she wanted to say. She hadn't spoken aloud and she wasn't even sure who she was speaking to but she reckoned it couldn't hurt and if there really was someone listening they would know what she needed to say.

She turned sharply and almost collided with Father Stephen who had come up silently behind her.

'Sorry. Did I startle you?'

'No. I just hadn't heard you.'

'Probably not a very good idea to sneak up behind a police officer like that. I might have ended up in a headlock or something.' He grinned and she returned his smile. She could see his glance at the candle she had lit but he made no comment about it.

'Any news on catching poor Marcus' killer?'

'It's still early days, I'm afraid. It's not like the movies where it's all solved in the space of a couple of hours.' She immediately thought she sounded very patronising. 'Sorry, Father. It can be very frustrating until we get some kind of a break.'

He nodded and she glanced down at the folder he was carrying. She saw rows of numbers on the top page.

'Still working on those parish accounts?' She nodded down to his papers and smiled.

'No. These are the Bible references for my next few homilies. See,' – he held the page out to her – 'OT 1 6 8, The book of Genesis, chapter 6, verse 8: "Yet truly, Noah found grace before the Lord." NT 1 6 27, Matthew, chapter 6, verse 27: "And which of you, by thinking, is able to add one cubit to his stature?"'

In her mind, she saw the numbers on Roberts' back.

'Is that how you set out your Bible references? What would 29 3 11 mean to you?'

'Well, I'm afraid I don't know the whole Bible word for word. Let's have a look.' He walked across to the lectern and leafed through the pages. 'Isaiah. Chapter 3,' and he turned another page. 'Verse 11, "Woe to the wicked. It shall be ill with him, for what his hands have dealt out shall be done to him." Sound right?' He turned a questioning look on her.

'Maybe. What about the New Testament?'

'That's easy. There aren't twenty-nine books in the New Testament.' He folded his arms across his chest, hugging his file to him. 'Any help, Chief Inspector?'

'It might be. That Old Testament reference could almost sound like a threat, couldn't it, if you sent it to someone? Would Mr Roberts have known about the way you write your Bible references?'

'Yes. I guess so. It's not a secret. I carried it on from my predecessor. He used the same format. It's a bit unusual but the parishioners were used to it.'

'Anyone else know about it?'

'Anyone in the parish, I suppose. Or who comes to a service where I'm speaking or who reads my parish notes online. I suppose you could say anyone in the world. However, I don't think my fanbase extends just that far.'

He laughed and Gawn thought his eyes looked tired although his words were upbeat. His work must be as draining as hers. 'I sometimes refer to the notation in my homily instead of naming the book, just to keep my parishioners on their toes. Makes them think.'

'Thank you, Father. You've certainly given me something to think about.' She held out her hand to him and was surprised when he took it in both of his. Then she turned and walked away. She didn't hear his parting words to her, spoken softly.

'Bless you, Chief Inspector. May the Lord guide you as you search for the wicked person who did this to Marcus and protect whoever you were lighting that candle for.'

Chapter 32

'So, what do you think?'

Gawn was sitting in Maxwell's office. Erin McKeown was there too. Gawn had just finished explaining to them what she had learned from Father Stephen.

McKeown was still finding her feet since her promotion and especially now the chief inspector was back too. Being taken into the confidence of her two superiors whom she had admired since joining Serious Crimes as a newly appointed detective constable and having her opinions valued was still a new experience for her. She ventured a response, 'It's possible.'

'If you think it's fanciful, just say so, Erin. I won't be offended. We have to be able to throw in ideas even if they do end up being discarded. And right now this is all I can come up with.'

She ran her fingers through her hair.

'Well, it's more than any of the rest of us have been able to suggest, ma'am.'

'So, what does it mean? Is our killer on some kind of mission to punish the guilty for something they did? If he is, what did Roberts do? Or is it a date? Does 29 March 2011 have some special significance? We haven't found anything in the man's past; anything to do with that date. And is there anyone else out there who he thinks deserves punishing? Could this turn into some kind of spree to kill people who he feels deserve payback? And none of this brings us any closer to finding him.' Maxwell's words showed he wasn't convinced by what Gawn had said but he couldn't provide any alternative suggestion.

'But it tells us at least a couple of things about him.' Gawn looked at the other two and waited to see if they responded. When nothing was forthcoming, she went on, 'It tells us Roberts wasn't just a random victim. It wasn't some sadist psycho picking a stranger up off the street to get his jollies by inflicting pain, thank God. Our perp knew Roberts. You saw them on the footage. They were friends or at least Roberts thought they were friends. And the perp had some reason to want to question him or punish him. And I'm thinking, question. Dr Norris suggested the cuts weren't meant to kill or even to seriously injure him. Roberts had a heart attack. Our perp couldn't have foreseen that, but he took the opportunity to leave a message.'

'For us?' Maxwell asked.

'No. I think more likely for someone else, Paul. It was a warning.'

'But no one else knows. We haven't released any information about the writing on his back,' came his quick response.

'No, we haven't and that's something we might have to think about. If we were to release it, someone out there might recognise it, get worried and come to us,' Gawn replied

'Or get worried and do a runner.'

'Well, that's always a possibility too, Paul. But if it was written on Roberts it could have been sent to others as well. But another thing we can conjecture is that our culprit could be, probably is, familiar with that particular church and specifically with Father Stephen's or his predecessor's reference system. Our perp didn't want to take the time or maybe didn't have the time to write the whole verse or even the whole reference out so he used the same format.'

'So Father Stephen would know him?' McKeown asked.

'Not necessarily. He might have seen him at Mass but it could be someone older who went to the church years ago.'

'The man on the CCTV footage didn't look older, ma'am. There was just something about the way he stood and the way he walked. I don't think he was older,' McKeown suggested.

'You could be right, Erin,' Gawn agreed.

'Anything else you've managed to deduce, boss?' Maxwell asked.

'I think whatever this is about, it all revolves around something that happened in the past.'

'On 29 March 2011?'

'Maybe.'

'I still don't see how this ties into Mr Mystery on the CCTV? He and Roberts looked on good terms. They were out drinking together. They seemed like mates. There was no suggestion of an argument or bad feeling. They might have known each other in the past but Roberts didn't seem to be afraid of him. How did he end up killing his friend?'

'I don't know, Paul. Yet. We just need to keep digging. Maybe the door-to-door will turn something up or Jamie'll find that newspaper clipping and it'll throw some light on things.' She believed the newspaper cutting was important but she didn't want to pin her hopes on it. There would be such a lot for Jamie to search through and, if he found it, it might turn out to have nothing to do with the case.

'He's been there all day. The Newspaper Library will be closed over the weekend. If he doesn't find something within the next hour or two we'll be stymied until Monday,' Maxwell said glumly.

'At least uniforms can continue the house-to-house over the weekend although it hasn't helped much yet. Nobody saw anything. Nobody noticed anything. Or, if they did, they're certainly not telling us. And the CSIs should be finished at the house too and might have something for us by then. Mark said they'd finished at the riverbank so they're all concentrating on the house and he reckoned they would be finished soon.'

A confident knock interrupted their discussion.

'Come.'

It was Jamie Grant. He looked very pleased with himself.

'If I never see another newspaper again, it'll be too bloody soon.'

'I take it you've been successful, Constable Grant.' She looked at him sternly, raising one eyebrow at him, a look they all knew and tried to avoid. He was doing his job; what he was paid for. She didn't want to encourage him to avoid the boring mundane jobs that often led to breakthroughs. She knew he loved the all-action door-kicking-down activities which seemed much more dramatic and heroic but in reality that depended on others doing the more boring, painstaking investigation to get them there.

'Yes, ma'am,' he replied, looking only slightly abashed. He was pleased with himself. He'd been lucky. He reached out and gave her two photocopied pages. '*Belfast Telegraph* from May 2006.'

'2006? Thank you, Jamie. Good work.' She smiled at him in encouragement as he left the office. She was surprised that the newspaper was not from 2011.

Maxwell and McKeown moved round to stand either side of the DCI so that all three could see the pages.

'We've got a half page ad on this one for a sale at an electrical appliances supermarket. I think we can leave that for the minute.'

'Unless someone bought a faulty washing machine in the sale and someone got electrocuted and they blame the owner of the shop.'

'At the risk of sounding like someone from *Dad's Army*, I think that might be in the realms of fantasy, Inspector.' She had missed their sparring and give-and-take. She knew he wouldn't be offended.

'What about this story, ma'am?' McKeown asked, pointing to a headline about a man being charged with dangerous driving after seriously injuring a pedestrian.

'Maybe. Worth following up. We can check up on the driver and the family of the victim and see if there's any connection to Roberts.'

Nothing else of interest caught their attention on the first page so Gawn turned to the second. A photograph of a group of young people along with a Mayor complete with his chain of office took up the top right-hand section of the page.

'Is that Dave Osmond?' Maxwell asked, peering closely at the picture.

'It could be.' Gawn thought of the man she had sat facing in Albert Mooney's. It did look like a younger version of him.

Maxwell read the caption under the photograph aloud. 'A happy group of young musicians from Youth Pop along with one of their tutors, Daniel Anderson, who entertained at the Summer Charity Concert at Hopewell House on Saturday. The concert raised over £1,500 for a variety of local charities.'

Gawn had reacted to the name Daniel Anderson and Maxwell had noticed. 'Does this mean something to you, boss? Do you recognise someone? I don't think anyone here is Marcus Roberts.' He peered closely at the photograph again.

'No. It's the name Daniel Anderson. I heard it recently. He was reported missing by his wife.'

They exchanged looks. This couldn't be a coincidence. It must be connected to their case. It could be the breakthrough they needed.

Chapter 33

Friday evening had been interminable. She had checked on her phone app that Seb's plane had landed safely at Newark. Then she checked when he was due to leave again and saw there was a two-hour delay due to weather conditions. She could picture him sitting around in the airport and had to resist the temptation to phone him. He'd probably have his phone turned off anyway. She was able to see when his flight was in the air and over six hours later that it was safely landed at LAX. By then it was long after midnight but she knew she was going to struggle to sleep. She got a text from him at 2am. 'Arrived safely. Good flight. Missing you already,' and a smiley emoji. She had texted back a heart. Eventually she did manage a fitful slumber hugging his pillow which still carried the fragrance of his aftershave.

On Saturday morning she headed into the office. She needed to be doing something. She couldn't just mope around the apartment. Seb would be phoning but not until 10pm. As she sat at her desk, she mulled over what she could do. If Maxwell had been there, they'd have discussed it and no doubt he would have advised her not to do what she eventually decided to do. She lifted the phone.

'Hello.'

'It's Gawn Girvin. Can we meet?'

'Same place at noon?'

'Fine.'

She used the time until she needed to leave by reading through the facts of the court case which Hill had already managed to pull together for her and had left on her desk. The driver had been seventeen-year-old Nathan Forsythe. He'd only passed his driving test the week before. He had been out with friends and was driving home at 1am along the Shore Road at Whitehouse on the outskirts of North Belfast. Traffic cameras had shown him driving erratically and speeding doing 70mph in a 40 limit. Sixty-eight-year-old Samuel Lee, a retired plumber from Rathcoole, had been crossing the road at pedestrian lights outside the Working Men's club where he had been drinking with friends. Forsythe had driven through the lights and failed to stop at the scene of the accident. He handed himself in an hour later to the local police station. When he was breathalysed, he was slightly over the drink driving limit but, according to his statement, his father had given him a brandy to steady his nerves when he got home before driving him to the station. Lee suffered a broken leg and a fractured skull. The report in the paper was from only day one of the trial. Hill had gone on researching and found that Forsythe had pleaded guilty and got probation and a fine. As far as the policewoman had been able to find out, Lee had recovered and was still alive.

Gawn decided it was possible that some relative of Lee's might feel the driver had got off lightly but she didn't see how Roberts fitted into it or why someone would wait fifteen years to do anything about it. She made a note to get Hill to check witness statements in case Roberts had been in the vicinity and witnessed the accident or been a character witness for Forsythe. But she didn't think what had happened to Roberts now had anything to do with a car accident. She just knew there was some connection to that music group in the other photograph and Hopewell House but what?

Chapter 34

The rooftop bar was busier today than their first meeting. It was Saturday and mostly women, laden with carrier bags from city centre boutiques, were availing themselves of the opportunity of a chance to sit, drink and rest their feet before continuing their assault on the shops and their credit cards. There was one group of six in their twenties, who had the unmistakable look of a hen party, and several couples. No chance to carefully select a table today, Gawn had to sit in the centre of the space but at least she was facing the door and could watch the comings and goings.

Just before the Albert Clock signalled noon, Donna Nixon appeared in the doorway. She seemed to have some difficulty identifying Gawn at first. Being Saturday, the policewoman was casually dressed in a pair of designer jeans and a new favourite shortie green tweed jacket she had picked up from a ridiculously expensive Champs Elysée shop on their whirlwind three-night honeymoon in Paris. Seb had insisted on buying it for her, saying the green matched her eyes perfectly.

Gawn waved and Donna walked over.

'Thanks for coming. I just got here myself. I haven't managed to order yet.'

'No problem. I'm not in any rush. This is a day off.'

'I thought journalists were like police – no such thing as a day off.'

'That's true. If I happen to stumble across a big story I'll be out of here like a shot. Or if you want to slip me an exclusive, I'll be only too grateful.'

The woman laughed and Gawn noticed for the first time how pretty she was. She was sure she would go far. She had little time for the press under normal circumstances. She always tried to avoid press briefings unless it was an absolute necessity and had never chosen to socialise with journalists as she knew some of her colleagues in the Met had done. Inevitably they had found themselves compromised when favours were called in.

They ordered two glasses of wine and, not wanting to spend too much time with the journalist in case she was spotted or to have to drink too much of her wine, Gawn came to the point of their meeting.

'What do you know about Dave Osmond?'

'Dishy Dave or Dirty Dave, depending on your point of view?' The girl allowed a smile to play over her lips. 'Everybody – no, make that every woman in the media knows Dave. He'll hit on just about anything in a skirt depending on how drunk he is.' She laughed. 'I must confess I've shared a glass or two with him but always in the company of his girlfriend, Kirsty.' Her eyes narrowed and she asked, 'Why do you want to know about Dave Osmond? Do you think he's involved in your case?'

'No. Of course not. His name came up in another case one of my colleagues is investigating and, because I already had a working relationship with you, I just wondered if you knew anything about him that I could pass on.'

'Other than his official bio, you mean?'

'Yes. I've looked up the radio station website and I've googled him on Wikipedia of course but I was hoping you might have heard some gossip about him.'

'You mean like he has a thing for underage girls or boys or he has a police record from when he was a teenager? But you'd know that already, of course, if he did.'

Gawn did already know he had no police record. 'I was thinking more about his time with Youth Pop. I couldn't find a lot about them on the web.'

'Youth Pop? I've never heard of it. What is it?'

'It was a youth band or some sort of youth orchestra in the early 2000s. I can't find any trace of it since about 2006. There's nothing on the internet and all I have is one photograph taken at a concert they played at.' She handed a photocopy of the picture to the journalist. 'I think that's Osmond in the back row beside the tutor whose name is Daniel Anderson. I wondered if your newspaper connections would be able to get me any more names of these other people.' Gawn waited and watched as Donna looked closely at the page.

'I can ask around. Most of the older staffers have retired but I could get in touch. Someone might remember the band or be able to point me in the direction of other times we covered their activities. I could maybe source you some more photos or info about it. But what's in it for me?'

Gawn took a deep breath. 'If you can and it proves helpful, I'd make sure you get a heads up on the case.'

Gawn felt she was doing deals with the devil and she didn't know exactly why. Yes, she did. She was pushing herself because she needed to make progress. But more than that she needed the thrill of the chase. She had missed the adrenaline rush she got from catching criminals, from pushing harder than anyone else, from doing whatever was needed. She had promised Seb she wouldn't do anything dangerous but consorting with Donna was only dangerous to her career – if it backfired.

The woman didn't quite laugh out loud but she seemed close to it. 'I don't even know if your colleague's case is worth my time. I'm more interested in the Marcus Roberts case. And we already have a deal about it, Chief Inspector, remember?'

How could she forget? Reluctantly Gawn felt she had to offer something, as little as she could get away with.

'Yes. I remember. Our forensics people are just finishing off at the victim's house and I should be getting a report from them on Monday.' She gave the journalist Roberts' address. It would soon be common knowledge anyway. The neighbours would talk and soon all the news outlets would know. Giving Donna Nixon the address now gave her a slight head start. 'You'll be able to interview his neighbours, get some background on him for your article. And I know they got a lot of fingerprints and genetic material in the house. If we get a breakthrough and identify anyone, I promise you'll be the first to know.'

'It's not much.'

'At the minute, it's all I can offer but it could be worth your while to check into Dave Osmond and see what his connection with Youth Pop was. That's all I can say.'

She hoped she had said enough to whet the woman's appetite and get her investigative senses engaged. But she feared she was already saying too much. She didn't even know yet who was investigating Daniel Anderson's disappearance and whether they were treating it as anything more than a missing persons case, a runaway husband. She doubted they would be working on it at the weekend. It would be low priority for them. She didn't know if Osmond had gone to the police about his friend Ronny at all. And she didn't know that any of this was anything to do with the death of Marcus Roberts; how he fitted into it all. All that was on her to-do list for Monday. What she did know was that she was playing with fire involving the journalist in any of it. Superintendent McDowell would blow a gasket if he ever found out and she knew Maxwell would disapprove. On top of that she wasn't sure she could trust the journalist. Donna was ambitious. If she discovered something, she could use it or sell it to the highest bidder, not pass the information on. But Donna would have sources she couldn't access. As Maxwell had said early in the investigation, sometimes people are keener to talk to the newspapers than the police. They weren't making a lot of progress and something told Gawn – that old chestnut 'the gut feeling' – that Roberts' death was not the end. In fact she suspected it was only the beginning.

Chapter 35

As soon as she and Donna Nixon had said their goodbyes, Gawn phoned Jenny Norris and invited her to meet up. She had been feeling guilty about not being in touch and even more guilty that she hadn't told her that she was married.

'Why don't you come to me? I've moved. I've got a penthouse apartment in the Bakery Building. I only moved in last week,' Jenny said.

'What was wrong with your old place? I thought it was really handy right in the centre of town.'

'It was, but I've bought this apartment. I got offered a permanent post here.'

'That's great news. Congratulations!' Gawn was delighted for her friend but she just hoped it would all work out for her. Jenny still hadn't met the chief pathologist, Professor Al Munroe, who was on sabbatical and she worried they would inevitably clash. They were such different personalities.

* * *

As she approached the red-brick building, Gawn's imagination carried her back to times she had passed this spot in her childhood. Then the smell of freshly baked bread had been pervasive, setting her taste buds salivating at the thought of the soft white centre, the crusty outside and her mother spreading lots of butter and jam all over it for her tea. Now an additional penthouse storey had been added to the building, all trendy grey metal cladding and floor to ceiling windows unlike the oblong symmetry of the original office windows over the bakery.

She entered the black and white checkerboard entrance hall and made her way to the elevator. Jenny's was a duplex apartment on the third floor. Gawn arrived with flowers, a bottle of wine and a personalised tassel keyring in Jenny's favourite aquamarine. She'd found it in a little shop near Cornmarket, not far from the bar where she'd met Donna, and had waited around until it was engraved with Jenny's name. The pathologist had buzzed her in and was waiting at her front door when Gawn exited the elevator. As soon as the two women had hugged and Jenny had put the flowers in some water, they had gone out onto the roof terrace with its view of the river and the park.

'This is fabulous, Jenny. It must be so nice on a good morning to sit out here and have breakfast.' Gawn thought she preferred her own sea view with its sense of infinity as the water ebbed and flowed and gave the promise of new adventures out there somewhere but this was lovely too.

'There haven't been too many of those recently and it can be a little noisy,' Jenny had to admit. The building sat directly on the main Ormeau Road. It was only a stone's throw from where Marcus Roberts' body had been found. 'Twilight is my favourite time out here. Then I light all my little candles. Take a seat and I'll get us some wine.'

'Just something soft for me, please.'

'Are they having another drink-driving push? I've got a spare room. You could stay over and save having to drive.'

'No. It's not that.' Gawn took a deep breath. 'I'm hoping to get pregnant.' She saw a look of surprise cross her friend's face followed almost instantly by a smile. This wasn't exactly the order she'd planned for telling her the news. She'd expected to tell her she had married Seb and then afterwards casually mention they were trying for a baby.

'Congratulations! How does Seb feel about it? It is with Seb you plan to have this baby?' Jenny added as an afterthought. She knew that their relationship had gone through various bumps along the way.

'Of course, it's with Seb. He's over the moon. Going for nominations for Dad of the Year already.'

'I expect he'll want you to marry him, make an honest woman of you.'

'Funny you should say that…'

'He does?'

'We're already married. A couple of weeks ago.' She wasn't quite sure how her friend would react. She thought she'd be happy for her but also very disappointed not to have been invited to the wedding. 'We organised it very quickly because Seb had to leave for America so soon and it was only close family. Just Seb's mother and sisters and their husbands and children.'

'Nobody from your side?'

Gawn hadn't even thought of that. She had no family at the wedding. The only family she had was her brother in Australia and her great aunt who had broken her leg and was in a nursing home. It said a lot about the lonely life she had been living all these years.

'It was very quiet, low-key, the way we wanted it. Just simple. All that really mattered to me was that Seb was there.'

Jenny was beaming.

'I always knew you two were made for each other, you know. Ever since that first time we went out for drinks at the John Hewitt and you told me about him. This calls for a celebration. Champagne and lemonade all round!' she laughed.

For a couple of hours, Gawn was able to forget about Marcus Roberts and what she would have to do next in the case. They'd eaten and talked and laughed and giggled. It had been good for her but when she looked at her watch and saw it was after nine and realised she'd need to leave now to be home in time for Seb's call, Gawn announced, 'I need to go now.'

'But it's early.'

'I know but Seb's phoning me at ten.'

'Take the call here. You can use the spare room. And then you can stay over and I get an excuse to open another bottle of champagne and you can have some more lemonade.'

'Are you trying to make me explode? Cause that's what'll happen if I have any more fizzy drinks.'

But she stayed. At ten, she was sitting propped up on pillows on the bed in Jenny's spare room when her phone rang. Seb's smiling face appeared.

'Hello, beautiful.'

'Hello, darling.'

'Hey, where are you? I don't recognise that wallpaper or those pillows.'

'I thought I was supposed to be the detective who was always suspicious.'

She explained then and even called Jenny in to say hello. Jenny had offered her congratulations and the pride on Seb's face said it all. Then they talked. For hours. Well, just over an hour. Jenny had said to take as long as she liked and Gawn took her at her word but Seb had a meeting later. They were working him hard but he was loving it and loving his apartment. He told her all about it and gave her a quick tour ending up with the view of Santa Monica beach and the ocean from his front window.

It had been hard to hang up and now Gawn was glad that when the call ended she wouldn't be alone. She was already counting down the days until they would be together again. But a lot would happen before that. She didn't realise just quite how much.

Chapter 36

Sunday turned out fun. The two women had breakfasted in a little bistro within walking distance of Jenny's apartment and then decided to play tourists for the day and head to St George's Market. They walked there. It was a nice morning. As they were passing the embankment where the crime scene tent would have been visible if it had still been in place, Gawn realised that they would be retracing some of the route Marcus Roberts had taken on his last day.

The area around the red-brick Victorian covered market was busy. On Fridays it was predominantly a fresh food market serving the local population as it had since its days as an open-air site in the late nineteenth century. But on Saturdays and Sundays, added to the smells of the fresh fruit and veg and the sight of the bloody cuts of red meat and the unmistakable tang of newly-caught fish transported from Portavogie and some of the other little harbours around the east coast, there was a Craft Market. Local artists displayed their latest creations. Often, and today was one of the occasions, there was live music and entertainers. Today it was a solo performer, a young man playing guitar and singing some Bob Dylan and John Denver covers, an eclectic mix which provided an unchallenging background for the browsers. A mime artist reminding Gawn of Marcel Marceau with his white painted face and straw hat was interacting with the passing crowds, amusing the children with his antics. She had barely given him more than a glance, more focused on looking for a present for Seb, a book perhaps, as if he needed any more. She was unaware that the figure had been watching her. Ever since she had walked into the market, his eyes had followed her, watching her every move.

Gawn and Jenny wandered down the aisles stopping at the stalls of handmade jewellery, enjoying the aromas of the scented candles, the produce of cottage industries and avoiding the trinkets and branded souvenirs for the tourists. There was obviously a cruise ship in port today. American accents were much in evidence all around and the stalls selling Belfast-related bric-a-brac were busiest. Gawn enjoyed leafing through some of the dusty old books mixed together in cardboard boxes which had once held baked beans or tins of soup. There was no sense of organisation, the haphazard collections an invitation to delve deeper for some buried treasure. She found a merchant navy seaman's manual from the 1940s sitting beside a 1960s Dandy comic book. When she was about to give up and turn away she came across a book of photographs of Belfast before the Troubles and stood turning the pages thoughtfully. This was a Belfast from before she was born but many of the places and buildings were still recognisable. Some, of course, no longer existed – either the targets for redevelopment and regeneration of the inner city or destroyed in the years of car bombs and nights of violence resulting in fires. She found a picture of her own school – not the building which she had attended but its predecessor in an Edwardian house which had once been a family home. She remembered hearing stories of classes taught in a draughty bathroom and remembered how as an imaginative ten-year-old moving to 'big' school she had thought it might have been fun to attend such an establishment no doubt peopled by all kinds of eccentric teachers, a bit like being in a real-life Enid Blyton adventure.

'Are you only lookin' or are you gonna buy somethin'?' The stallholder's brusque question and broad Belfast accent brought her back to the present. Customer service was not part of this man's vocabulary, she thought. Then he burst into a smile and added, 'Only jokin'. Take as long as you want, love.' Just a blunt Belfast character. She was sure the tourists loved his gritty demeanour and his deliberately broad Belfast banter.

She bought the book. She wasn't sure what she would do with it. She imagined Seb might see it as a source for one of his stories. He regarded everything as inspiration – even the time he had been arrested for murder.

As the two women were leaving the market, they passed the mime artist on the way out. Gawn glanced briefly in his direction but he spun round quickly away from her.

'Thanks, Con, for standing in at such short notice. The kids loved you.' The man accepted an envelope from the market trader, no doubt his payment for the day.

'You're very welcome, monsieur.' They heard the response in a thick French accent. The trader had laughed loudly at the clown.

The women lunched on the balcony of a French-themed restaurant directly across from the imposing City Hall building with its green cupolas and Portland stone frontage. The restaurant building had once been a well-known department store. She remembered her mother talking about it and especially its wide imposing staircase but the shop had closed before she was born, its famous staircase auctioned off. Now the building housed a trendy restaurant and offices.

By this time, the shops were open in line with Sunday trading hours and more people were in evidence on the streets – couples, families, groups of teenage girls out shopping together giggling over their purchases under the stern gaze of Queen Victoria on her plinth. Gawn had always enjoyed people watching and she and Jenny had lingered over their light lunch and coffees. She had treated her friend to a selection of macarons. They had eaten one each and then asked that the rest be boxed up. Jenny promised she would do them justice later. They took a taxi back to Jenny's apartment and then said their goodbyes. It had been a brilliant distraction from both missing Seb and from her case. But she knew she wouldn't be able to put off thinking about both for long and especially about Marcus Roberts. Tomorrow they needed to make some progress.

Chapter 37

On Monday, Gawn felt the need for action. She had enjoyed her Sunday night call with Seb but they had arranged they wouldn't speak again until the following weekend. He was busy and was going on a trip to the film set on Vancouver Island for a few days and she was busy with the Roberts' investigation. So now she needed to be doing something, not just sitting at her desk waiting for others to unravel the circumstances of his death.

As soon as Maxwell had briefed the team, the two headed to the Holylands. She knew the CSIs had been working at Roberts' house for days, meticulously going over it, inch by inch. They were nearly finished. She had wanted to see it for herself but she didn't want to interfere with their work.

The street was parked up. A white CSU van was still there sitting directly outside the house but Gawn drove past – she wasn't going to pull rank to get them to move. Instead, they had left her Audi in the university car park, flashing their IDs to gain admittance. The porter on duty at the barrier was ex-army and keen to help the police. He found them a spot beside the McClay Library.

'I wonder how many normal people live around here now?' Maxwell asked, looking around at the terraced houses, many sporting 'Let' signs or with bags of rubbish and pieces of broken furniture taking up all the space in their tiny front gardens.

'I take it you don't class students as normal people?'

'You know what I mean, Gawn. You've read some of the reports of what goes on round here especially at the weekends, same as I have. Can you imagine trying to bring up a baby with a rowdy party going on next door till all hours of the night?'

She found it difficult trying to imagine bringing up a baby anywhere.

'No, I know what you mean. Most students are fine but when they get together and get a few drinks in them—'

'And some drugs,' Maxwell added.

'Yes and drugs, it can all go to hell very quickly.'

They had reached the front of their victim's house. A young PC stood up straighter as he watched them approach, recognising the DCI's red hair.

When they reached him, he opened the door for them.

'Do we need to suit up?'

'No, sir. Inspector Ferguson and his team are finished but he's still inside.'

The hallway was narrow and dark, the wallpaper peeling off in some places and there was the rancid smell of discarded fried food still lingering in the air, clinging to the curtains and furnishings and adding to the stench of the blood and vomit. When they reached the back room, they found Mark Ferguson still there packing away some of his equipment. The bright working lights were gone but even in the semi-gloom the marks left by the fingerprint powder were visible everywhere. A few spots were circled on the walls, probably blood spots. Sections of carpet had been cut away and were, no doubt, already being worked on back at the lab.

'Good morning, ma'am. Paul,' Ferguson said.

'Anything useful, Mark?'

'Not an awful lot more than I reported before.'

Gawn didn't believe him. She recognised his satisfied demeanour and knew he must have found something. He was just waiting to tell them.

'We'll just need to wait for the results of all the tests now. This is obviously where the business went on.'

He moved his head to gaze around the room and the two detectives followed suit, taking in the old-fashioned furnishings and the obvious signs of violence. A battered two-seater red moquette settee, an old leatherette armchair with wooden arms already covered in preparation for being removed to the lab and a fold-down table against one wall was all the furniture. There wasn't space for anything more. A three-bar electric fire sat in the open grate. The only picture – a landscape print of a hunting scene – was askew on the wall. A mirror hung over the fireplace reflecting back at them their own images as they scanned around the room trying to get some sense of the man who had lived and presumably died here. There were no personal photographs, nothing to show them the personality of their victim.

'You can see where Roberts was tied to this chair.' Ferguson indicated marks on the wooden arms and they could see staining on the seat of the chair through the plastic covering. 'The house-to-house confirmed that he'd only lived here a matter of months. He bought it from an elderly woman who had to go into a nursing home. The neighbour across the street says he bought it lock, stock, and barrel – all the woman's furniture, curtains, the lot.'

'Nothing very personal here to give us any leads then?' Maxwell observed.

'There was an old photograph album. It had obviously been sitting out during the attack because there was some blood smeared on it and some of the photographs had been taken out of their mountings. They're missing. We searched for them, of course, before you ask. They're not anywhere in the house. Now, whether they were taken out by our perp or whether they were taken out a while ago, and the album just happened to be sitting out I don't know but the fact that someone with bloodstained hands – presumably the perp – looked at it would seem to indicate it had something to do with what went on here. And there were captions on the pages. The missing photos all seem to have had something to do with Youth Pop.'

Gawn was excited to hear this. To her it was clear that the motive for Roberts' ordeal lay in the past and Youth Pop was at the centre of it but she couldn't work out what connected their victim to it all. How was he involved with YP?

'Where's the album now?' she asked.

'Gone for fingerprinting and testing. You should get it back maybe tomorrow.' He paused, then added, 'you might want to see out here too.'

Ferguson led them through a tiny kitchen area with dishes stacked up in a stained Belfast sink and a greasy pan providing evidence of the victim's last meal still sitting on the cooker. They stepped out into a backyard. The high walls had been whitewashed, a white which had turned to a mournful grey. Gawn noticed the line of broken bottles strategically placed along the top of the wall, an old-fashioned deterrent to unwelcome visitors. She sniffed the air.

'You smell it?'

'Cannabis?'

'Yes. Some of the neighbours. They were at it last night when we were working here.'

'Any sign of cannabis or drugs in the house, Mark?'

'Just prescription drugs. Roberts must have had high blood pressure. There was a box of lisinopril in the bathroom cabinet. My dad's on that for his blood pressure.'

Gawn was looking around the tiny space as she listened. One tub of half-dead flowers sat in a corner alongside a wheelie bin liberally covered by fingerprint powder and what must have been originally planned as a flower bed or maybe to grow vegetables signalled by a row of red bricks dividing it from the rest of the yard. Now it was just a heap of soil. Roberts had been no gardener.

'Here' – Ferguson pointed to an area to the side of the bin – 'my men are just arranging to collect the bin along with the armchair but you can see where someone has been sick. We've already removed it, of course. And here,' – he indicated a white patch in the soil – 'someone stood here. Just a partial footprint, the front of their foot where he stepped into the muck, probably reaching over to the bin. It was a man's shoe. We used Shoeprint Image Capture software and we should get a match with any luck.'

Gawn was always impressed with the latest innovations and technology that Ferguson and his team employed. She knew he was in a constant battle to purchase new and ever more ground-breaking, but also very expensive, kit and she always supported him when he was trying to make his case for more funding.

'Thanks, Mark. I'd appreciate getting a look at that photo album just as soon as possible and the results of all the tests, of course.'

'Of course, ma'am.'

Some progress at last. Gawn left the Holylands happier than when she had arrived. She wouldn't have been so happy if she had known how close they had been to their quarry. Even as they walked out the front door and made their way up the street back to her car, they were being watched from the window of the house opposite. The man was hanging back making certain not to be seen, even though she had already seen him. He smiled. He was feeling very clever and rather pleased with himself. It hadn't gone exactly to plan but it would. Soon. He had been promised.

Chapter 38

Hill and McKeown were sitting looking intently at a page which Grant had just passed to them.

'I suppose it could be our Mr Mystery. What do you think, ma'am?'

Hill had looked up at the sound of the door opening and now walked across and handed the paper to Gawn who had just come into the office followed by Maxwell. They both examined it closely.

'Is this the artist's impression from Father Stephen?'

'Yes, ma'am.'

'There's not enough on any of the footage to know, is there? We can't get a look at his face, only his back and a bit of his head from the side and even that's covered in a scarf. Did you ever trace the scarf? Is it a school one?'

'Yes, ma'am. I got the tech boys to enlarge the badge on the scarf and get it a bit sharper for us. It turns out it was a school badge.'

'Which school?'

'Newtown Grange.'

'Where's that?'

'Cheshire, ma'am. Just outside Manchester,' McKeown replied.

'Looks like we have our link then. Roberts was working in Manchester when he had his accident. They must have known each other from there.'

Gawn wasn't sure what this piece of information meant for their investigation. The Manchester police had no record of their victim. He had never come to their attention.

'I'm not sure how much further this gets us. This man could be anyone – a former work colleague, a neighbour, a friend from the pub that he used to play poker with. If we could get a clear image of his face we could run facial rec or maybe Manchester would be able to get an identification for us. What about the reflection from the off-licence window? Any luck?'

'No, ma'am.'

Jack Dee had walked in behind them and had glanced at the drawing Gawn was holding as he was about to pass her.

'There's something familiar about the eyes.'

'Do you think you've seen him, Jack?'

'I don't know. We've been talking to so many people from the area. Maybe one of the homeless men we questioned that Roberts used to hang around with? I don't know.' He shrugged and moved on to his desk.

'Mr Mystery didn't look like one of the homeless men and the others didn't seem to know him, and he obviously had plenty of money to throw around. He gave Roberts the cash to pay for the whisky and Guinness and he paid for all the drinks in the Crown.' McKeown stated in a despondent voice. She had hoped to be able to offer her boss a breakthrough.

Gawn felt her mobile vibrate in her pocket and took it out. It was Donna Nixon's number.

'I have to take this.' She answered, 'Hello, just a minute please.' She didn't speak again until she was safely in her own office with the door closed behind her. 'Sorry about that. Can I take it you've discovered something useful for me?'

'I don't know how useful it is, but I have made some progress on your Youth Pop and I think you might find it interesting.'

Gawn waited. Maybe this was a complete waste of time, a blind alley she was working her way up. It had happened before in other cases and now that it seemed

Roberts' attacker was linked with Manchester, it was less likely that it had anything to do with YP. That was why she was keeping it to herself. Not just because she knew Maxwell would be critical of her involving the journalist any further in their case.

'It was a youth group started up by a man called Arthur Courtney. Professor Courtney, he called himself, although I haven't been able to find out where he was a professor. It was just young people, between the ages of about fifteen and up to twenty-five, who liked playing pop music and didn't get the chance to do it at their schools or with their own music teachers. It was a cross-community sort of thing and got funding from Community Relations. They used to meet up once a week for rehearsals and then in the summertime they'd play a few concerts for charity. It all seems to have ground to a halt in 2006 when Courtney left the country.'

There was something about the way Donna Nixon had said 'left the country'. Gawn just knew there was more to come.

'The professor was charged with sex trafficking and exploitation in Thailand and died awaiting trial in prison in Bangkok in 2009. There was nothing reported about it here, nothing in our local papers because he was English, not originally from here and by that time he wasn't associated with any group or people here. I only know about it by a fluke. One of my colleagues, Gerry, remembered Youth Pop because his daughter had been in it for a short time and then when Courtney was arrested one of his friends had been in Thailand on holiday, recognised the name and told Gerry about it.'

'That's certainly interesting and helpful.'

'He was able to find a couple more news reports for me from here when the group was in operation, and his daughter was in it. I can email them over to you.'

Gawn hesitated. Maxwell might see an email in her inbox from Donna Nixon and wonder what was going on between them.

'I'd prefer to meet and get them from you personally.'

'OK. By the way, you were right. Dave Osmond did belong to YP. Gerry remembered he was an irritating wee poser even then.' The woman laughed.

Chapter 39

It felt a bit like a scene from a James Bond movie. They had arranged to meet in the car park at a fast-food restaurant across from a local shopping centre on the outskirts of South Belfast. Gawn got there early – of course – combat parked and waited for the journalist to arrive. It was mid-afternoon so the restaurant wasn't overly busy. A few cars were queueing in the drive-thru section, children being given a treat after school or flustered parents buying takeaways because they didn't have time to cook.

About half the parking spaces were filled but Gawn had chosen one close into the hedge with enough room for Donna Nixon to park alongside. Neither would need to get out of their cars. She lowered her window to get some fresh air and was met instead with the smell of chips wafting in, making her feel hungry. She was trying to eat healthily, avoid junk food and takeaways.

Donna Nixon was late. Ten minutes. Gawn was growing impatient. Then she saw an elderly silver Fiat Punto with a scrape down the driver's side turn quickly into the car park and then immediately come to a halt. The journalist scanned the parked cars, spotted Gawn and drove slowly across pulling the car into the space beside her. She let the window down and pushed her hair back out of her eyes as she spoke.

'Sorry I'm a bit late. I got called into a meeting with the editor. He wants me to do a series of articles on powerful women in business and civic life in Northern Ireland. He mentioned he knew you. I might be calling on you for a favour.'

Like hell you will, thought Gawn.

'Have you got the information for me?' She wanted to keep this meeting short. And she wanted to see what Donna Nixon had turned up. She knew a lot of the older papers weren't digitised. It could have taken them weeks to trawl through paper copies of years of daily papers to find anything on Youth Pop. And she hadn't even been sure until Donna came up with this information that there was anything there to find. She didn't think she could have justified having some of her team ensconced in the recesses of the Newspaper Library for that length of time. Manpower was always at a premium and finances were always tight. And they wouldn't have had access to Donna's colleague who knew all about it from personal experience.

The journalist handed a large brown envelope across into Gawn's eager hand.

'Thank you.'

'Now your turn, Chief Inspector. How does Dave Osmond fit into all this?' With her journalist's natural radar, she had homed in on the crucial question.

'I don't know if he does.' Then seeing the disbelieving look on the other woman's face, she hurried on, 'If and when I find that Dave Osmond has anything to do with my case, I'll let you know. At the minute it's still my colleague's case I'm concerned with.'

'Excuse me if I don't believe you, Chief Inspector. I've made a few inquiries about you. You get results but sometimes you take chances.' Gawn couldn't deny it. 'And sometimes you bend the rules.' She couldn't deny that either. 'But the word is you can be trusted.'

'I'm not lying to you, Donna. I'm not aware that Dave Osmond has anything to do with Marcus Roberts. I doubt they've even met.'

Before she could continue, the journalist cut across her and what she said shocked the policewoman. 'Oh, they did more than meet. My colleague, Gerry, remembered taking his daughter to rehearsals and chatting with the caretaker who looked after the building. He remembered his name because it was a bit unusual – Marcus. I followed it up and it seems your victim was that caretaker. He was employed by Professor Courtney.' She could see her words had had an effect. 'What do you have to say now, Chief Inspector?'

It wasn't often Gawn was lost for words but she hadn't seen this coming.

'I'll be in touch.' Without another word she engaged drive and headed out of the car park, her tyres squealing in her haste to get away.

Chapter 40

'How did you get hold of this again?' Maxwell asked.

They were in Gawn's office. She had called him in and told him she had new information. Then she had opened the envelope and the two had read through the pages. There were reports of charity concerts in Bangor, Larne and Ballymena. There was a profile of three of the members, up and coming musicians who were expected to make careers in music. One she recognised. He was a violinist and she knew he was a member of a chamber orchestra in London which had played at a concert she'd attended in the Wigmore Hall some years back. The second was Daniel Anderson. She knew that name and now she had to tell Maxwell how, and how she had got the information.

'From Donna Nixon?' He was incredulous. 'You got it from Donna Nixon? And what did you give her in return?'

'A heads up when we make a breakthrough.'

'If this gets out McDowell will implode.'

'It won't get out. You're the only one who knows.'

'Me and Donna Nixon. You don't think she might drop you in it if you don't come up with the goods for her?'

'I intend to keep my word. Whenever we're about to make an arrest, I will let her know. Just enough to give her a head start on her rivals. Nothing more.'

'Good luck with that, Gawn. You know what they say about lying down with dogs.'

'I'll take the consequences, whatever they are. But we need to follow up on this. Roberts was involved with Courtney and he ended up dying in a Thai prison as a suspected paedophile. Makes you think. We need to have a talk with Dave Osmond, officially this time. No friend of a friend bullshit.'

'And we should probably trace that third young musician. What was her name?'

Gawn looked at the page again. 'Kellie Beale.'

'Right. I'll get Jo on it.'

Chapter 41

Osmond had started out all friendliness and confidence. He had been getting ready to head out to a drinks event in a Belfast hotel, the launch of a new local gin. Then he was due to meet his mystery caller afterwards. He was behind schedule, and he'd been surprised when he had answered his door and found Gawn and Maxwell standing there. Of course, he'd invited them in. What else could he do? But he quickly realised this was an official visit and he became wary.

'Mr Osmond,' Gawn began.

'Dave.'

'Mr Osmond,' she repeated pointedly. 'Did your friend ever turn up?'

The truth was he didn't know. After speaking with Gawn at Albert Mooney's, he had decided he had done his bit and should stay out of it. Ronny had probably run off with a boyfriend, maybe even with Anderson. He couldn't afford to get involved in any scandal or gossip. His agent was in negotiations for him to get his own show on one of the big Irish radio stations. A move to Dublin, a penthouse apartment overlooking the quays and a salary considerably larger than he was earning now, were too important to risk.

'I'm afraid I don't know, Chief Inspector. I got caught up with work and I assumed if anything had happened to her I would have heard.'

'Have you tried phoning her again?'

Sheepishly he confessed he hadn't.

'And was she a member of Youth Pop too?'

He had been pouring himself a drink, the two officers having refused his offer of one for themselves, when his hand froze mid-air at the mention of Youth Pop. It was only a momentary pause and his voice, when he spoke, sounded normal.

'My God, that's a blast from the past. I haven't thought of Youth Pop for years.'

Gawn knew he was lying. Although he had his back turned to them, she had seen his reflection in the glass of a painting hanging over the drinks cabinet. She had seen the look which had crossed his face when she mentioned the name.

'Yes. Yes, she was.'

'So Daniel Anderson who is missing and Ronny Fisher who is missing were both members of Youth Pop. And Marcus Roberts who was the caretaker for the hall where you all practised was found dead.'

'You think it has something to do with Youth Pop? It all closed down years ago. The Prof moved away to England or somewhere and we all just went our own ways. Why would they go missing now because of Youth Pop? And why would anyone kill Marcus Roberts? All these years later, why?'

'We were hoping you could tell us, sir,' Maxwell said.

'Well, I have absolutely no idea, Inspector. Now, if you'll excuse me, I'm expected at an event in about twenty minutes time. The press'll be there and I'm supposed to have photographs taken with some new distillers and their products.'

'Before we go, where were you the weekend before last, sir?'

'When exactly?'

'Let's say midday Saturday until Monday morning.'

'You think I had something to do with what happened to Marcus?' When they didn't respond, he continued, 'Saturday and Sunday I was with my girlfriend. We went out for dinner on the Saturday evening. You can check. We were photographed for the Out and About feature in the newspaper. I was on air on Monday morning so we went to bed early on Sunday night and we were up about 4am and in the studio for just after five on Monday morning.'

'Your girlfriend can corroborate that? She was with you all night?'

'Yes, Chief Inspector. She most definitely was with me *all* night and we made the most of it, I can assure you.' A smirk passed across his face. Gawn recognised this tactic for what it was. He was trying to divert attention by embarrassing her. 'Now I really must ask you to leave and let me finish getting ready.'

Reluctantly they left. When they were back in the car, Maxwell turned to Gawn.

'He knows something.'

'Oh yes. Did you see his face when I mentioned Youth Pop?'

Maxwell nodded. 'We should get his alibi checked.'

'His girlfriend might lie to back him up but if he was photographed out and about in Belfast he probably isn't our man. But get it checked anyway.'

Chapter 42

The whole team was gathered for a briefing. Billy Logan, notebook in hand, was standing beside the board reporting what he had discovered. 'I checked the Out and About feature from the paper, ma'am. They had two photos of Osmond and his girlfriend. In one they were having dinner in a new restaurant in the Cathedral Quarter and then later they were snapped listening to a jazz trio in another bar off High Street.'

'Any idea exactly when the pictures were taken? Are we sure it was *that* Saturday night? Sometimes they use photographs from previous nights, Billy, as fillers.'

'I thought you might want that checked, ma'am. I talked to the photographer. He knows Osmond well. He said they were definitely taken that Saturday and by the time he was leaving the bar, Osmond was pretty drunk. His girlfriend was having to help him into a taxi so I don't think he'd be in a fit state to drive over and torture Roberts or dump his body in the Lagan.'

'Unless his girlfriend helped him,' chipped in Grant.

'Let's leave that thought for now, Jamie,' Maxwell said in response to the young detective. He didn't think the boss was in the mood for any levity. 'Any update from Inspector Ferguson, Erin?'

'They weren't able to lift any prints from the photo album other than Roberts' own, sir. No joy with the DNA either but they've identified the shoe print so Inspector Ferguson says, get him a suspect's shoes and he can match them.'

'All we need is a suspect then.' Maxwell caught Gawn's eye. She wasn't impressed with what they had discovered so far. 'Who was checking into our third musician?'

'Me, sir.' It was Jo Hill. 'It's rather a sad story really. She was a brilliant musician for her age. She played piano, violin and clarinet to a really high standard and everyone said she had a beautiful singing voice too. Everyone expected her to have a career as a professional musician.' They waited, wondering what Hill thought was rather sad. 'She died in June 2006 when she had only just turned sixteen.'

'That is sad,' Gawn agreed.

'Yeh, but she didn't just die. She committed suicide.'

'At sixteen?' Maxwell was shocked. Anything to do with children always affected him. He had two of his own of whom he was immensely proud but whom he worried about all the time.

'I got hold of the coroner's report. The girl slit her wrists. Bled out. She was found in the bath.'

'Awful for her family. A parent would never get over losing a child like that,' Maxwell stated solemnly.

'Did they find out why she did it?' Gawn asked.

'According to the report, everyone said she seemed really happy.'

'They always do,' threw in Dee from his seat at his desk in the corner.

'Her mother said she'd been looking forward to starting on her A levels. She was going to apply to the Royal

College of Music in London and her music tutor was going to help her get a grant and a scholarship. Apparently, she talked about it all the time. They had no warning at all that she was worried or upset or was contemplating suicide.'

It seemed Hill had finished her report and Gawn was about to speak, when the constable added, 'There was one thing that came out at the inquest. Kellie was pregnant. Now, she'd only just turned sixteen a matter of a few days earlier, so it seemed someone had been having underage sex with her but they never seemed to follow that up – not that I could find anyway. I guess they thought it must have been one of the boys she hung around with who were around the same age, and they didn't think it was worthwhile raking it all up when she was dead anyway.'

'Did she hang around with a lot of boys?'

'No. That was the funny thing. Her mother said she wasn't much interested in boys and other than school and her musical activities she never went out much.'

'What sixteen-year-old girl isn't much interested in boys?' Logan asked sarcastically.

'We're not all sex maniacs like you, Billy,' Hill retorted sharply.

Gawn had moved to the front of the room. She addressed the whole team.

'So, we have a girl who committed suicide around the time this Professor Courtney, the man behind Youth Pop, left the country and now fifteen years later, we have two missing adults, one of whom, Daniel Anderson, we know was a member of Youth Pop.'

She pointed to his photograph now pinned up on the board.

'And another one, Ronny Fisher, who Osmond has now confirmed for us was a member too.'

Her finger strayed across to a photograph of a smiling Ronny Fisher holding up a cocktail glass obviously at some party.

'And, finally, we have Marcus Roberts, the caretaker for the professor, tortured, we're now thinking, to get some information from him.'

She taped the photograph of Roberts' body taken at the riverside.

'Quite a little web but who's the spider in the centre of it all? I don't think it's a coincidence that it's photographs of Youth Pop that were taken from Roberts' house by our perp. Could our Mr Mystery be another ex-member of Youth Pop? Dave Osmond would fit the bill if it wasn't for the fact he was drunk. What we need to find out is what information Roberts had that he died rather than give up. We have lots of questions, people. Too many. Let's get some answers. Quickly, before anyone else gets killed.'

Chapter 43

Gawn hadn't intended to visit the church again. She had no good reason to. They had got the likeness of the man looking for Roberts from Father Stephen. McKeown had told her the only working CCTV in the church was in the sanctuary for transmitting services and, according to the priest, the man had only come as far as the front door. He hadn't been inside so he wouldn't be on that camera and the one outside the church had been broken for weeks. He apologised that he hadn't got around to having it repaired. They had also been disappointed to find that the CCTV camera on the building opposite worked on a seven-day loop and would already be over-taped, so no joy there for them either. There wasn't anything else to be found out here and it was unlikely he would come back to the church if he was their Mr Mystery. Yet, still, she was drawn back.

She had just reached the top of the stone steps when a figure rushed out of the darkened doorway, knocked against her and had to grab at her to stop her falling backwards. She steadied herself against him and then stood back.

'Jeez, I'm sorry, ma'am.' The American accent was unexpected. The church was part of many tourist trails with its interesting history and architectural quirks but there would be no tours at this time of day. She had half expected that it would be locked up and had only come as an afterthought.

'Are you OK?' The man flashed a smile at her, his row of perfectly straight bright white teeth dominating his face. It couldn't be the man from the airport? That would be too much of a coincidence. She hadn't really looked that closely the day in Dublin airport and she hadn't been in the best state of mind, still upset at Seb's departure.

She found her voice and spoke, 'Yes. I'm fine. No harm done.' He smiled again, nodded and headed off along Alfred Street.

Gawn straightened her jacket and walked into the church. Once again she immediately felt enveloped by an almost cocoon-like sense of warmth and peace. She spotted Father Stephen kneeling before the altar and when he stood up and turned around he saw her too and walked over.

'Good evening, Chief Inspector. I'm surprised to see you again. Do you have more questions for me? I really think there's nothing more I can tell you.'

'No, Father. I just wanted to sit a while and think. I'm actually on my way home but it's been a stressful day and I–'

'I understand. We're always here. You're always welcome. I'll leave you in peace.'

As he started to move away she asked, 'I was almost knocked off my feet by a man rushing out just now. Do you know who he was? I think I've seen him before.'

'That must have been Kevin. An American accent?' She nodded. 'Yes. I'd never met him before tonight but he used to be an altar boy here years ago, so he told me. He's home for a few days and called in for old times' sake, I think, but here's the woman who could tell you all about him.'

She looked around to see who he meant. It was Rose O'Hare who had just entered from the side door.

'Rose, Chief Inspector Girvin was asking about Kevin.'

'Ach, Kevin.' The woman nodded her head and smiled. 'Yes. I remember him as a wee lad playing about the street. His family lived close to me. He was a lovely-natured child with the most beautiful smile.'

'What's his second name, Mrs O'Hare?'

'Donnelly. Kevin Donnelly. He was a brilliant singer. He would have brought a tear to your eye. When he and wee Kellie Beale sang together it was just like heaven on earth. The voices of angels.' Gawn tried very hard not to react to the mention of Kellie Beale's name. Obviously unsuccessfully.

Chapter 44

When Father Stephen had seen the look of surprise and the blood drain from Gawn's face he had immediately suggested that all three of them needed a cup of tea.

'Sorry. I think I must have been a bit shocked. He nearly knocked me down your front steps.'

'Then a nice cup of hot sweet tea will be just the thing, won't it, Rose?'

'Absolutely, Father.'

For one absurd moment Gawn was reminded of *Father Ted* and his housekeeper. The older woman bustled ahead of them and then straight into the kitchen with the ease of long practice and familiarity. The priest took Gawn's arm to steady her. She was embarrassed. She'd had nothing to eat all day, just a few cups of coffee. So much for her healthy eating plans. She had felt light-headed once or twice but put it down to that, hoping it wasn't to do with anything else. She didn't want to find herself pregnant now in the middle of an investigation. It would be… inconvenient. But then she was always going to be in the middle of some investigation or another, wasn't she? She wondered what that meant for them starting a family. Just at the minute she didn't want to have to be consulting doctors and informing McDowell. And she wanted to get this case closed. She could think about everything else afterwards.

Once comfortably settled in an armchair by the fire which had already been lit and was providing a cheery glow as well as heat to the room, with a cup of tea in one hand and a delicious home-made piece of shortbread which Rose had thrust upon her in the other, Gawn began to feel better.

'I'm so sorry to put you to all this trouble.' She included both Rose and the priest in her look.

'Rose loves to be the wee mother hen, don't you, Rose?'

'Sure, it's no trouble. You had a shock. You need to be careful in your condition.'

'My…' and then she could get no further. 'What do you mean?'

'I've been around pregnant women and babies all my life, dear. I was a midwife for over twenty years. I noticed the way every now and again you touch your stomach.'

She would have to watch out for that.

'I'm not pregnant.' She said it but she didn't know whether it was true or not. 'Tell me about Kevin Donnelly.' She changed the subject. Enough about her.

Father Stephen sat down on the armchair across from Gawn and took a sip of his tea, while Rose settled herself on the sofa and started her story.

'Kevin was brought up here in the parish. He lived with his parents just round the corner near me. They were good people. His daddy worked on the buses and his mammy worked in Anderson and McAuley's. You won't remember that, either of you. You're too young. It was a fancy department store across from City Hall.'

The woman smiled at her own memories and then continued, 'A bit out of my price range. C&A was more my style and you probably don't remember it either.' She chuckled. 'They were like wee angels, Kellie Beale and him, God rest her soul. They used to sing at concerts in the church and everything. Then he started getting into a wee bit of trouble. I don't think he ended up in court. If he did, I didn't hear about it. But anyway, he went out to live with his uncle and aunt somewhere in the States. I think his parents probably sent him away before he got into something more serious.'

Gawn didn't ask whether Donnelly had been involved with the paramilitaries. The woman probably wouldn't tell her anyway. The Good Friday Agreement might have been signed but the paramilitaries on both sides had not gone away. Donnelly could have got caught up in their drug activities.

'I'm not sure where exactly. Maura Donnelly used to show us pictures he sent home and tell us how well he was doing. He even went to university out there. Then his daddy died and his mammy moved back to Cookstown where she'd grown up and still had family. I never heard any more about him until tonight when he showed up here out of the blue. He told me he was home for a few days to see his mammy. He's got some big fancy job in Washington and he's doing really well for himself, so he says.'

'Was Kevin a member of Youth Pop?' Gawn asked.

'Youth Pop? I've never heard of that,' Rose replied.

'Oh well, I can check that out for myself. You don't happen to have an address for Mrs Donnelly in Cookstown, do you?'

'I'm afraid not but it's getting more and more like old times round here these days. Takes me back.'

Gawn threw a quizzical look at the woman. Rose explained, 'First it was Connor Beale and now Kevin too.'

'Connor Beale?' Gawn realised her voice seemed to have risen an octave. This was a new name but he must be something to do with Kellie.

'Yes. Kellie's wee brother. He was a lot younger than her. He's been back about two or three months, I think. I haven't seen him in church, just about the street. I don't think you've ever met him, Father.' The priest nodded. 'He's renovating his parents' old house. He was a wee imp when he was young. Used to follow his sister around like a wee lost sheep. She was very good to him. Awful what happened to her, to all of them really. Very sad.'

Gawn's mind was working overtime. 'Thank you both for your help and your kindness. And the shortbread, Rose.' She smiled at them as she stood up.

'Did you get what you came for, Chief Inspector?'

'I think I got a lot more than that, Father.'

Chapter 45

Gawn had just got back into her car. Over a week had passed since Roberts' body had been discovered and she felt she was getting more confused instead of beginning to see her way clearly to a motive and a perpetrator. What she was beginning to sense was that at the centre of it all was someone manipulating all these people and events, drawing them all together. So far Roberts' death seemed to have been unintentional, an unfortunate outcome of the beating. Anderson's and Fisher's disappearances might simply mean they were hiding but she couldn't shake off the feeling that there was something more to come; that they hadn't reached the endgame yet, whatever it was. It was a strange coincidence that Connor Beale was back in Belfast but maybe no more than that. If he was a lot younger than Kellie then he would have been too young to be a member of YP. But she didn't really like coincidences. She would get Hill to do a background check on Connor and see what he'd been up to all these years. It might be worth sending someone to have a word with him and they needed to find Donnelly too and speak to him, although if he'd only arrived in Dublin when she'd seen him he couldn't have been in Belfast to be their Mr Mystery.

Her mobile rang. Donna Nixon's name appeared on the screen. What did the woman want now? Gawn wasn't in the mood for a confrontation with the journalist.

'Ms Nixon, I'm afraid I don't–'

The woman's voice, fast and breathless sounding excited, maybe even a little frightened, broke into her words.

'I think something's happened to Dave Osmond.'

'Like what? I'm afraid I don't have time to listen to wild theories.'

'If you don't believe me, check with the radio station. His show wasn't on air this morning. They said he was ill and his assistant stood in for him.'

That would be easy enough to check. There wouldn't be any point in the woman spinning a lie about that. She would realise they could verify it very quickly.

'Perhaps he's ill or…' Gawn thought of the meeting she and Maxwell had had with Osmond the previous evening when he was getting ready to go to some event or other. She couldn't remember where he had said he was going but no doubt he would have been partying late into the night. 'Perhaps he simply had a bit too much to drink at some PR event. I know he was going to one last night.'

'Yes. I know that too. I was there. I followed him afterwards.'

There was a pause as Gawn took in what Donna Nixon had just revealed.

'You followed him?'

'Yes. That's what I do. I'm an investigative journalist,' came the cocky reply, her confidence returning.

'You've done a few reports for radio, not undercover exposé work. You don't know what you could have got yourself into.' Gawn was feeling guilty and that made her speak more harshly than she had intended. Donna Nixon was young and ambitious. She obviously saw this case as her chance to progress her career. But she had no idea what it was all about. Neither did they yet, of course, but Gawn had used her. She had been happy to encourage the woman to investigate in the hope it would turn something up to help her case. Now she was feeling guilty about that decision. But the pragmatist in Gawn won out. Donna Nixon had already followed Osmond. She shouldn't be in any danger now. It was still daylight so Gawn might at least find out what she had learned.

'So why do you think something has happened to him?'

'I followed him to Ravenhill Road after the party last night. I saw him park down an alleyway between some warehouses. I waited but he didn't come out. I was tired and a bit fed up. I thought maybe I'd missed him somehow so I went home.'

Some tough investigative reporter, Gawn thought to herself, but said nothing.

'Then, when I turned on the radio this morning and it said he was ill and wouldn't be on the show, I decided to drive down to the warehouse after work and have a look around and his car is still here, parked down the alley.'

'Where are you now?'

'I'm parked just across the road from it. I can see his car in the alley now.'

'Stay there. I'm on my way.'

Gawn knew she should probably phone Maxwell and tell him what was happening. If she phoned now, he should still be in the office but she decided to hold off. The girl might be mistaken or making something out of nothing. Instead, she drove to Ravenhill Road as quickly as she could and then slowed down keeping an eye out for Donna's battered Punto. It wasn't hard to spot. She pulled in behind her, got out of her Audi, walked up to the passenger door of Donna's car and got in.

'Anything happening?'

'No. Nothing. The building looks as if it's not in use.'

Both women jumped as a firm tap came to the side window. They looked up and saw a uniformed policeman bent down looking in at them. Gawn put the window down.

'Can we help you, officer?'

'Can I ask what you two ladies are doing here?' He was polite but obviously suspicious.

The women looked at each other. They almost burst out laughing. It seemed they looked to be up to no good. Gawn reached into her pocket and withdrew her warrant card. She offered it to him. She saw his expression change from mild interest to shock. He handed the wallet back and then straightened up.

'Sorry, ma'am. We had a call. Someone spotted this car here last night and then again this evening. They've been having a bit of trouble with some prost...' He stopped speaking and looked flustered, unsure how to go on.

Gawn realised what he was going to say. He had thought he was approaching a couple of prostitutes on the lookout for clients. She almost laughed. It was the first time she had ever been mistaken for a prostitute.

'I just wanted to check out the reports. I didn't think you were going to... or...' He didn't finish his sentence.

Gawn stepped out of the car. 'Don't apologise for doing your job, Sergeant Moore,' she said, reading his name badge and smiling at him. 'I was just about to take a walk down that alley to inspect a suspicious car myself. It's been sitting there since last night and this lady is worried about the driver. You can accompany me.'

'Yes, ma'am. Of course.'

She turned back and spoke to Donna Nixon. 'You stay here.' It was an order. She didn't care what Maxwell would think if he heard her speaking to the journalist like this. The woman needed to keep back.

Gawn leading the way, she and Moore crossed the road and walked down the narrow alley. It ran between two tall warehouses and was only just wide enough for one car. Osmond's empty dark blue BMW was sitting parked near the open back door of the nearest building.

'Is this building occupied, Sergeant?'

'That one is.' He pointed to the one on the other side of the alley. 'But this one's been empty for a couple of years, I think. It was a store for one of the carpet warehouses further up the road and prior to that I think it was a gym, and years ago it was a mission hall or something. Maybe your man out of this car is inside.'

That was what Gawn was afraid of. She was even more afraid of what condition he might be in if he was inside. Thank God Donna Nixon hadn't followed him into the building. Moore was beginning to sense something of Gawn's wariness.

'Do we need backup, ma'am?' Moore seemed a little tense now.

'I think you and I can handle anything we find, don't you, Sergeant? Just keep behind me.'

He couldn't really do anything other than agree with her even though his instinct told him to call it in and wait.

The musty smell of years of disuse filled their nostrils as soon as they stepped over the threshold. It was surprisingly light inside and an ocean of dust flecks swam before their eyes. This was obviously a foyer or maybe, from the empty bookshelves lining one wall, an office or preacher's study in its mission hall days. Another door faced them. It must lead into the main part of the building. Gawn opened it slowly just a crack and listened. Only the noise from the passing traffic outside. Nothing from inside. She pushed the door fully open. Inside the big empty space it was not so bright. The street-level windows had all been boarded up to save them from being vandalised but there was still some light making its way inside from other smaller windows higher up near the ceiling, forming square patches of light on the dusty floor. They spotted Osmond straightaway, or at least a figure who Gawn took to be Osmond. She recognised the cream linen jacket he had been wearing when she and Maxwell had interviewed him. Now it was spattered with blood. He was lying in the centre of the floor, curled up, his knees drawn up almost to his chin, one arm flung above his head and the head was lying in a pool of dark liquid. Off to the side, Gawn spotted a heavy metal torch.

Moore went to rush past her but Gawn put her hand out to stop him.

'Call it in, Sergeant. Ask for an ambulance and my team. Tell them I'm already here. They'll get here fast. Then stay back and don't let her in.' Gawn had looked behind them and saw Donna Nixon standing holding on to the frame of the outer door with one hand, her other hand over her mouth. The journalist turned away just then to be sick, the scene in front of her, and perhaps a growing realisation of what she could have walked into last night and what could have happened to her, taking hold. They could hear her retching.

'Let her sit in your car until the ambulance arrives. And don't let anyone down this alleyway until my team comes.'

'Right, ma'am.'

The policeman moved back and Gawn was left alone taking in the scene before her. There was no one else here.

That was evident. There was nowhere for anyone to hide. The room was bare. The dusty floor bore signs of disturbance.

She made her way carefully over to the prone figure. She would have liked to stay back, not disturb the scene, leave all the evidence intact. She cursed that she didn't have any shoe covers. But there was just a chance Osmond was still alive and she couldn't prioritise the scene over the victim. She made her way carefully over to him and hunkered down trying to disturb the area around the body as little as possible. She felt for a pulse in his neck. His skin was warm to her touch and there was a pulse, weak but it was there. He was unconscious and there was nothing she could do to help him. She stepped back trying to take the same route back to the door as she had walked to reach him. When she arrived at the outside door, she stepped through the opening and took some deep breaths.

Was Osmond number two on the list after Roberts or were there two others – Anderson and Ronny Fisher – out there somewhere dead or dying? And was there going to be a number five?

Chapter 46

While she waited, Gawn went back to her car and got a stack of evidence markers she kept in the boot. She couldn't stop the paramedics walking over to Osmond to help him but she could try to prevent them messing up the crime scene too much. She marked out a pathway that they could keep to, avoiding as many of the marks already on the floor left by whoever had attacked Osmond and following the trail she had already made.

Maxwell and the rest of the team arrived quickly, beating the ambulance crew by seconds. She had heard their approach, the blues and twos signalling their arrival. She watched as they went into action, organising the uniformed officers who had arrived simultaneously, getting the area cordoned off, beginning to question people in the neighbouring buildings. She saw McKeown walking up the road looking at the outside of buildings for security cameras. This part was mostly commercial before the residential section began past the entrance gate to the park. There should be plenty of cameras. They should be able to get some good coverage. She hoped.

The CSIs weren't far behind. They couldn't start work inside the building but they quickly suited up, moved everyone else back and began work on Osmond's car. They would all have to wait until the paramedics stabilised Osmond before anyone could go inside.

Eventually a white-faced unconscious Osmond was wheeled out by two paramedics. Much of his head was swathed in bandages but they were already quickly becoming bloodstained.

'How is he?' It was Maxwell who spoke to them.

'He's taken a bad blow to the head. Lost a lot of blood too and he's still bleeding. He's breathing on his own which is a good sign but what internal brain injuries he might have you can only guess at this stage. We're taking him to the Ulster.' The paramedic had named one of the largest local hospitals. Then he shrugged and moved on.

Gawn had spent part of the time, after she had briefly spoken to Maxwell and filled him in with some meagre details of how she had ended up discovering Osmond in the warehouse, sitting with Donna Nixon in the back of Moore's car. The woman was still shaking. She was obviously suffering from shock. There was no sign now of the tough hack she had claimed to be. Gawn was sitting with her arm around the other woman's shoulder, trying to provide some sense of security as the implications of her near miss sunk in. She didn't try to question her. She didn't say anything at all. She was glad to be able to hand her over to a second ambulance crew who had arrived and would check her out. Then she had to face Maxwell. She had been avoiding meeting his eye. She wasn't looking forward to their conversation. As she approached him, he took her firmly by the arm and drew her aside where none of the others would be able to hear them.

'For God's sake, Gawn. What were you thinking? She could have been lying dead in there, too.' His voice was urgent and angry but he was keeping it lowered and watching around making sure no was listening.

'Osmond isn't dead.'

'But he could have been and she could have been too.'

'He probably would have been if we hadn't discovered him, if he'd been there much longer. It was only because she followed him and called me, he's got a chance. And I didn't ask her to go playing detective. I suggested she do a bit of digging into Osmond. I thought she would ask around, speak to some of their mutual friends in the media, not go following him around the country like a Jessica Fletcher wannabe.'

She was trying to assuage her own guilt as much as convince him. She realised Nixon could have been lying in there in the same condition as Osmond… or worse. She didn't need Maxwell to tell her.

'Anyhow, we are where we are. She's OK and hopefully Osmond will be too. If he regains consciousness he should be able to tell us who attacked him or at least what this is all about. Now let's get on with our job, Paul. Time for any recriminations later.'

He hadn't said 'I told you so' and anyway when he had warned her about Donna Nixon he had meant that dealing with the journalist could land her in hot water, not that the woman would nearly get herself killed.

Chapter 47

Gawn decided to leave them all to it. Paul was capable of taking any decisions that were needed. It would be hours before the CSIs would have anything for them. She had dispatched a team under McKeown to Osmond's apartment to search it too. Then, without discussing it with Maxwell, she decided to check out Ronny Fisher herself.

She drove to Fisher's house in a row of neat terrace houses just off Lisburn Road, not quite what she had been expecting. From all she'd heard, Ronny was a party girl, liked the high life, was usually seen in flashy cars and even flashier designer clothes in the company of some rich man or propping up a bar looking decorative at some party. Her house was almost on the edge of student bedsit land. At first glance, as she sat in her car, Gawn thought it looked empty. While other houses in the street had lights on, Fisher's house was in darkness. It had the air of somewhere that hadn't been occupied for a while. In the past, when Gawn's father had walked the beat in Belfast, missed milk deliveries would have meant old milk bottles sitting outside to give a clear sign that the occupant either was away or was incapacitated in some way. Now there was no such easy signal.

Gawn peered through the front window, as Osmond had told them he had done. Like him, she could make out signs of disorder but whether this was from someone searching or someone simply making a quick getaway not worried about leaving a mess behind, or whether it was evidence of some kind of struggle, she couldn't know without getting inside and taking a closer look. There was no body in sight and no sign of blood that she could see so that was a positive at least. She had feared finding the woman's body lying on the floor as she had discovered Osmond's. On her drive over, she had checked with the nearest police station. No one had been looking for Ronny Fisher.

She turned away, deep in thought. What was going on with these people? As she made her way down the short pathway from the front door and closed the gate behind her, a woman came out of the house directly across the narrow street. Gawn knew it wasn't just by chance. The woman had obviously spotted her looking in through the window and had come out either to ask her something or to offer some information.

'She's away somewhere, I think. We haven't seen her about for a couple of days. But you're not the first one looking for her. There was a man here looking in the window too.' The neighbour, a forty-something with trendy designer tracksuit and carrying a sports bag as if on her way to the gym, must have seen Osmond looking around too.

The woman was staring at her, obviously dying to ask for more information. She looked Gawn up and down.

'Are you from the landlord?'

'No. What makes you think that?'

'Just Ronny was saying she might be moving soon. I assumed maybe you were here to look around the house and check it out for re-letting.'

'You've no idea where Ms Fisher might have gone?'

'No. Not really. I don't know her all that well. We tend to keep ourselves to ourselves round here. All I know about her is she works at a charity shop down Botanic Avenue. You could try there. Some of her friends there might know where she is.'

'Thank you.'

Back in the car, Gawn watched as the woman walked away towards the Lisburn Road. Then she dialled the nearest police station and reported Veronica Fisher as a possible missing person. She could have left it there, let them follow it up, but she knew she wasn't going to do that. It was too late now to start trying to interview anyone at the charity shop. It would be closed. Tomorrow. First thing.

Chapter 48

Clutching her venti Americano tightly in her hand – good intentions of being careful and not taking too much caffeine far from her mind now that she felt they were getting closer to finding the attacker – Gawn walked purposefully up Botanic Avenue from the vacant parking spot she had managed to find. She felt the excitement of the chase, a feeling she knew from the past, a feeling that was an important part of her life. Like a junkie, she craved the exhilaration that came from the challenge of pitting herself against the worst of humanity – the rapist, the violent robber, the murderer. She just knew they were getting closer, closer to solving this puzzle, closer to finding their perp, closer to preventing anyone else being hurt or killed.

The roadway was busy as usual. She barely registered the car fumes she was breathing. A van, its driver's window wide open blasting loud music out into the street, sat at the traffic lights. Commuters using this as a rat run to avoid the busy Lower Ormeau Road sat revving their engines ready to make a speedy getaway. Two lorries delivering to a supermarket and offloading fresh produce to a Chinese restaurant were double parked causing traffic build-up and blaring horns. Tourists on their way to visit the Ulster Museum or grab a photo opportunity at the front gates of the university mingled with chattering students clutching files and textbooks heading to their lectures. All around was life and activity. The area was filled with cafés and restaurants and bars which made Queen's Quarter, as they were now calling it, such a lively and busy place. Only in Belfast could you have more than four quarters, Gawn thought to herself.

She passed the famous crime bookshop, her husband's idea of heaven on earth. He could spend hours inside the tiny shop, just browsing, and leave carrying yet more crime fiction to add to his heavy bookshelves. When he got back from America and they moved into their new permanent home together, he had promised himself a real study with floor to ceiling bookcases and promised her that his books would not take over every inch of spare space in their living room and bedroom as they did now.

A moveable metal noticeboard sat outside the charity shop. It was swinging in the light breeze and squeaking slightly declaring it open for business and inviting passers-by to stop and support their work. She paused to take a final swallow of the hot coffee and disposed of the cup in a bin. A bell tinkled, triggered by the door as she pushed it open. Inside the shop a couple, probably students, were stocking up with crockery, not really concerned with matching sets of cups and saucers, just needing something to eat and drink out of. A woman with a colourful headscarf and a baby tied around her front was browsing through a rack of baby clothes. The child was sleeping blissfully unaware of everything around her.

'Can I help you?' The voice came from behind her. Gawn spun round and came face to face with Rose O'Hare.

'Rose!'

'Chief Inspector! Do you need to ask me more questions?'

'No. Yes. I mean, I didn't know you worked here. I do need to talk to someone about Veronica Fisher.'

Rose made her way over to a curtain which separated the shop from a storeroom behind and offered some privacy to the volunteers working on the latest donations. She called to someone inside.

'Mairead, could you look after the shop for a wee minute till I speak to this lady?'

A middle-aged woman, her grey hair pulled tightly back into a bun giving her a school marmish look, emerged through the curtain untying an apron as she walked.

'Of course.' She smiled and nodded at Gawn as she passed, no doubt wondering who she was and what she wanted to talk to Rose about.

Rose led the way through the curtain to a packed storeroom. Bags of donations were piled up – black bin bags, green refuse sacks and store shopping bags identifying the shopping preferences of their donors – forming a mound against the wall. There were three chairs in the cramped space, one an armchair, its stuffing escaping from the side of the cushion and two upright dining room chairs with scuffed wooden legs, which Gawn surmised had probably all been donated. There was a sink with a tray of mismatched cups upturned on a draining board and a kettle with a jar of coffee beside it. Against the other wall stood a table where Mairead had obviously been sorting through donations dividing what they could sell in the shop from what they could sell for rags or anything they would need to dispose of.

'Sit down. Take the weight off your feet, dear.' She could see that Rose fell naturally into mothering mode and she wanted to discourage that. This was business.

'I'm fine, Mrs O'Hare.' She thought she'd better get this interview onto a more formal footing. She'd called the woman by her first name because she had been totally blindsided to see her there. Now she needed to make this official. 'I'm making a few inquiries about Ronny Fisher.'

'Veronica?' So, the woman used her full name here. She couldn't really picture Rose chummy with some socialite flitting from event to event and man to man so probably Rose would have little to tell her that would help. Ronny would hardly confide in the homely little Belfast woman, salt of the earth as Father Stephen had described her.

'She hasn't been into the shop since last week. Is she alright?' Rose's concern seemed genuine, not just the result of curiosity.

'You were expecting her then?'

'Oh, yes. She's the manageress, I suppose you would call it. She has the keys and opens the shop every morning. Most of the rest of us are just volunteers who help out a day or two a week. When she didn't show up we had to contact the big boss to get the shop open and she asked me to take the extra set of keys and take over until Veronica's back.'

'But you don't know when that will be? Or where she might have gone?'

'Do you think she's alright? Has something happened to her?'

'I don't know. That's why we're checking. Do you have any reason to think something might have happened to her?'

Gawn had detected something in the woman's voice. She couldn't quite interpret what it was but she thought Rose either knew or suspected something about Veronica. Rose seemed to hesitate as if she was making up her mind whether she should say something or not.

'Look, it was just something that happened last week. It probably has nothing to do with anything but it was the last time I saw her.'

Rose sat down on one of the wooden chairs and straightened her skirt over her knees, flattening it out with both hands before continuing.

'It was first thing last Monday morning. We both arrived at the same time and there was a black bin bag sitting outside the shop. Now that happens quite often. People are on their way to work and if we're not open and they want to donate something they'll just prop it up against the shutters. Anyway, I lifted the bag and some stuff fell out of it and Veronica started screaming. At the top of her voice. It scared the life out of me. I didn't know what was wrong with her. I thought she was in pain or something. Anyhow I got her settled and I opened the shop and then she said she wasn't feeling well – and she certainly didn't look well. She looked really awful, as if she'd seen a ghost. She said she'd have to go home and that was the last time I saw her.'

'What do you think set her off screaming? Was it something in the street? Did she see someone going past in a car?'

'I don't think so. I think it was the doll that fell out of the bag.'

Gawn remembered Dave Osmond's account of his friend being spooked by a freaky doll.

'Do you still have the doll?'

'No. I threw it away.' Rose shook her head and pursed her lips. 'It was a horrible looking thing. We could never have sold that in the shop. We'd have had complaints from parents even if we'd tried to sell it at Hallowe'en, I think.'

'What was it like, Rose?' Gawn slipped back into using the woman's first name. It just seemed natural.

'It was just an ordinary doll. I looked at it. It wasn't expensive. Just made of that hard plastic stuff. Made in China. It had quite a pretty face if you could get past its arms.' The woman shuddered.

'What was wrong with its arms?'

'The arms had been ripped open and something red had been smeared all over them and over the mouth. It looked like something from a horror movie. Not that I've watched any horror movies but that's what I think they would be like.'

An image of Kellie Beale came into Gawn's mind and she was sure it had been the same for Ronny Fisher when she'd seen the doll. All she could think of was what Donna

Nixon would make of a grotesque doll mimicking a bloody suicide and how she would weave it into her storyline of Satanists and black magic.

'Anything else you noticed about the doll, Rose?'

'Well, before I threw it in the bin, I took the clothes off it. It was wearing a nice wee cotton dress and matching floral panties and I thought we could sell them in our toy corner. Some wee girl would probably like them for their doll, I thought. And I was right. We did sell them.'

Gawn was getting impatient.

'But there was nothing else on the doll. It was the note, I think, that upset Veronica. She'd hardly looked at the doll.'

'What note?'

'The note I found on the floor after she'd gone. I thought she'd dropped it but I'm not sure. Maybe it was one of the customers, but I just thought I would keep it in case it was hers. Give it to her whenever she comes back.'

'Have you still got it?'

'Yes.' She bustled over to the corner and extracted a note from her coat pocket. She handed it over. Gawn took a set of gloves from her pocket before unfolding it and read 'Hopewell'. Underneath was a row of numbers, the same numbers which had been on Roberts' back and the same slightly threatening drawing too.

'I don't know what it means, I'm afraid, Chief Inspector.'

'I do.'

Chapter 49

Gawn felt she was on a roll. She had found out more important information in the last few hours than in the last week. At least she thought she had. She was beginning to form theories in her mind; make connections. She just wasn't totally sure yet where it was all leading. She wanted to talk it over with Maxwell but decided to visit Daniel Anderson's wife first before heading to the office, just to complete the row of missing musicians from the photograph and ensure he hadn't turned up safe and sound already, in which case he might be their perp. If not, that would just leave Kevin Donnelly and Connor Beale to check up on. She wondered if Beale could be some kind of catalyst; if his return had triggered something, brought back memories or roused guilty consciences. But about what? It had to be something to do with his sister's suicide. Was it a suicide? Could it have been murder? There had been no suggestion of that at the inquest.

The drive to Holywood, the little town bypassed and often overlooked sandwiched as it is between big city Belfast and the ever-spreading commuter town of Bangor, took a little longer than she had anticipated. Eventually she pulled into a cul-de-sac of neat, detached houses and bungalows. The Andersons lived in number six. A mini sat on the paved driveway. As she climbed out of her car and walked up to the front door she was aware of someone watching her from inside and wondered how many other eyes were following her from behind their vertical blinds and trendy wooden shutters. As she reached out to ring the bell, the door was jerked open.

Eva Anderson was pale. Her eyes were moving restlessly looking at Gawn and then away, darting from side to side, searching for something; someone.

'Yes?' Her voice was surprisingly firm.

'Mrs Anderson.' Gawn pulled her ID from her pocket but before she had raised it to the woman's eye level, she could see her expression change.

'I thought you were a reporter. I didn't think you were police. You weren't with the others who came.'

'No. I'm not from your local station. My name's Gawn Girvin. May I come in?'

She didn't mention that she was from the Serious Crimes Squad. She didn't want to freak the woman out, upset her so that she wouldn't be able to answer any questions.

'Of course. Sorry.' She stepped back and made room for Gawn to walk into the hallway. 'Just in there.' She indicated a room to the right. 'Sit down. Do you have some news for me?' Her natural good manners had disguised her nerves but her voice betrayed her anxiety.

'No. I'm sorry. I don't.'

Eva Anderson's expression changed then. Her anguish became very evident. She didn't try to disguise it. 'Where in God's name is he? Something must have happened to him. He wouldn't just go off and leave me and he wouldn't leave his beloved Jag either in that car park where anybody could have taken it. That car was his pride and joy... *is* his pride and joy. I used to joke he cared more about that blasted car than me sometimes.' A tear trickled down her face and Gawn waited while she wiped it away with the back of her hand. Then the woman's natural good manners and sense of hospitality kicked in.

'Can I get you some tea or coffee?'

'No. I'm fine. Thank you.' Gawn didn't want to prolong the interview.

'I was just going to have a cup of Dan's favourite. He's very particular about his tea. He loves that new strong brew. He makes me go all the way to Knock to get him the Belfast blend in the yellow packaging, you know, like the cranes. He says he should have been a shipyard worker getting his tea in a big mug so strong you could stand on it.'

She had almost laughed but then her voice was caught again in a sob. Gawn thought she better get on with her questions before the woman broke down completely.

'I apologise if I ask you anything my colleagues may already have asked but I'm coming to this afresh.' Eva Anderson nodded. She was clinging to the hope that a new police officer meant they were doing something more about Dan's disappearance. So far, she'd had the impression they weren't taking it too seriously. But maybe she was being unfair to them. They had told her there was no indication that anyone had abducted Dan; no signs of foul play as they had called it and no trace of his body. They tried to suggest he would probably turn up of his own volition when he had worked out whatever crisis he was going through.

'Was your husband under any pressure? At work? Or about money?'

'He's a teacher. It wasn't what he dreamed of doing. He wanted to be a professional musician when he was younger – a performer – but it just never happened for him and with a mortgage and everything he needed a secure job with a reasonable salary. Teaching can be stressful. I've heard lots of teachers complaining about their workload and their pupils. Dan was the same and I know he sometimes had run-ins with some of his colleagues too. Not everybody rates music as very important. He had to fight his corner against the scientists and the mathematicians and the others who felt their subject needed more time and a bigger share of the budget. There were disagreements sometimes. And it's concert time again.'

Seeing the puzzled look on Gawn's face, she explained, 'He gets very stressed every year when all the orchestras and soloists have to perform for the public, all their doting parents and the Board of Governors and everybody. He puts a lot of pressure on himself but this was no different to any other year.'

'And, sorry to have to ask, Mrs Anderson, but what about your relationship? Were there any problems in your marriage?'

'We were… we *are* very happy,' she replied with conviction. But Gawn knew just because a wife thinks all is well, it doesn't necessarily make it so. Men can get itchy feet. A new young teacher at school, a sixth form student with an attractive smile. It had happened before. He wouldn't be the first. Gawn was sure the local police would be checking at the school. 'My husband was not having an affair and before you ask, neither am I.'

'Well then, had anything happened or was he acting out of character in any way?'

'No. We were booking our holiday for the summer. In the Bahamas. We were both looking forward to it.' Then she stopped. 'There was something.'

'Yes?'

'He got a letter.'

This sounded promising. Osmond must have been contacted to get him to the warehouse at Ravenhill. Veronica Fisher had got a message of sorts with the doll.

'Did you see the letter? Read it?'

'No, he took it away with him but it upset him. He said, what would I think about moving to Australia. Then he tried to laugh it off as just his joke. But he wasn't joking, I know.'

'And you have no idea at all what could have been in the letter?'

'No. He took it with him, I told you.'

'How soon after this did he disappear?' Gawn asked. If he had received some kind of warning or threat, then he might simply have chosen to run away.

'Two days.'

It seemed she had learned all she could about Anderson's disappearance and what might have triggered it. The local police were searching for him. She knew they had made extensive searches of woodland near where his car had been found and they had searched the Lagan towpath. There had been no sign of a body and no sightings of Anderson, either alone or with anyone else.

The next step would be to send divers in to look for his body in case he had simply decided he'd had enough.

'My colleagues are continuing to look for your husband. From what you say he may have decided he needed to go away for a few days if he felt pressured at work and he could just turn up on the doorstep tomorrow.' Even to her own ears, her words sounded trite. Eva Anderson needed something more definite just to know her husband was still alive.

Gawn hesitated before she asked the question she really wanted an answer to. What did Eva know about YP? Osmond had obviously wanted to hide his involvement with the group. Maybe she would be more forthcoming. She hoped Eva Anderson might be able to provide a link to help identify the person behind all this.

'Mrs Anderson, were you a member of Youth Pop along with your husband?'

'Youth Pop? Me? No, I'm not very musical, I'm afraid. I haven't even heard anyone talking about Youth Pop for years. Dan used to talk about it sometimes when we were first married. I think it was a very happy time for him. He was hopeful then of making a break into a band or some orchestra. But recently he hasn't mentioned it at all. He still has a box of mementos and music from that time.'

'Do you think it would be possible for me to have a look at it, maybe take it away for a few days? I'd make sure you got it back.' She smiled to convince the woman of her good intentions.

'I don't see why not. If it'll help.' Eva Anderson would do anything if it would help get her husband back.

While she was out of the room fetching the box, Gawn took the opportunity to have a look around. Her colleagues had once thought she was merely a 'nosey cow' as she had overheard one of them describing her but in fact she had taught Maxwell how useful it could be to get an idea of a suspect or a victim from their home surroundings. You could learn a lot from what they liked to read and how they organised their home. This room was neat and tidy. A family Bible lay open on the coffee table. There were a few ornaments and lots of photographs. The obligatory wedding picture of Eva and Dan looking suitably happy standing outside the church was joined by one of them in front of the Taj Mahal and another showing Anderson standing looking out of place in a suit and tie among a group of leather-clad bikers.

Mrs Anderson returned surprisingly quickly with a cardboard box filled with sheet music and at least one photograph album.

'I suppose you should have this too. I should probably have given it to the others but I was too flustered then.'

She held out an envelope.

'The letter Dan got came in this.'

Gawn took a plastic glove and evidence bag from her pocket and reached for the envelope, holding it by the corner. She placed it carefully into the bag.

'Has anyone else but you and your husband touched this?'

'Well, I suppose the postman but no one else.'

'Thank you, Mrs Anderson. I may need to get someone to come along and take your fingerprints. Just for elimination purposes. If that's alright?'

The woman nodded her agreement.

'Thank you again. You've been a great help.'

Chapter 50

Gawn had phoned Maxwell to check progress at the warehouse and about Dave Osmond's condition.

'Where are you? I was expecting you down here this morning.'

He sounded annoyed. She didn't want an argument and she wasn't going to be spoken to like some newly promoted detective who was still learning the ropes so she simply said nothing. When she didn't respond, he seemed to take the hint and began telling her what was happening.

'The CSIs are doing their thing, the rest of the team have just been finishing off interviewing the neighbours and so far no one admits to seeing or hearing anything except for one lady who was at that church just across from the warehouse. She noticed Donna Nixon's car sitting two nights in a row and was suspicious. She said the pretty girl inside seemed nervous and jittery, as she put it, so she confessed to being the source of the phone call which had Moore out to check up on you.

'Erin's managed to amass a fair amount of CCTV footage and she's just waiting now for access to the traffic cameras at the bottom of the road. Then she and some of the others will begin trawling through it all but they're not sure what they're looking for.

'As for Osmond – he's stable, but he's still unconscious and the doctors aren't making any predictions about the outcome. Early days, they say.'

'Right. Good.'

She gave him a very brief resume of where she had been and whom she had spoken to. Details could wait until the morning. She wanted to run some of her ideas past him but not over the phone.

'I'll meet you tomorrow at eight so we can talk before the briefing and I'll fill you in on what I've found out.'

She ended the call before he had the chance to ask any questions or make any comments. She realised she would have to mend a few bridges with him when they did speak. She didn't want to be doing it over the phone.

She had noticed a coldness in Maxwell's manner towards her. She really couldn't have missed it. She thought she might have deserved it. Maybe she should have taken him into her confidence. Maybe she should have taken him with her. But he wasn't her sergeant anymore. He didn't need to follow her around like a puppy as he had once told her his wife, Kerri, had accused him of doing. He had plenty to do without babysitting her. And she didn't need him tagging along and feeling his disapproval at some of the things she might do. She didn't want him falling into the role of her conscience either. She knew she sometimes had to set her conscience aside to get results. She could live with that, but she wasn't sure he could.

Then she headed home stopping at the forensic laboratory at Seapark on the outskirts of Carrickfergus on her way. She handed over the note Rose O'Hare had retrieved from the floor in the charity shop and the envelope Eva Anderson had given her to Joe Lester. Maybe he would be able to lift a fingerprint from one or both of them. Maybe. They needed some hard evidence.

'As soon as you can, Joe.'

Her voice sounded tired and he must have noticed for he replied with, 'You know I always do my best for you.' And she remembered the rush job he had done on the hoax device which had been left outside her apartment by the Perfume Killer. 'I'll get back to you asap.'

It had been a long and busy day. A lot had happened since Donna Nixon's phone call last night. Although they hadn't arranged to speak tonight, she had succumbed to the need to hear Seb's voice. They had talked for nearly two hours. She didn't go into details about the case, of course. She was determined never to do that, but she tried to explain about involving the journalist in her investigation and hoped he would offer her some absolution for what she had done or at least some encouraging remarks. Instead, he had asked what Maxwell had thought about it. For one second she had a suspicion that Seb had spoken with her inspector before he left, perhaps telling him about their situation and asking him to keep an eye on her. The two had struck up a sort of distant friendship since a rocky start when Seb had been their person of interest in a murder investigation. Then she thought not. He wouldn't do that. And Maxwell wouldn't be capable of knowing and not dropping at least a hint or being oversolicitous of her. And he hadn't been.

Then she had changed the subject and instead they had talked about his work and what he was getting up to. He said she looked tired and hoped she wasn't overdoing it. He looked fabulous. He had a tan, of course, already. He had grown some designer stubble. She didn't know if she liked that or not but his eyes were sparkling and his excitement with his life was obvious. She just hoped that was all that was producing the sparkle. She knew he could be impressionable and easily led although he would deny that. But he wasn't stupid enough to get caught up in the drug scene. It was just he was loving it all – the work, the creative people he was working with, the beachside apartment, the lifestyle, surfing in the morning before breakfast. All the things he had dreamt about as a boy in East Belfast growing up on a council estate. And Gawn wondered if he would ever want to come back. What if she went out to California and she did get pregnant? Would he want them to stay there after the baby was born? Could she make a life there? She knew the answer to that question all too well and she hoped Seb knew her well enough to know the answer too without ever asking the question.

When they had said their 'goodnights' and 'I love yous', she was left with a feeling of loneliness. Technology was wonderful and she wouldn't suggest not facetiming. Those few hours seeing him, if only on a screen and being able to talk with him, were a highlight. But it only made the hours alone seem even more lonely and she needed her work to fill that emptiness.

She went to bed looking forward to the day ahead. They were making progress. They had found out things today that they hadn't known yesterday. It was just how the pieces of information fitted together that they had to work out now. And there was still one missing piece, the figure behind it all, the one who had orchestrated it. Orchestrated, she thought, like a piece of music. But who was the conductor? They needed to find him or her to prevent another death. She sensed that and also sensed that, whoever was behind it, it was all coming to a climax. Soon.

Chapter 51

She had carried the battered cardboard box in from her car as if it held the Holy Grail. For this case, maybe it did. At 8am sharp the knock on her door told her Maxwell was there for their meeting.

'Come.'

He walked in. Normally he would have walked in without knocking. The expression on his face told her a lot. There was no smile; no greeting; no proffered cup of coffee, a normal forerunner of their chats about a case. She took a deep breath. Apologising did not come easily to her. It never had. And she wasn't totally convinced she had anything to apologise for.

'Look, Paul, before we begin, we need to clear the air. Sit down.' When he didn't move, she added in a quiet voice, 'Please.'

He sat on one of her armchairs but he didn't relax back into it. She positioned herself perching on the edge of her desk facing him.

'If you think I've done something wrong, I need to know what it is. We need to be honest with each other.'

She waited and watched his face. It might tell her more than his words would.

'You're having clandestine meetings with a journalist and making God knows what arrangements or promises to her. I don't know and quite frankly, Gawn, I don't want to know. You used to avoid the press like crazy. You wouldn't even give them a comment when they asked for one. Now you're best buddies with Donna Nixon. And she could have been killed, Gawn. I don't like her but I don't wish her harm.'

'Neither do I, Paul. What do you think I am? I had no way of knowing she would be so silly as to start following Osmond around playing detective. I only asked her to do a bit of digging; see what she could turn up. If I'd wanted Osmond followed, I'd have put someone onto him.'

'And then yesterday you went AWOL. No word. I didn't know where you were, who you were interviewing. You could have run into our perp and we wouldn't even have known where to start looking for you. We're supposed to be a team, for God's sake. You're not the bloody Lone Ranger.'

Gawn didn't think she'd seen him so angry before. His words reminded her of a confrontation she'd had with her commanding officer in Afghanistan. He had told her she wasn't the Lone Ranger too.

She was silent for a moment, her head bowed. Then she looked up and spoke. 'You're right, Paul. What can I say? Sorry. This case has got to me. Or rather the lack of progress in this case has got to me. I suppose it might be because Seb's away in the States and I have nothing else to focus on when I get home at night. I can get fixated on a case, you know that. You've seen it before and I'm a bit obsessive I suppose and I can lose perspective. You know me. I should have told you where I was going yesterday. But it just started out as one thing and that one thing led to another and it just made sense to keep going.'

She smiled at him trying to look suitably contrite. Eventually, after a moment's hesitation, he returned her smile, weakly.

'So, you and Seb are still an item.'

This was the moment to tell him – some of it anyway. She took a deep breath.

'We're married.'

He didn't quite splutter but he came close to it. She was just glad then that he didn't have a cup of tea in his hand. It might have ended up down his shirt front.

'You're married! Wow. I certainly didn't see that one coming. Congratulations. Mrs York, is it?'

'No. DCI Girvin for work as usual and we're the Girvin-Yorks. Seb says he's always wanted to be hyphenated but he was afraid it would be too painful.'

Maxwell laughed then and the ice was broken. He could believe that. It sounded just like Seb's sense of humour.

'Is it a secret?'

'For now. I don't want it broadcast all over the office. I haven't told them upstairs yet.'

'OK. It's your business. I can keep a secret. But I'm pleased for you, Gawn. I always thought he was good for you.'

'That's not what you said when we first met him.'

'Well, you hated him then too.' Maxwell stood up and kissed her on the cheek and gave her a hug. 'Am I allowed to tell Kerri?'

'Of course. I thought husbands and wives weren't supposed to have any secrets from each other.' She laughed. She thought she knew everything about Seb by now but he certainly didn't know everything about her. And she wondered about Eva Anderson. Were there things about her husband she didn't know? Things from his past? From YP?

'Now talking about husbands and wives. Let's see if this one had any secrets hidden away from his wife.'

She lifted the box from her desk and set it on the coffee table in front of Maxwell's seat. 'Provided by Mrs Anderson. This is her husband's memento box from YP.'

The two began to work their way through the contents, item by item. There was lots of sheet music, the tunes of the day which the band must have played. The titles brought back memories. There was a keyring model of the Eiffel Tower, a trashy tourist trinket.

'The group must have played in Paris or at least been there on a trip. A keepsake of a fun experience?' Maxwell speculated.

There were programmes from concerts the group had played.

'They were quite busy, weren't they? They got around. The City Hall for a cross-community event, the Waterfront Hall as part of a celebration of Belfast's Youth Initiative.' She read off the front covers of the leaflets as she lifted them out of the box.

'Here's one for a Charity Concert at Hopewell House,' Maxwell said as he lifted the next programme out.

'Where was Hopewell House?' Gawn pounced on the name and then explained the note received by Ronny Fisher.

Maxwell turned the leaflet over. 'It doesn't say. I suppose if you were there with a programme in your hand, you knew where you were. You didn't need directions.'

'We need to find out, Paul. Something happened there. Ronny Fisher was being reminded of it and it scared her.'

A knock interrupted them and McKeown's head appeared around the door. 'We're all ready for the briefing.'

'Thanks, Erin.' Gawn stood up, collected all the material back into the box and carried it into the squad room.

Chapter 52

The detectives of the Serious Crimes Squad were sitting and standing around the office space.

'Right, what's the latest on Kevin Donnelly and Connor Beale?' Gawn waited for her sergeant to answer. She had asked McKeown to find out where they were.

'You were right about Donnelly. He was in Washington when Roberts died. We've traced him to his mother's in Cookstown. He's staying there with her. I wasn't sure if you wanted someone to go and speak to him?' McKeown waited for an answer.

'If he wasn't even in the country he can't be our perp. He might be able to give us some more info on YP but it's not urgent. What about Beale?'

'He doesn't seem to be at his parents' house. The neighbours haven't seen him for a couple of weeks.'

'OK. Leave him for now. Our top priority is to find out where Hopewell House is and what happened there. I think that's what links these people and these attacks together. It must have been around 2006. And someone needs to check on Osmond at the hospital. There is still a guard on him, isn't there, Erin?'

'Yes, ma'am.'

'Good. Our attacker may think he's killed Osmond but if he realises he's still alive he might try to come back to finish the job. We need to know as soon as he regains consciousness and can be interviewed. We have two missing persons, maybe witnesses, maybe potential victims or maybe even one could be our perp – Veronica Fisher and Daniel Anderson. I've spoken with the officers in charge of their misper cases and they're both happy for us to go ahead and look for them. It seems more sensible for us to take the lead and not go trampling all over their cases and duplicating their work.'

'You mean do their work for them. I'm sure they are happy.' Logan spoke in a voice just loud enough to be heard by all. Neither Maxwell nor Gawn reacted.

'Jack and Jamie, you speak with the team from Finaghy and get up to speed on what they have on Ronny Fisher so far. Billy, you and Jo do the same for Dan Anderson with Holywood. Erin, you're on the CCTV footage?'

'Yes, ma'am.'

'If you get a chance you could have a look through the box of stuff I got from Mrs Anderson. But prioritise the CCTV.'

'Right, ma'am.'

'Any word from Forensics?'

Grant had taken the call from Ferguson just before the briefing started.

'Yes, ma'am. The torch found beside Osmond was the weapon used to hit him.'

'Any fingerprints?'

'Yes. Osmond's and an unidentified set. But they're smudged and they haven't been able to match them.'

'OK. So either they struggled over the weapon or Osmond handled it too.'

'Inspector Ferguson said Osmond's prints were consistent with him having held the torch in the normal way, not smudged as if he'd been struggling and trying to grab it from someone else.'

'So, it may have been Osmond's own torch,' Maxwell suggested. 'He might have brought it with him in case it was dark inside the warehouse. The perp took it off him and used it to hit him.'

'Which means, again like with Roberts, killing may not have been the perp's intention if he didn't bring a weapon with him,' Gawn added. 'Now, Hopewell House, where is it and what happened there? Something did and I want to know what it was.'

As the others moved back to their desks, Gawn turned to Maxwell. 'I'm going to see Donna Nixon.'

She saw his raised eyebrows.

'Bloody hell, Gawn, can you not keep away from that woman?' he hissed, keeping his voice low so the others wouldn't hear. 'It's like a moth and a bloody flame.'

'No, it's not. I haven't questioned her since we discovered Osmond in the warehouse. It was a shock for her. I want to make sure she's alright and find out if there's anything else she knows that's useful for us. No one's questioned her, have they?'

He nodded.

'And then I'll warn her to keep well out of it.'

'In that order?'

'Yes. In that order. Why not come with me if you're concerned I'm going to send her undercover or something?' There was just a slight spark of annoyance in her voice. She was used to a Maxwell who always followed her lead, never questioned her decisions, and trusted her instinct. She preferred him to this Maxwell.

'I think I've got better ways to use my time than babysitting an experienced chief inspector.' He paused and then added, 'who knows what she's doing.'

The look in his eyes didn't quite match his words.

Chapter 53

Gawn hoped she did know what she was doing. This case was getting to her and she couldn't have said why. It wasn't that there was a victim whom she felt sorry for and for whom she wanted to get justice as there had been in other cases in the past. She didn't think she was on some sort of personal crusade. Then she thought again of the Lone Ranger who righted wrongs and saved the innocent. That wasn't how she saw herself. She didn't particularly like any of the victims or potential victims in this case. Roberts was at the very least a voyeur, if not worse. Osmond could be rather obnoxious and was the type of narcissistic womaniser she despised and Ronny Fisher was a typical party girl for whom the years were going to be an ever-increasing enemy in her bid to find a rich husband. Dan Anderson was a bit of a loser – a sad figure whose dreams of a life in music had been reduced to a mundane job he probably hated, a mortgage to pay, and a yearly holiday to keep him going. His wife seemed like an ordinary woman who was somehow caught up in this nightmare drama and was out of her depth.

The only person in all this YP story that she had felt a moment's sadness over was Kellie Beale and she was long dead and nothing to do with the case. Or was she? A thought flitted into Gawn's mind. The doll Rose O'Hare had described to her, the one which had upset Ronny Fisher so much, had had cuts and red marks on its arms, like Kellie's suicide. The girl's suicide must be involved in this. But how? And why? Nearly fifteen years after it happened. She shook the thought away. She had enough live suspects to think about.

A phone call had tracked Donna Nixon down to Clarendon Dock, a mixed office and residential development on the edge of North Belfast within view of the *Titanic* slipways and the much-visited Titanic Museum. She was covering a story about changes to the examinations system. Hardly ground-breaking investigative journalism, Gawn thought to herself with a wry smile. Donna was interviewing the Chief Executive of the local examinations board at their headquarters and then there were to be photographs of students who had achieved top grades in the last set of exams.

Gawn had parked in a new multistorey car park near another new hotel. They were sprouting up all over the city and all over the country, needed to cope with the increasing volume of tourists who wanted to enjoy a bit of the famous Ulster hospitality and a delve into its past whether it was the tragedy of the stately ship on its maiden voyage or the years of bombings and killings which had blighted the place and caused Gawn, among many others, to stay away.

The walk from her parking space to her destination was pleasant although she did struggle a little with the paved walkway in her black Louboutins. Perhaps they hadn't been such a great choice this morning although they did compliment her formal black trouser suit. The sun was out and sparkling off the water. She could hear the jingling from the rigging of the little yachts moored alongside the SSE Arena. She passed a boat tied up beside the river walkway and was surprised to see a German flag on its mast and several young men in navy uniforms, not British, working on its deck. She was struck as she walked towards the Titanic Museum, its outline designed to mirror the tragic vessel, by the vibrancy of the city all around her. Behind her, traffic whizzed ceaselessly over the M3 bridge heading into North Down. Above her a plane was making its final descent into George Best City Airport and in front of her she could see one of the ferries from Scotland approaching its berth not far from where another of the monstrous cruise liners which had become regular visitors to Belfast was already tied up having disgorged its passengers into the city or onto tour buses to head to the North Coast.

She spotted the journalist standing watching while a photographer was posing three young people all dressed in their best school uniforms alongside a smiling woman in a smart business suit who she took to be the CEO. She was within touching distance when something, probably her footfall or her shadow falling on the cobbled path, must have caught Donna Nixon's attention and she wheeled around.

'Oh. It's you. I'm still a bit jumpy from last night. I didn't expect to see you again now I'd outgrown my usefulness.'

Was she really such a monster, Gawn thought to herself? Did she use people and discard them? Maybe. Sometimes. But for good reasons, she told herself.

'I just wanted to check how you are. I didn't get the chance to talk to you much yesterday after… everything.'

'Excuse me if I'm a bit cynical about that. I don't see you as some sort of Mother Theresa taking care of the innocent wee mortals who get themselves caught up in her business. Maybe more like a black widow spider.'

Ouch! The sarcastic tone was clear to hear. But Gawn felt she was being unjustly judged. She did care what happened to people, otherwise why did she do this job?

'I didn't ask you to follow Dave Osmond, you know. I only asked you to try to find some useful information. And I didn't have to exactly twist your arm to get you to agree. You wanted to play in the big league. You were willing to deal with me to get what would help your story and your career, remember?'

The girl looked slightly uncomfortable at her words.

'You're right. Sorry. But it was awful seeing him lying there like that and all that blood, and knowing if I'd followed him I could have been lying there too. How is he, by the way?'

'Still unconscious last time I checked.'

La Cucaracha blared out on a car horn making both women turn to look, as a little red mobile coffee wagon pulled into a lay-by outside one of the office blocks and a dark-haired woman stepped out and began opening up the side of the vehicle to reveal a coffee machine and food for sale.

'Time for a coffee?' Gawn asked.

'Johnny, are we finished here?' Donna Nixon called to the photographer.

'I'll be done in two minutes. But you can go on.'

'Yes. Definitely. I could do with a strong coffee.'

They joined a queue of office workers, mostly girls and women, who had spilled out of the surrounding buildings chattering and gossiping as they waited for their coffee fix. Eventually they reached the top of the queue and Gawn ordered an Americano for herself and a latte for her companion. They spotted a vacant bench alongside the water's edge and made their way over to it.

Any passer-by would have seen only two women sitting in the sunshine enjoying a break from the office and chatting pleasantly together, probably discussing curtains or the latest fashion or the cost of childcare. Instead, these two were engrossed in discussing what had happened to Dave Osmond.

'You followed him from the party. Did he seem worried or frightened about anything?'

'I'd been watching him all evening at the launch event from when he arrived. He kept looking at his watch all night, checking the time, like he had somewhere important to go or maybe someone to meet, not just that he was bored and couldn't wait to leave.'

'And when he did leave, did he seem to know where he was going or was he looking out for someone or trying to find somewhere?'

'Oh, no. Definitely he knew where he was going. He went straight to the warehouse and he turned into the alleyway no bother. I was trying to hold back a bit so he wouldn't spot me following him and when he turned off I almost missed the opening to the alleyway. It's quite narrow and very dark at that time of night and I was almost past it before I realised.'

'Right. That's useful to know. Osmond must have been there before if he was familiar with it.' Gawn didn't think it was likely he would have been there when it was a storage facility for carpets but it might have been used for something else. She made a mental note to check with Organised Crime and Vice and see if they knew anything about it.

'How long do you reckon you sat outside watching, Donna?'

'I don't really know. It's hard to judge. It seemed like a long time when it was happening but I was home in my bed by just after two and he'd only left the party at twelve, so I suppose it couldn't have been all that long.' The woman looked rather sheepish before adding, 'I'd had a few drinks, you see.' Gawn almost commented on Donna's drinking and driving but decided that what the woman might tell her was more important than a reprimand. 'And I was dying for a pee by then. How do you do it?' She saw Gawn's quizzical look and said, 'Long stakeouts.'

Gawn smiled then. 'With great difficulty sometimes. It's another of those occasions when it's easier to be a male.' They both laughed. 'In the time you were watching, Donna, did you see anyone go in or come out of the alley?'

'No. But that part of the road isn't very well-lit. I might have missed someone.'

'And no one else was around or walked past?'

'There were a few people who came out of a building on my side of the road. I think it's a sort of church or something. I remember thinking it was a funny time of night to be at church.'

Gawn thought of the witness who had reported spotting Donna's car. 'So, you would have looked away at them?'

'Well, yes, I suppose so but only for a few seconds.'

'And nobody else?'

'There was a group of young men. I couldn't see their faces. They had hoodies on but they were carrying on like young men.'

'Carrying on?'

'You know, laughing and shouting and shoving each other. Macho men.'

'Which side of the road were they on?'

'The alley side.'

'Is it possible someone could have slipped out of the alley and joined the group without you seeing?'

'Wouldn't they have done something, said something to him if he just appeared and joined them?'

'Not necessarily. Anyway, he might have known them.'

'Then I suppose it is possible. I'm not much of a detective, am I?'

'You're not supposed to be. You're a journalist and I think you have the instinct to be a good one, Donna. But you stick to your job and I promise I won't start writing articles for the *Telegraph*.'

Chapter 54

'Well, anything?' Maxwell greeted her as she walked into his office.

'Yes and no. Osmond was familiar with that building. Donna Nixon followed him and he had no difficulty finding the alleyway. He may have been expecting to meet someone there. She said he was looking at his watch all evening so it seems he had a time arranged to be there. But, unfortunately, she didn't see anyone else so she can't help us with that.'

'The CSIs have been over every inch of the alley and there's nothing to indicate that our perp made his escape any way other than out onto the main road,' Maxwell informed her. 'There's a wall running along the back but it's over 14' high and there's steel prongs built into it to stop anyone climbing over. They checked and there was no evidence of anything being put over the spikes, no fibres and no blood where anyone had injured themselves climbing. Either he was an Olympic pole vaulter or he must have just walked out.'

Gawn thought of the young men Donna had seen. She told her inspector.

'Or he could have left later. Donna didn't stick it out too long. If he'd waited for an hour or two he could have just walked out and there wouldn't have been anybody around to see him.'

'More work for the CCTV search then.'

'Yes. They could concentrate on trying to find the group of young men Donna saw and if we could identify them we might get some more info from them. They might have noticed something.'

Through the glass which divided Maxwell's office from the main squad room, they both noticed a burst of activity around McKeown's desk. Jo Hill had been sitting beside her as they had trawled the camera footage. They had now been joined by Grant. It was Grant who walked over and poked his head into the office.

'Sarge has got something.' At almost the same time, the phone rang on Maxwell's desk. Gawn followed Grant out of the office while Maxwell held back to answer the phone.

'I picked up a group of people leaving a supermarket opposite the park at 12.40. About ten minutes later here they are again at Bridge End caught on the traffic cameras, which would have been the time it would have taken them to walk that distance. They split up here. Someone could have joined them from the warehouse and then slipped off into the industrial complex opposite or one of the wee side streets. Anyway no one extra was with them when they got to Bridge End.'

It seemed her theory was possible. Their mystery man could have simply slipped out of the alley and joined the group of men or he could have waited and left later. They had no way of knowing.

Maxwell was standing behind her now.

'That was the PC from the hospital on the phone. Osmond's regained consciousness.'

Chapter 55

Gawn and Maxwell had driven to the Ulster Hospital together. They walked to the Critical Care Complex and took the stairs to the second floor.

Once through the double doors all exterior noise ceased. The lighting was subdued. There was a palpable sense of calm which reminded Gawn of Father Stephen and the church, although the two detectives were immediately aware of the gentle beeping of monitors all around them and nurses moving purposefully from patient to patient. But there was no rush, no bustle, little in the way of talk. Most of the patients seemed to be sedated or at least asleep.

A round-faced woman in blue scrubs walked towards them, a serious expression on her face.

'No visitors allowed,' she announced in a voice which brooked no contradiction.

Gawn read her badge. Helen Mitchell, Ward Manager. She took her warrant card from her pocket and held it out.

'I'm DCI Girvin. This is DI Maxwell. We're here to see Dave Osmond. He was brought in during the night. We were told he'd regained consciousness and we were hoping to have a quick word with him.'

The Ward Manager looked down her nose at the proffered card but didn't touch it as if it was a smelly dead fish.

'I see.' It seemed she was on the verge of denying them entry and then thought better of it. 'He's back with us but he's very weak and any stress could have serious consequences. It's important he's kept calm.'

'We're not here to harass him. He was attacked and we want to find who did it. Stop them hurting anyone else. I'm sure he would like that too.' Secretly Gawn was doubtful if he would. If Osmond was caught up in something illegal either in the past or currently he might well prefer to keep it quiet. 'I promise we'll only take a few minutes.'

'He's in the last bed. But you can only stay a few minutes. I'll be back to see you out.'

'Thank you.'

They wasted no time in heading towards Osmond's bed. They knew the nurse had not been joking. She would be back and they needed to get whatever information he could – or would – give them as quickly as possible.

As they approached the bed, Osmond seemed to be asleep and Gawn worried he might have lapsed back into unconsciousness but as she moved nearer he slowly opened his eyes. She was shocked at the change in him. His head was swathed in bandages. She'd been expecting that. It reminded her of seeing Seb in the ICU when he had hit his head during the debacle in Donegal. Osmond seemed to have shrunk into the bed and he looked older too. His eyes were bloodshot and seemed sunk down into his head and he was attached to all kinds of leads and drips. She took all this in in one quick glance.

'Dave, do you remember me? From Albert Mooney's? Gawn Girvin? Jonah's friend?' She kept her voice low. Maxwell hung back.

'Yes.' His voice was barely above a whisper.

'Do you know who did this to you, Dave?'

For five seconds he made no response and she wondered if he did remember and was debating with himself whether to tell them.

'No. I was hit from behind. I'd set my torch down and someone must have lifted it. Couldn't see who it was. I tried to get it off him but he pushed me down and hit me.' The words came out jerkily, each one taking an obvious effort. If he was lying to them, he could just have said 'no' and saved himself a lot of trouble, Gawn thought to herself.

'He?'

'I think so.'

'Why were you there, Dave? What was in that warehouse?'

This was an important question. Osmond could be caught up in something else; something totally different. He might have been meeting someone for any number of reasons which had nothing to do with her case. If he had been, she needed to know. She didn't want to waste time chasing after shadows.

He closed his eyes but then he opened them suddenly and looked straight at her.

'Hopewell.' One word, forced out from between dry lips.

'I think that's long enough now. Time for you to leave.'

It was the Ward Manager back. She looked like she meant what she said and Gawn wasn't going to start a row in the ICU with all these seriously ill people around. Anyway, Osmond's eyes were closed again. She thought they had probably got as much as they could have hoped for on this visit.

'Thank you.' She turned and walked out, followed by Maxwell.

'Hopewell again,' he said once they had passed through the swing doors and were standing in the brightly lit corridor.

'Yes. Hopewell again. What happened at Hopewell?'

'Maybe one of the others will have found something. We need some sort of a break.'

Chapter 56

And one of the others had found something. Jack Dee smugly announced, 'We've found Hopewell,' as soon as the pair walked into the squad room.

'Hallelujah!' Maxwell couldn't help letting his relief show. He was getting as consumed by this case as Gawn seemed to be. It was a puzzle and he had never been a fan of jigsaw puzzles, especially with missing pieces, which was what Hopewell had become. Both detectives hoped that having found it, all the other pieces would begin to fall into place and they would know what they were dealing with.

'Go on, Jack. Stun us with your brilliant discovery.' Maxwell joshed him, prepared to let him enjoy his moment of success.

'It's up the Glens. Near Carnlough.'

'I wasn't expecting that. I assumed it must have been somewhere in Belfast, maybe where YP met or something,' Maxwell responded.

'No. They met for rehearsals every week in that warehouse at Ravenhill,' McKeown cut in. 'Sergeant Moore says his granny remembered after the mission hall closed down it lay vacant for a while and then it was rented out to a youth group that had a sort of orchestra.'

'Youth Pop.'

'Yes, ma'am.'

'So Osmond would have been familiar with the Ravenhill building. But what about Hopewell? How does it fit in?'

It was Jack Dee again, relishing being the bearer of good news. He stood up, walked across the room, and pinned a photograph to the board.

'Hopewell House, ma'am. Or rather Acton House or even The Charles Lamont Memorial Home.' He was enjoying seeing her reaction. 'It was built in the mid-nineteenth century by a local businessman called George Acton, later Sir George. It was his family home. Very grand. He owned a lot of land all around the Glens. After his death, the family line seems to have died out and the house and estate went through various incarnations. It became the Charles Lamont Memorial Home in the late 1940s after the war when a Trade Union bought it and redeveloped it as a holiday home for injured or retired members. Then in 1973 it was bought by the local education authority as an outdoor pursuits centre for school groups and it ran as that for over twenty years. Then they built a new all-singing, all-dancing outdoor pursuits centre and Acton House as they called it again was taken over by a commercial company who wanted to run it for youth groups and church groups and the like. It had all been kitted out by the education people so it had dormitories and kitchens and all the stuff needed for a residential centre. But it didn't do very well. There wasn't much of an uptake. According to the man I spoke to at the local council, they were charging too much and why would groups pay big bucks when they could use the newer purpose-built education place down the road which was cheaper.'

Gawn was getting impatient. 'Get to the point, Jack.'

'Anyway, it closed down after a couple of years and then lay vacant before it was taken over by an American Health Food company called Hopewell. They never officially changed the name of the building and most people still called it Acton House. Then they got a grant for allowing its use for community and charity purposes.' Dee caught Gawn's eye and hurried on. 'They started using it for cross-community groups and conferences and the like. And for charity concerts.' He finished, allowing his voice to trail off lamely.

'And that's it?' Maxwell asked. 'No murders, no missing musicians, no problems at all?' He couldn't help his disappointment sounding in his voice.

'Not that I could find. It was closed up when the company shut up business in Europe and it's just been sitting there ever since.'

'It's still there?' Gawn asked, surprised.

'Yes. Probably derelict but, yes, it still seems to be there.'

Both Gawn and Maxwell were disappointed. They had at least hoped if not expected that finding Hopewell House would fill in what they needed to know to solve the case. Gawn had assumed something had happened there which was the source of all the current events. Instead, it seemed nothing had happened there, at least nothing that was ever reported to the police.

'Fancy a wee run along the coast to take a look at this Hopewell House?' Gawn asked Maxwell.

'I don't think there'll be much to see.'

'Maybe not or maybe we'll get some inspiration from being out of the office.'

Chapter 57

It was late afternoon. Gawn was in no hurry to get home. There was nothing waiting for her but an empty apartment and whatever Martha, her part-time housekeeper, had left in the fridge for her evening meal. Maxwell, she was sure, would be keen to get home to his family; they had travelled in separate cars so that he would be able to head straight back after they'd had a look at the famous Hopewell House.

She had chosen the coastal route, passing within sight of her own apartment, under the protective eye of the Norman castle. Maxwell followed dutifully in her wake. This would take a little more time, but she never failed to be awed by its majestic beauty, by the sacrifice of the men who had died hewing the rock to make way for the road. Passing through the Black Arch, Gawn led their two-car cavalcade along the Antrim Coast Road which was looking at its best in the late afternoon light. There was still some sunlight playing on the water which was beginning to look a little choppy. A fishing boat was working not far offshore; Gawn could glimpse the men on the deck gathering their nets.

The drive took over an hour. She had listened to some classical music and enjoyed just allowing her mind to roam aimlessly not thinking about the case. When they reached the pretty seaside town of Carnlough, they had driven through, the house being on the far side. Eventually her sat nav told her she was about to arrive. She slowed and began scanning for an opening in the overgrown stone wall which edged the landward side of the road. Thick bushes and trees formed an almost intransigent barrier to whatever lay beyond. Suddenly she came upon the entrance. The tall stone pillars which would have supported gates were standing bare now on either side of a tarmacked driveway which meandered into the distance up the hill. This had been some estate. She drove, her eyes darting from left to right at what would once have been carefully tended gardens with mature trees and huge rhododendron bushes. She couldn't help but be impressed. The grounds would have been a perfect setting for all sorts of outdoor activities and she imagined concerts held on the rolling lawns here would have been spectacular, with a view from the top of the hill out over the North Channel towards Scotland.

Gawn pulled her Audi to a stop and parked facing the old house. Maxwell drew in alongside her. They both got out and stood looking up at the building, taking in its size and obvious former grandeur. It still impressed even in its reduced state. Gawn thought with amusement that she was in danger of being mistaken for an estate agent or landlord again. The house bore the obvious signs of its neglect and disuse – boarded up windows on the lower floor, greenery overflowing the guttering, ivy allowed to grow unchecked taking over the frontage and almost covering some of the upstairs windows, and weeds poking from between the stone steps which led up to the impressive double front door – but still its one-time grandeur was easy to imagine.

They walked across and tried the door, but, as they had expected, it was firmly locked. Then they walked around the building looking into the one window at the back which was uncovered. This had been a kitchen or probably closer to what would now be called a utility room or in earlier times a larder or pantry. It had shelves which would have held all manner of foodstuffs. Now all that stood on one solitary shelf was an upturned cup and a tin caddy, its lid lying beside it.

'Nothing much to see here.'

'You didn't expect there would be, did you, Paul? Whatever happened here was over fifteen years ago. And whatever it was attracted no attention at the time. But I'm still glad I came. It's good to get a picture in your mind, a feel for the place.'

'Sometimes I wonder if you're going to go all new-age on me and feel vibrations from crimes in the past.' He laughed. She didn't. She remembered all too clearly the palpable sense of evil she had experienced twice during her investigations in the Netherlands. She believed evil was very real just as she had sensed the opposite of it when she had been with Father Stephen. 'There have been a few people up here recently.' He pointed to some tyre tracks.

'Probably a favourite spot for couples, I would think.'

'What about the motorbike?' He pointed to a set of motorcycle tracks across the grass.

'Never heard of a pillion passenger?'

'Yes, of course, but you wouldn't have a warm back seat to do your courtin','' Maxwell responded with a smile.

'There are some people who like sex in the open air. I've heard it's supposed to be a turn-on.' She grinned and thought of what she and Seb had got up to in the moonlight in the sand dunes opposite their holiday apartment on the North Coast and wondered if there were any dunes on Santa Monica beach. When she noticed him turning slightly pink with embarrassment unused to having this type of conversation with her, she quickly added, 'Time for a quick drink before we start heading back?'

Maxwell checked his watch. 'Yes. Why not? Go on.'

Chapter 58

He had heard them coming. The sound of their car engines had sliced through the sounds he had become accustomed to from the old house – the squeaks and creaks that he had come to know and expect, their familiarity comforting. He had watched the cars drive slowly up towards the house and two people get out, a woman from the grey car, a man from the black. She was tall, had an air of authority and her expensive-looking black trouser suit suggested she was the boss. Her red hair made her easily recognisable. The man was smartly but more casually dressed with a black leather jerkin. He wondered if they were from the estate agents hoping to sell the property or perhaps from some company interested in buying it. He didn't care. Soon it wouldn't matter. Soon it would be all over. Only a few more days.

They wouldn't interfere with his plan. He wouldn't let them.

He watched as they gazed up at the house. He felt secure behind the grimy window and dust-laden curtains. They wouldn't see him. When they moved towards the building, he had backed away and made his way onto the landing. He listened as they tried the front door, holding his breath even though he knew he had locked it securely. They wouldn't be able to get in.

He listened to their footsteps on the gravel pathway below and caught glimpses of the top of their heads as they walked around the building. He realised they would be going to look at the back of the property. He was confident he had secured everything there too. But he still rushed across to a back bedroom and watched them again as they rounded the corner. The window in this room was broken, one of the few episodes of vandalism the house had endured, so he could hear their voices.

'Nothing much to see here.' The man's deep voice displayed his disappointment. The watcher wondered what he had been expecting to see.

'You didn't expect there would be, did you, Paul?' The woman's voice had a slight English accent. 'Whatever happened here was over fifteen years ago.'

He had stepped back at those words, shocked at what she had said.

'And whatever it was attracted no attention at the time. But I'm still glad I came. It's good to get a picture in your mind, a feel for the place.'

It was the woman. She knew. No, she didn't know. She suspected. Now it would be a race against time and against her. He wouldn't let her spoil his plans.

As he watched, the two climbed back into their cars and drove away. His face was set. He bared his teeth in a grin which had nothing to do with happiness and everything to do with the anticipation of his ultimate success. He would get his revenge and nothing and no one – he thought of the red-haired woman – would stop him.

Chapter 59

Gawn and Maxwell drove back to the village. She had spotted a bar in the main street on the way through and headed back there now. They walked together into the old-fashioned public house, probably not much changed in the last fifty years or more. This was an authentic local pub, no national chains with their makeovers trying to provide a faux atmosphere, no pandering to tourists with folksy clutter bought by the metre from some bric-a-brac shop. Instead, this was as it had always been. A fire was lit in a blackened cast iron fireplace. The wooden floor was not highly polished but rather carried the marks of years of feet coming and going enjoying the camaraderie of this place. Gawn would not have been surprised to have seen it strewn with sawdust to soak up the split beer and globs of spittle which she could remember her father describing from his childhood. The smell of peat hung over the room and evoked for Gawn past visits to the local Folk Museum where recreations of nineteenth-century country life centred round smoky turf fires once used for griddle cooking as well as heat. Gawn recognised the yellow and white flag hung prominently over the fireplace – the county GAA flag with a row of team photographs hanging either side of it.

A buxom brunette stood behind the bar. A welcome smile spread across her face when she looked up from polishing a pint glass and saw her new customers.

'*Fáilte*. What can I get you now?' Her accent reminded them they were no longer in Belfast, if they had needed any reminding.

'I'll just have an orange juice, please.'

Gawn noticed Maxwell's puzzled glance in her direction.

'Have you any low alcohol beer?' he asked, following her lead.

'God, I'm certainly not going to have to be throwing you two out at the end of the night because you're drunk, am I now?' the barmaid asked with a laugh. She looked them both up and down and Gawn realised she was sizing them up. She imagined it wouldn't be long until she had sussed them out as police.

'Not too busy today,' Maxwell said just to make conversation.

'Sure it's early yet. The usuals will be in soon enough. Tourists, are you?'

'Just passing through. We were looking at that big house up the road.'

'Hopewell? Are you thinking of buying it?' The woman had cast an eye over Gawn's outfit and obviously reckoned she was well-off.

'No. We were just looking around.'

Gawn realised the barmaid must know the house and she knew it as Hopewell. 'It's very impressive. Have you ever been in it?'

'Sure, isn't it an awful shame? It's been lying there going to wreck and ruin for years and it used to be so lovely. I was at a few concerts there years ago.'

'Oh, it wasn't someone's private house then?' Gawn asked, hoping she sounded only mildly interested, not that she was hanging on the woman's every word.

'I'm talking years and years ago but, when I was there, it was a sort of youth hostel and they held charity concerts there. It used to be great for all of us local girls with the young fellas down from Belfast or across from Derry around the town. I even got a few dates out of it.' She smiled at the memory. 'The man who organised it all, Professor somebody or other, I don't remember his name, his assistant asked me out. He had a car and everything. We didn't have a car then. He took me dancing in Ballymena. Aye, Marcus was good fun. And then they stopped coming and I never heard anything more from him.'

Gawn had thrown a warning look at Maxwell to stop him reacting to the name Marcus. It had to be Marcus Roberts.

'When would that have been?' she asked.

The woman sucked in her lips and thought. She rested her chin on her hand and let out a sigh. 'It must have been about 2006. I think. God, time flies, doesn't it? It seems like yesterday. It would have been summer, August. I remember because I was heading off to the Catering College in September. That was the last time any of them were here, I think.'

And September 2006 was when Professor Courtney had suddenly packed his bags and left Northern Ireland. They mightn't have got much from visiting the house but their trip to Carnlough had still proved useful.

Chapter 60

Gawn knew the weekend would drag if she hadn't made some more progress by the end of the day. They were getting more information but it was coming in dribs and drabs and it was all so tantalising. She thought it had been useful to visit Hopewell House yesterday and she was sure they had nearly everything they needed to know now and yet one major piece of the puzzle was still missing and one major player was still shrouded in mystery.

'Penny for them.' Maxwell broke into her thoughts. She had been a million miles away, well 6,000 approximately.

'What are we missing, Paul? *Who* are we missing? There has to be something we've overlooked.'

The two made their way into the squad room where everyone was gathered. Mark Ferguson was there too and Gawn noticed him and turned to him first.

'Got something for us, Mark? Please.' She tried not to sound too desperate.

'We found a fragment of an earring in the alley and we've tested it for DNA. The results are just back. We got a match. It belonged to… well, it was worn by Veronica Fisher. We matched it with DNA we got from a search of her house.'

'So, one of our other missing persons had been there as well as Osmond. How recently, Mark?'

'Difficult to tell precisely but within a day or two.'

'We need people back there with her photograph questioning neighbours. See if anyone saw her and especially if we can pin down when she was there and if she was with anyone. A woman could have hit Osmond. It wouldn't have needed that much strength, just the element of surprise. Osmond says he struggled with his assailant, but I'd take that with a pinch of salt. More likely he was ambushed from behind.'

'But could she have done that to Roberts and transported his body to the river?' Maxwell asked.

'She might have had an accomplice. Maybe Anderson. Maybe even Osmond and then they had a falling out and she turned on him. Jack, you were checking with the hospital. How's Osmond?'

'You know what they're like, boss. Cagey. Won't commit themselves but they did say he's stable and making progress.'

'Did they give you any indication when we might be able to question him again? Properly this time,' the chief inspector cut in impatiently.

'No, ma'am.'

'Has anyone managed to turn up anything more about Hopewell House? No crime reports?' She was losing patience as much with herself as with her team. She knew they were all doing their best but sometimes your best didn't cut it. And she didn't want that to be the situation this time. They had two missing persons, either or both of whom could turn up dead at any time or one or both of whom could be their attacker, and a man seriously injured in ICU as well as one in the morgue. The body count could rise.

Heads were shaken. Logan spoke up. 'I contacted the local cop shop. The sergeant has been there for nearly twenty years and he has no memory of any major problems associated with the house when it was running as a hostel and nothing about YP.'

'OK. Let's forget Hopewell House for now then. Maybe that's just a red herring. Let's go back to these people.' She had walked across to the murder board and was pointing to a blow-up of the photograph taken of the young musicians at the Summer Concert. 'I want everything we can get on them. Before they were in YP and ever since. And this writing and drawing.' She indicated the numbers and angel drawing which had been on Roberts' back. 'We think we know what the numbers refer to – the perp is redressing some sin he thinks has gone unpunished but does the angel with the smile have any special significance?'

'Other than freaking you out?' asked Logan.

Gawn didn't rise to his comment. 'See if you can find it on any database or associated with any other crime scene. Erin, did you have a chance to look through the box I got from Mrs Anderson?'

'Not yet, ma'am. I've been concentrating on the CCTV.'

'OK. I'll take another look myself.'

Before she could lift the box to carry it through to her office, Maxwell appeared beside her. He had just taken a phone call and she wondered what he was going to tell her.

'McDowell wants an update. I've to go up now.'

'*You've* to go up? No offence, Paul, but this is *my* case.' Apart from the terse few words at the very beginning of all this when the superintendent had rung to tell Paul about the body in the Lagan, Gawn had had no communication with her superior. '*I'll* go and speak to him.'

'Do you think that's wise, boss?' That seemed to be a question he was posing to her too frequently for her liking. 'He asked me. I can give him an account and take any heat that we haven't nabbed anyone for it. You don't need to face him yet. Wait until we've got our man and then present it to him and there'll be nothing he can say.'

'No, Paul. That's not the way I work. I'm not going to hide behind you and McDowell has to realise he can't use you as some kind of ping pong between us either. You don't want to get caught in the middle here. I'll deal with it.'

As she walked out of the office, she knew she was much less confident about the coming confrontation than she had sounded to Maxwell. McDowell had usually been fair in his treatment of her in the past, but she knew from office gossip that he'd had his own preferred candidate when she was appointed. They had clashed once or twice and she knew he regarded her as a pain in the arse because he had once told her that to her face. Mind you, that was after she had accused him of being stapled to his desk and buried under paperwork and that he had forgotten what real police work was like. Up to now she had always had the comforting cushion of her godfather ACC Smyth to fall back on. Not that she had ever run to him for help, but she knew McDowell would always have thought twice before acting because he knew Smyth held her in high regard. He had never actually known that Smyth was her godfather. No one had.

She stood outside McDowell's office and hesitated for just a second before knocking.

'Come in.' McDowell's gruff response gave her some indication of his mood and the welcome she should expect.

She started speaking as soon as she opened the door and before she had stepped into the room.

'You wanted an update on the Roberts case, sir?' Then she became aware there was someone else already there. It was a woman and an ACC from the insignia on her tunic. It could only be ACC Wilkinson, all the others she knew. 'Sorry, sir. I didn't realise you already had someone with you. I can come back later.'

'Don't let me hold up your good work. Chief Inspector Girvin, isn't it?' The woman walked across to her and held out her hand. 'Sandra Wilkinson. We haven't met yet, but your reputation precedes you.' Gawn couldn't figure out whether she was being serious or sarcastic. 'Norman Smyth spoke very highly of you.'

'Nice to meet you, ma'am.'

'Perhaps when you're finished with the superintendent here you could spare a few minutes to come and see me.'

'Of course, ma'am.' Gawn would have preferred not to. Apart from the fact that she was expecting a sticky meeting with McDowell which might leave her in a bad mood, she wanted to get on with the case.

Chapter 61

Her meeting with McDowell had gone better than she'd anticipated. Perhaps he was waiting for his opportunity to pounce later when she made a mistake or the case went cold and they never found their perp but for now he simply listened and nodded as she recited what they had done and what they knew so far.

'And what's your take on it all, Chief Inspector? What do you think it's all about?'

What did she think it was all about?

'I think we're dealing with someone who's on a mission. I don't believe they're random attacks so the general public isn't at risk. It's very much targeted on one small group of people and we know what links them – their membership of this youth group. Now all we need to find out is what they did that someone thinks they deserve to be punished for.'

'And you've found no criminality linked to YP?'

'No, sir. Only Professor Courtney. But that was in Thailand and none of these others were anywhere near there so they couldn't have been involved.'

'I would guess someone like your professor didn't just start his funny business when he went to Thailand. I'd be very surprised if he wasn't involved in some kiddie diddling here too. He just wasn't caught. Hence his speedy departure. Talk to Vice – that would be my suggestion.'

'Yes, sir.'

'And you haven't traced anything that happened to any of the group here which might have involved the professor?'

'The only suspicious thing was a death, a suicide. One of the members of the group. But there was no suggestion that it was anything other than a suicide or that it had anything to do with Professor Courtney. And anyway, why would anyone wait fifteen years, and if it was the professor who did something to her, well, he's dead. Why attack these other people who were only young themselves at the time?'

'That might all be worth finding out, Chief Inspector.'

Gawn came away from McDowell's office with a clearer idea of where she wanted to take the investigation. She admitted to herself it had been unexpectedly useful to talk it over with him; to have him bring a fresh perspective to it all. And she'd been pleasantly surprised at his attitude. Maybe she had rushed to judgement. Maybe he had simply been trying to let her work herself slowly back in after her last case which had almost broken her.

The few minutes she spent in ACC Wilkinson's office put her in an even better mood. The woman, whose accent she found slightly difficult to make out at times, seemed down-to-earth and practical and her time spent reading herself into her post had paid off because she certainly seemed to be on top of everything. Even how to pronounce her name. She had been prepared to explain it was Gawn to rhyme with Dan but didn't need to. Gawn was impressed and sure she could work well with this woman. So it was a DCI with a new spring in her step and a lighter mood who returned to the squad room.

Chapter 62

Things had obviously been happening while she was with McDowell. Maxwell and Dee were gathered around McKeown's computer.

'Find something?' she asked as she approached them.

'What she didn't find is more important,' Dee replied enigmatically, which wasn't like him. He saw Gawn's eyebrow raised in query and explained, 'My bloody witness, ma'am.'

'I've been going over everything again, ma'am, watching all the comings and goings on foot or in vehicles from midnight until 6am. There was quite a bit on the main road, mostly taxis but virtually nothing turned onto the embankment and very little foot traffic.'

'So where did Walter naffin' Plinge spring from?' Dee added, his voice betraying his annoyance.

'Could he have come from a different direction?'

'He told me he was coming from town and he'd come up the Ormeau Road.'

'Yes, but he was drunk, wasn't he, Jack? Maybe he got confused.' Gawn tried to sound reassuring.

'I've watched the Malone, University and Lisburn Roads, ma'am, which would all have been very long ways round and still wouldn't have put him anywhere he could have seen what he said he saw. I'm nearly cross-eyed. Nothing. There was a group of men, looked as if they'd been doing some heavy drinking. They came up Ormeau Road from the direction of the city centre about 2am and stood at the corner for a while passing round a bottle before heading on up the road, but no Walter Plinge with them and no pram.'

'His pram,' Gawn repeated.

Gawn looked at Maxwell and he returned her look.

'Are you thinking what I'm thinking?' Maxwell asked her.

'Maybe. It would be a handy way to transport a body, wouldn't it?'

Dee's face looked like thunder. He didn't like being made to look a fool. 'Why would he offer himself up as a witness if he was our attacker? He could have stayed well out of the way. We wouldn't have known anything about him.'

'Maybe he was worried that someone had seen him or he would turn up on some camera somewhere that he didn't know about. If he is our man, he's very camera aware. He managed to keep out of the way when he was with Roberts so maybe this was a way to allay suspicions, convince us he was an innocent witness with nothing to hide and have us wasting our time chasing some non-existent van.'

'Or maybe he just likes playing games,' Maxwell chimed in. When he saw Gawn's face, he wished he hadn't spoken. The Perfume Killer had liked games too and it had nearly cost her her life.

'Find him, Jack.' She didn't have to issue that order twice. Dee had grabbed his coat and stamped out the door before she had finished speaking.

'That's not all.' Maxwell took her by the arm and led her towards the door to the corridor. 'Donna Nixon tried to contact you.'

'Did she say what she wanted?'

'She would only talk to you. I suppose she doesn't know that I'm aware of your little arrangement.' His lingering doubts about how she had involved the journalist were reflected in his tone.

'I'll call her back. Give me a minute, Paul, and then come in. We can go through the rest of Anderson's mementos together.'

Chapter 63

'Donna? It's Gawn Girvin.'

She could hear noises in the background. The sound of chatter and clinking glasses. There was low music too.

'I've found your missing woman.'

'Veronica Fisher?'

'Yes.'

'How? Where?' They had half the PSNI out looking for her and the journalist had found her. Gawn was livid. If Nixon had got to her first, no doubt she would have interviewed her before letting them know. Gawn knew that's what she would have done. She would probably be able to read the report in the paper before she'd get speaking to the missing woman herself.

'She's staying in a wee B&B in Portrush.' Nixon had named a seaside resort on the North Coast, once popular with families but now more well-known for its nightclubs and occasional drugs busts.

'How did you find her?'

'I talked to some of her friends.' So had they, but all had claimed not to have seen her for years.

'A few expensive cocktails, a bit of chat and it appears Veronica came to a particular B&B in the Main Street here with her family every year for holidays ever since she was child. She used to talk about it all the time. She even referred to the owner as Auntie Annie and apparently the woman was the closest thing to family she has left. I thought it was worth a look and I drove up this afternoon. And here she is, sitting in the Portside Bar and looking a bit sorry for herself.'

Maxwell had been right. The journalists could splash the cash and schmooze in a way they couldn't.

'Have you spoken to her yet?'

'Not yet.'

Gawn didn't know whether to believe her or not.

'Don't!'

She heard a faint snort in response. Gawn moderated her voice then. She couldn't order her not to speak to Veronica and if she pushed too hard it might only drive her to do it.

'I mean, you'll scare her off. Wait and I promise you can get your interview after we speak to her.' Gawn had her fingers crossed metaphorically. There was no way she could force Donna to hold off her interview and no way she could force Veronica to give Donna Nixon an interview if she didn't want to. If the journalist put the phone down now, she could take Veronica off somewhere and interview her before Gawn could have the local police alerted to pick her up. She just had to wait for her response.

And it didn't come immediately. There was silence at the end of the line for what seemed like a very long time. Donna Nixon was no doubt balancing the pros and cons of waiting for the police to pick Veronica up versus pushing ahead for a scoop. It could be a big break for her if Veronica was able to identify Roberts' and Osmond's attacker. It could be a front-page article with Nixon's name on the by-line. On the other hand, Northern Ireland was such a small place. Falling foul of a senior police officer could mean you'd be blocked and thwarted at every turn, never get a break, the last to get any information.

'You better keep your word.'

Gawn had been holding her breath. Now she spoke. 'I will. Sit tight. Keep watching her but don't let her know. I'll get someone there as soon as possible.' She realised she sounded as if she were addressing one of her own officers and wondered what Maxwell would think if he could hear her. 'Just sit tight.'

Chapter 64

After phoning the police station in Coleraine, Gawn went into the squad room and took Maxwell aside and gave him the news about Veronica.

'Bloody hell. I told you that journalist would be trouble.'

'She found our missing woman for us.'

'Not for us. For herself. Do you trust her not to speak to her?'

'If she'd wanted to do that, she could have done it before she rang.' But she wasn't really sure, and she was worried that somehow Nixon might scare their witness off.

The office phone rang just then and McKeown answered it.

'That's Coleraine, ma'am. They've picked up Veronica Fisher. They're bringing her down.'

'Thanks, Erin. Let's get the rest of this box gone through before she arrives.'

* * *

Gawn and Maxwell had gone back into her office and begun digging through the last few items in Anderson's box of memories. There was a lot in it to go through.

'Either he's a natural hoarder or it must have been a very important time in his life for he seems to have kept almost every shred of paper. Look, even old birthday and Christmas cards.' Maxwell held out a pile of cards to her. She took them and opened the top one.

'This one's from someone signing himself Kev the Rave.'

'Kevin Donnelly?'

'Probably.'

She flicked open the next one and Maxwell saw the look on her face.

'What is it?'

She turned the opened card around so he could see it too. The greeting read, *Happy Birthday, dearest Danny* and it wasn't signed with a name but a drawing – an angel with a smiley face.

'So, our angel was someone to do with YP too.'

'Did you ever doubt that, Paul?'

'A girl?'

'Looks like it. There's an X after the drawing.'

'Could still be a male.'

'Well, yes. What age was Anderson when all this was happening?'

Maxwell took time to calculate his answer.

'Osmond told us he was one of the tutors and a bit older than the others in their little clique. They were between about fifteen and twenty-five. I think Anderson was more like about thirty-five.'

'A bit of grooming going on, do you think?'

The inspector just shrugged.

'Anyway, Veronica Fisher should be able to tell us who this is,' he added.

'Maybe it was her.'

'So you're saying she tortured Roberts, dumped his body in the river signing it with her drawing and then attacked Osmond at the warehouse having lured him there somehow?' Maxwell's scepticism was showing.

'She disappeared after Roberts was found. We've assumed it was because she was scared of something happening to her. Rose O'Hare kind of led me in that direction by describing her reaction to the doll and the note. But she could have planted them herself. Then she contacted Osmond and told him about the note. I assume that she told him what was in it and about the doll, which he didn't tell us. Why? Because he had something to hide? Or to protect her? We know she was in that alleyway at the warehouse because of the earring. She could have set Osmond up and attacked him. It wouldn't have taken much strength, just the element of surprise and that would have been easy if he didn't suspect her and had turned his back on her.'

Maxwell didn't react. He had listened carefully. It was a reasonable hypothesis.

'If something happened to Veronica over fifteen years ago which she blamed some of the others for, why has she waited until now to do anything about it?' he asked.

'Good question. I can't wait to ask her.'

Chapter 65

The two detectives were observing Veronica Fisher on a monitor. They had watched as McKeown had brought her into the sad little interview room which was sorely in need of repainting and then arranged for a cup of tea to be brought to her. A uniformed constable was now standing silently in the corner trying and failing to be unobtrusive. The woman glanced at him from time to time as she sipped at the tea, cradling the disposable cup between her hands as if she needed to get some heat into them.

They had seen photographs of her both as a teenager in her YP days and a more recent glamour shot which she had posed for at the opening of an upmarket hairdressing salon in Belfast. The figure before them now looked very different. She was haggard. There was nothing glamorous about her appearance. Her blonde hair was scraped back starkly from her face, emphasising her paleness without make-up. Her eyes were puffy, the result of crying, and when Grant had opened the door suddenly to bring in the tea, she had jumped in her seat.

'We better get in there before she has a heart attack from stress, like our other victim.'

'Don't even joke about that, Paul.'

Veronica Fisher looked up when they walked in. Her eyes moved from Gawn to Maxwell and then back to Gawn again, searching their faces, looking for a clue as to what to expect. She didn't speak but she licked her lips and patted her hair into place, in a gesture which was probably second nature to her when an attractive man was about, and then she tried to raise a smile. Not very convincingly.

'Ms Fisher, I'm DCI Girvin and this is DI Maxwell. You're not under caution but we would like to ask you some questions. You were reported missing and we believe you may have information which is pertinent to our inquiry.'

'You're not arresting me?'

'No.'

'I can get up and walk out anytime I want?'

'Yes.'

But Veronica didn't move.

'What's your inquiry?'

'We're looking into the unexplained death of Marcus Roberts. I think you knew him,' Maxwell stated. They both watched the woman's face closely. She tried desperately not to give anything away. Unsuccessfully.

'I knew *a* Marcus Roberts, but that was years ago.' She took another sip of her tea, waiting to hear what they would ask next.

'Roberts lived in the Holylands, which is only a stone's throw away from the charity shop where you work. We thought you might have bumped into him; seen him around the area,' Maxwell said, hoping that making that suggestion would encourage her to admit to having seen him.

'No. I haven't set eyes on that man for over ten years, maybe nearer twenty.'

Was there something suggestive in the way she had called him 'that man'? Gawn thought there might be. Veronica had sat back into her chair. She was getting herself more comfortable. Gawn decided to switch things up a bit.

'Why did you decide to go missing; to run away, Veronica?'

'I wasn't running away. Whatever gave you that idea?'

She was bluffing. Gawn could see it in her eyes.

'I just wanted to get away for a few days. It's all been a bit hectic recently. I've been very busy. I thought some nice sea air would do me good.'

'Nothing to do with the doll and the note you got, then?'

Her face changed instantly, betraying her. She couldn't conceal her shock that they knew about the doll, although she tried.

'How did you…' she began and then realised the answer to her own question. 'Rose told you.'

'And Dave Osmond.' Gawn waited before asking, 'Why did the doll scare you so much, Veronica?'

Would she provide the missing piece of their puzzle or would she try to lie and bluster her way out? She said nothing. She didn't speak so Maxwell decided to press her a little more.

'And why did you follow Dave Osmond to a warehouse on Ravenhill Road?'

'Follow him? I didn't follow him.'

'But you were there.'

'Yes, but he wasn't. Not when I was there anyway.'

At least she was admitting to being there. That was something.

'When exactly was that, Veronica?' Gawn asked.

'Last Sunday night.'

'And why were you there?'

Suddenly all the fight seemed to dissipate out of her body. She was no major criminal or even a good actress. She had probably never even been in a police station before never mind been questioned. Veronica Fisher seemed to crumple before their eyes. She set the cup down, careful not to spill any of the still hot liquid, her face creased up, her tears started again and she buried her head in her arms on the table. The two detectives watched her shoulders rise and fall as sobs racked her body. They left her for a minute until the loud sobs had begun to subside and she regained control of herself.

It was Gawn who spoke first. She reached across and seemed as if she was going to pat the woman's arm in a gesture of concern, then pulled her hand back.

'Whatever happened in the past, you'll feel better when you tell us about it and we might be able to help you.'

Then they waited. Minutes seemed to pass although in reality it was only seconds. Gradually she raised her head and faced them. Her face was streaked with tears and her lips were quivering. Her eyes locked with Gawn's.

'We never meant for it to happen. Never. We didn't mean for her to die.'

Chapter 66

Maxwell turned to Gawn at Veronica's words. His face reflected his shock. They had killed someone? He hadn't been expecting that and he didn't think Gawn had been either. Whom had they killed?

'Take your time, Veronica, and tell us exactly what happened.' Gawn spoke softly. She was working very hard to keep any hint of judgement out of her voice and she offered the woman an encouraging smile.

'She–'

'Who?'

'Kellie. Kellie Beale.'

Now Gawn was beginning to get some idea of what this was all about.

'Kellie was the youngest of us all, our wee group, and a bit naive too. She'd never been with a boy.'

It was on the tip of Maxwell's tongue to say 'she was only fifteen' thinking of his own daughter who wasn't that much younger, but he didn't speak. He knew Gawn would be furious if he said or did anything to antagonise their witness or stop her cooperating with them.

'She fancied Kev. Kevin Donnelly, another one of our gang. A lot of us did. He was pretty fit, a real looker. But she told me about liking him. One night when we were talking. I thought it was funny. I knew he was a bit of a lad. He had an opinion about himself. He had plenty of girls to choose from. He used to boast about it.'

Veronica's words were coming in spurts. She couldn't help herself smiling as she talked about Kevin Donnelly. She must have had quite a crush on him. Gawn wondered if she detected a slight touch of spite or jealousy. Veronica had obviously fancied Kevin too and maybe he hadn't responded to her advances as she had hoped.

'I never thought he'd be interested in her. I only told him for a laugh. She was only a kid. They practically grew up together. They were more like brother and sister. At least that's how he'd always talked about her and anyway, he always used to say "you never shat in your own bed".'

Maxwell couldn't hide his disgust at her words.

'But when I told him what she'd said, he was so pleased about it. He asked us to set her up for him.'

'What do you mean "set her up"?' Maxwell asked.

'We were to invite Kellie to meet us at our special place. The building on the Ravenhill where the band used to practice. Kev had stolen a key and we could get in any time we wanted. We'd meet there sometimes on nights when there wasn't a rehearsal and just smoke and talk and maybe have a few drinks and make out a bit. Nothing too heavy. She thought it was the four of us just going to be messing around together as usual. But Dave and I didn't go. At least we did but we kept out of sight and watched her arriving. We saw Kev arriving too and then we slipped inside and listened to the two of them from behind the stage.'

'What about Anderson?'

'Danny? He didn't know anything about it, until later when she told him. He would have stopped it if he'd known.'

At least someone had shown a bit of decency and care for the girl who was barely more than a child, Maxwell thought to himself.

'So what happened?' Gawn asked.

'I don't know for sure. Not all the details. As far as we could hear from where we were hiding they had a few drinks. Kev always had a stash of drink and drugs he could produce. He might have slipped her something. I don't know. I heard her slurring her words but she didn't usually drink much so I thought she was just a bit drunk. Kev never said exactly what happened and I never asked him. Anyway, we heard noises and we knew what was going on.'

'What?' Gawn needed her to spell it out for them.

'They were having sex and she was crying. Kev boasted about it later. He liked to think he was her first. But afterwards she freaked out. She was sure she was pregnant. She was afraid her da would kill her. She thought she would lose her scholarship to Music College. Kev just laughed it all off. He didn't want to know then. He said she had nothing to worry about. But she was ringing me all the time. Every night. Sometimes more than once a night.

Eventually I told her to grow up, she was a big girl now and I stopped answering her calls.'

She paused and seemed to gather her courage to speak again.

'A couple of weeks later she committed suicide. They found her in the bath with her wrists slit.'

A sob caught her voice again and took it from her for a minute.

'She'd told Danny too afterwards, and he'd tried to talk to Kev. As if that would do any good. Kev wasn't going to listen to him. He always called him old Granny Danny because he liked to look out for us like a wee granny. Danny tried to help her. He spent a lot of time with her afterwards. I know he advised her to tell her parents but she wouldn't, of course. At least I don't think she ever did.'

'And the only people who knew about this were you, Dave Osmond, Dan Anderson and Kevin Donnelly?'

'Yes. I think so.'

'What about Marcus Roberts or Professor Courtney?'

'I don't think so. Kellie wouldn't have told them and Kev certainly wouldn't have. Marcus might have guessed something. He was always hanging around, watching us all and listening. He was a bit creepy, but I don't think he would have known. If he did, he kept it to himself.'

'Then who sent the doll and note and wanted you to meet up at the warehouse? Could it have been Anderson? Did you see anyone there?'

Veronica shook her head at the suggestion Anderson might have been involved.

'Why would Danny have done that? It doesn't make sense. And I didn't see anyone. There was just a tape recorder sitting in the middle of the floor when I went inside. It was dark and I was afraid whoever had sent the doll and note might have been watching me so I did what I was told. There was another note on the floor signed with Kellie's wee angel signature. That was her. Everyone said she had the voice of an angel so she used to draw that stupid angel with a smiley face on everything. The note said to press the button. I pressed it and it played but it was a weird voice, like a dalek or something.'

'A voice distorter,' Gawn suggested.

'Yes. I suppose so. It said to explain what happened to Kellie Beale; what I had done. So I pressed record and I told it what I just told you.'

'Then what?' Maxwell asked.

'I waited. I expected someone to appear but no one came. I waited an hour like the voice on the tape said and then I left. I thought someone would appear every time there was a noise. I expected to be attacked. I'd even lost one of my earrings out of a hole in my pocket and I was too scared to look for it. I got out of there as soon as I could. I was petrified.'

'But you didn't see anyone?'

'No. Nobody.'

Chapter 67

'Do you believe her?' Maxwell asked.

They were back in the comms room and watching Veronica on the monitor still sitting, wiping her eyes with her handkerchief.

'About what happened to the girl?'

'Yes.'

'Maybe, although I suspect there might have been a bit more to it than Veronica's admitted. I think they probably witnessed a rape and did and said nothing. The girl was underage and drunk. She couldn't have given consent even if she'd wanted to. Maybe there was a bit of jealousy, setting the younger, innocent, more talented girl up with bad boy Kevin knowing something would happen. Bad boys always hold a certain attraction for some women, even innocent wee things like Kellie.'

'Not you?' he asked with a grin, trying to lighten the mood after the revelation about the teenager's suicide, which he had found unsettling.

'Not anymore.' And with that enigmatic answer he had to be content, for Gawn quickly went on, 'I do believe her about the tape recorder. Someone wants to know what happened to Kellie and to have all those involved admit what they did. I think that's what all this is about. Roberts must have had some information about it or at least our perp thought he did. I'm pretty sure it's not Veronica or Osmond, they already knew, and it's definitely not Kevin. It would be no advantage to him to rake everything up now. He's made a good life for himself in America. He wouldn't want old stories about underage sex or possible rape allegations surfacing. That only leaves Anderson. Maybe he's had some kind of crisis of conscience that he didn't do more to protect the girl and he wants to exact some sort of revenge on the others, make them suffer, maybe even try to lead them to commit suicide like Kellie did.'

Maxwell wasn't so sure. Her hypothesis seemed a bit fanciful to him.

'But he got a letter too, ma'am,' Maxwell pointed out to her.

'Ye…ss,' she was thinking. 'You're right. That doesn't make sense, does it?'

But she couldn't shake her suspicions about the teacher.

'Using the tape recorder was quite clever. Low tech. Fairly easy to obtain. There's still quite a few around in older people's homes or attics. I wouldn't be surprised if Anderson owns one. It might be worth getting someone to check with his wife and see if he does and if it's still there. They're not expensive and it means the perp didn't have to meet anyone face to face. He could set it up well in advance and pick it up any time later and listen to it. And he would have a permanent record of their complicity in whatever happened to the girl,' Gawn said.

'Her rape.'

'Yes. The tape recorder was probably how Osmond was caught off-guard too. He might have been leaning down to pick up the instruction note or press some button when he was hit. Check with Ferguson if they found any trace of a recorder, any void in the dust on the floor.'

She tried to cast her mind back to what she had noticed that night but she couldn't picture a space in the dust and she certainly hadn't seen a tape recorder.

'It seems like we might have some kind of a motive. Someone wants to punish this group of people for how they drove Kellie to suicide but who and why now? If it's not Anderson, who else could it be? Fifteen years is a long time to wait to get revenge or justice or whatever you want to call it.' Maxwell's mystification showed in his voice.

'Whatever Veronica admitted to on the tape, it was enough to get her off the target list, at least for now. Osmond might have said something more or been aggressive, and we just don't know what happened to Anderson yet if he isn't our perp.'

'Just as well Donnelly was safely away in America.'

'But he isn't now, is he?' Gawn responded.

'Bloody hell! Too much of a coincidence, isn't it?'

'Our avenger probably sent him a message too. In fact, I'm sure he would have and whatever it said it was enough to have him scurrying back to Belfast. But Donnelly's a different proposition to the others. By all accounts he has connections both here and maybe stateside too. He mightn't be just so easy to intimidate and if our man does want to take him on, he wouldn't be such a soft target. We could be facing another dead body, either Donnelly or our mystery avenger.'

Chapter 68

The Andersons, it turned out, did have a tape recorder but although she searched, Eva Anderson couldn't find it anywhere in the house. She suggested to Grant when he phoned that her husband might have taken it into school to use there.

'Doesn't prove anything one way or another,' Maxwell stated. 'I'll get Jamie to go to the school and ask to search Anderson's store and classroom. They might be willing to agree without a search warrant.'

'We actually don't want him to have it there. If he is our perp, the tape recorder should be with him complete with the recordings of Fisher and Osmond. Anyway, it's getting late. I'm sure the school will be closed for the weekend. He'll have to leave it until Monday. A more pressing issue is what are we going to do with Veronica Fisher?'

'We can't arrest her. She hasn't committed any crime so far as we know.'

'But if we let her go, she'll do a runner. I'm sure she won't agree to go back to her own house. She's scared.' Gawn hadn't told Maxwell about her arrangement with Donna Nixon and wondered if the woman would agree to give an interview and how she was going to put it off for as long as possible. If Donna Nixon heard Veronica's story, it would be on the front page on Saturday evening. And who knew how the Avenger would react to that?

'We could put her up in a hotel for the weekend,' Maxwell suggested tentatively.

'But we couldn't leave her alone. We'd have to put a guard on her, for her own protection.' Gawn could see pound signs before her eyes and hear McDowell's voice in her ear complaining about expenditure on the case. 'Well, it has to be done, we need to keep her safe no matter what. Can you imagine what the press would do to us if we sent her off and something happened to her?'

They explained to Veronica their plan to send her and a police officer to a Belfast hotel for the weekend. She seemed relieved. Maxwell had asked McKeown and Hill to divide the duty between them. McKeown would start tonight with Hill taking over in the morning. Gawn had taken them aside before they left.

'She's not under arrest. You don't need to be trying to question her or get her to confess to anything but chat to her; be friendly. She may give some more away about what happened fifteen years ago or about what happened at the warehouse. I'll call in sometime during the day tomorrow to make sure everything's all right. We don't anticipate any problems. You'll really be there more to stop Fisher running off. I'll need to question her again. Probably not until Monday.'

Before she left, Erin McKeown turned to Gawn and Maxwell. 'I noticed while I was rereading Kellie Beale's inquest report that the thirtieth, tomorrow, is the anniversary of her suicide. Do you think that could have any significance, ma'am?'

'I most certainly do. It would be perfect timing, wouldn't it, for our Avenger if he could mete out his punishment on that date, the anniversary. Well spotted, Erin.'

The three women left, Veronica looking a lot happier than when she had arrived.

'OK, Paul, what Erin suggested means that we may be coming to some kind of endgame. By tomorrow, our Avenger, let's call him, may have done whatever he's aiming to do. We've got Veronica. We've got Dave Osmond. What about the guard on Osmond, Paul?'

They had checked on the radio presenter's condition to find he was out of intensive care and had been moved to a private room in the new wing of the hospital.

'You think he's still in danger?'

'I don't know. Maybe the Avenger has finished with him. Maybe not. Can we risk him coming back to finish the job? Make sure the uniforms are still guarding him anyway. We need to find Daniel Anderson, one way or the other, and we need to find Kevin Donnelly too. Put the whole team on it.'

Gawn's next task, to get it out of the way so she could concentrate on the case, was to ring Donna Nixon. She had already arranged that the team would work overtime during the weekend. McDowell would only permit expenditure for guards on Fisher and Osmond for a short time. They needed to find the avenger, soon and preferably before he struck again, and in her own mind she was thinking tomorrow.

'Donna Nixon.'

'Donna. It's me.'

'Well, did she tell you what you wanted to know?' The journalist didn't need any introductions. She got straight to business eager to hear what the woman had told them. She had a deadline if she wanted to get her story into the Saturday paper.

'She's provided some useful information which has helped the case but we'll need to question her again.'

'Before you can let me speak to her.' A mixture of disappointment, anger and resignation all filtered through her voice.

'I can't let you talk to her in the middle of us questioning her.'

'So, I can't make tomorrow's paper.'

'No. Sorry. You can report we're making progress and hope to make an arrest soon.'

'And do you? Are you really going to make an arrest soon? Play fair, Chief Inspector. I've kept my side of the bargain all along. Give me something.'

Gawn admitted to herself that Donna had been straight with her. She had provided useful information about YP and now she had found their missing woman for them. Gawn's sense of fair play made her want to offer something.

'We're focusing our investigation now on a number of members of Youth Pop. We believe that events from some time ago may have some bearing on the events which led up to the death of Marcus Roberts. He wasn't murdered, Donna. It wasn't deliberate. Whoever did it didn't mean to kill Roberts so we're not looking for any cold-blooded murderer as you might call him in your headlines. We would simply like to speak to Daniel Anderson who has been missing from his home since Tuesday.'

'Do you think he was the one who attacked Roberts?'

'At the moment he's a person of interest but also a possible witness. We need to speak with him so if you wanted to ask around, check with your sources, see if anyone has seen him and ask them to get in touch with the police that would be helpful.'

'Or I could try to find him myself.'

'Keep away from him.' Gawn had spoken with some vehemence. The young woman had been lucky when she had followed Osmond. She mightn't be so lucky if she went investigating again.

'You have until Monday, Chief Inspector. Then I expect something. Last chance. If you don't come through for me, I'll publish what I have and put my own spin on it. Remember you gave me your word.'

Chapter 69

Gawn had woken with a headache and the feeling that some crisis was at hand. Everything had been leading up to today. She just knew it although she couldn't have explained how. She arrived in the squad room to find the whole team busy at their desks, all except Hill who was with Veronica.

'We got the results back from Veronica Fisher's note and the envelope sent to Daniel Anderson,' Dee informed her as she walked past his desk.

'That was quick work. Anything?'

'There were two sets of prints on the note – Fisher's and another which they've identified as Rose O'Hare's. They got hold of her prints for elimination purposes.'

'So whoever wrote the note wore gloves. Not a surprise really. And what about the envelope?'

'Just Anderson's prints where he opened it and held it. They got hold of his prints from his bedside table and matched them. Then Mrs Anderson's were on it too and an unknown set, probably the postman delivering it but it could be our perp. If it is we don't have a match.'

'Not much use then.'

'There was something a bit weird, ma'am.'

'What?'

'The DNA on the envelope where someone had licked the seal is Anderson's own.'

'Why would he be sticking the envelope closed?'

'Unless he wanted to make sure his wife couldn't get to read it,' suggested Maxwell walking out of his office to join the conversation.

'But he didn't put it back in the envelope. He took the letter with him and left the opened envelope behind. It doesn't make sense… unless he sent it to himself,' Gawn said slowly, thinking aloud, remembering her earlier suspicions about the teacher. 'What if he *is* our perp? He sends a threatening letter to himself which means he can disappear and everyone will assume either that he's hiding or the perp has got him. Which is what we have been thinking. Then he can get on with finishing whatever he wants to achieve and he can then reappear with some story of having managed to evade his attacker who has miraculously escaped.'

They had all listened carefully to her theory. No one spoke immediately.

'Do we know where Anderson was the weekend Roberts was attacked?' Gawn asked Logan. He and Jo had been looking into Anderson's disappearance.

The veteran detective flicked back through his notebook until he found his interview notes. 'Yes. He and Mrs Anderson were at a church weekend in Fermanagh.'

'All weekend?'

'From Friday evening until Sunday teatime. He was playing the keyboard for all their activities so it would have been kind of obvious if he wasn't there. Then they drove home and Mrs Anderson said they went to bed early because they both had to get up for work the next morning.'

'No chance he could have slipped away?'

'No, ma'am. She says she's a light sleeper. And he couldn't be our man on the CCTV with Roberts anyway. He's too small. I've seen photos of him with his wife. He's only about 5'6". Our Mr Mystery is nearer six foot.'

Gawn was disappointed.

'That only leaves Kevin Donnelly and it doesn't make any sense for him to bring this all up.' Maxwell's voice showed his disappointment too. He had thought Gawn's theory about Anderson fanciful at first but gradually had come round to her view. He had seemed like the only suspect they had left, until they heard his alibi.

'There is someone else,' Gawn said.

Every eye turned on the chief inspector.

'Connor Beale. What do we know about him?'

Chapter 70

The next three hours were spent gathering as much information about Connor Beale as they could. Being a Saturday some agencies they contacted were closed for the weekend but by early afternoon they had enough that Maxwell decided to call them all together.

Just before Gawn joined them a text came through on her phone. It was from Donna Nixon.

Ran appeal in morning edition for Anderson's whereabouts. Got a tip-off. Following it up now.

No. What was the woman doing? She tried ringing her but her phone went straight to voicemail. She left a message.

'Whatever you do, don't go near Anderson. Keep away. It's too dangerous. I'll speak to you tomorrow.'

If she met up with Anderson she could end up caught in Beale's plans and in danger again. Maxwell noticed how pale she looked as she joined the rest of the team in the squad room but he didn't know why.

'Connor Beale found his sister's body in the bath.' McKeown's revelation shocked them all.

'How did we miss that?' Maxwell asked.

'It wasn't mentioned in the coroner's report, sir. Jo didn't miss it. It wasn't there. I suppose everyone was trying to shield him from having to give evidence at the inquest. It just said her family had found her when her mother returned from visiting a friend and Mrs Beale gave evidence of finding the body. It was only when we questioned the neighbours today that they mentioned it,' McKeown explained. 'That must have been pretty traumatic for him. He was only ten and he and his sister seemed to have been very close. I talked to Rose O'Hare this morning and some of the other neighbours and they all spoke of how good Kellie was to him and how close the two were. After Kellie's death the family seemed to just fall apart. I managed to get talking to a social worker, the one assigned to the Beale family.'

McKeown didn't explain how many phone calls she'd had to make and how many favours she'd had to call in to get speaking to this woman on a Saturday.

'She's retired now but she remembers the problems they were having. Mrs Beale took ill and died within a year. Mr Beale developed a drink problem and lost his job. Connor was in danger of running wild so his father decided to send him away to an uncle in Manchester.'

Gawn and Maxwell both reacted to the mention of Manchester.

'Where he could have known Marcus Roberts,' Maxwell stated although they were all already thinking it.

'He knew Roberts anyway,' McKeown continued. 'He went everywhere with his sister including her rehearsals. He would have known Roberts from there.'

'And he would have known the rehearsal room on Ravenhill Road too then,' Maxwell added.

'I looked into his time in Manchester, boss,' Grant announced. 'He seems to have got in with a bad crowd there. He did a bit of shoplifting and criminal damage. The local police knew him. Eventually he was offered the choice of three months in a juvenile rehabilitation centre or taking his chances in court and ending up with a criminal record. That's where it turned around for him. He joined the drama group there run by some charity and found he had a talent for acting, especially accents. When he was released he took himself off to London and got odd jobs in theatres, until eventually he started getting small acting parts. He got his Equity card and has never looked back.'

Grant walked across and pinned a photograph up on the board. It was a posed headshot obviously used for publicity purposes.

They all looked round as Dee slammed his fist down on his desk.

'Walter naffin' Plinge.'

'Is that your witness, Jack?' Gawn asked. She remembered the homeless man from that first morning by the side of the Lagan but she hadn't really paid him much attention, more focused on trying to get used to being back on duty.

'I think so but look here.' He strode across the room and held up the drawing of Father Stephen's visitor, the man who had been looking for Roberts. 'Look at the eyes.'

'It was Beale,' Maxwell stated simply. 'But Father Stephen said the man had a Liverpool accent.'

'He's an actor. He's good at accents. Good enough to fool the priest and good enough to fool us too. Do we know where he's been staying?' Gawn asked.

Grant spoke up.

'Up until about two weeks ago he was staying at his dad's old house. Several people saw him there. He was renovating it. Then he simply disappeared. We showed his picture around and the lady in the house opposite Roberts' recognised him. He's been leasing her front room for a couple of weeks. Probably so he could watch Roberts. But they've not seen him for the last couple of days.'

'And he could watch us too from there,' added Dee.

'Right, get round to the house he was renovating and take the place apart,' Gawn said.

'If he hasn't already done that,' Logan added, not able to resist a joke. Gawn directed a steely stare at him. She was in no mood for levity.

'See if you can find anything that would show us where he is now. He may have been holding Anderson there or even Donnelly. See if there's any trace of either of them. And have a look around his room opposite Roberts' too.' Gawn issued the orders, her voice trying to instil a sense of urgency.

'Should we get Ferguson in first?' Maxwell asked.

Gawn hesitated. If they ploughed in ham-fisted they could destroy precious evidence and it could prove problematic for any case if it came to court. But they couldn't afford to wait around until forensics had gone over everything. It would take too long and she was convinced that time was something they didn't have or, to be more specific, time was something Beale's target didn't have.

'No. We go now.'

Chapter 71

The little terraced house had obviously been undergoing extensive refurbishment. The plaster had been taken off the walls, the floorboards had been lifted in many of the rooms to reveal old pipework. The walls had been tracked for electrical connections. It seemed Beale had been working to do up the house. So, what had happened? What had changed? A little over two weeks ago he had diverted his energy to finding out who had been involved with his sister and what they had done which led to her committing suicide. At least that was Gawn's read of the situation and Maxwell now agreed with her.

The two detectives were standing in the gutted living room when her phone rang and she saw Ferguson's name on the screen.

'Damn! Did someone tell Mark about the house?'

'I don't think so.'

'Mark. Have you got something for me?' She tried to make her voice sound neutral.

'That photograph album we took from Roberts' house. We've finished our tests and I thought you'd like to see it. It's full of snaps that he must have taken clandestinely of young people, well, girls really. One or two were taken in a changing room. But there are three photographs missing from it. Roberts was obviously a very well-organised man. He had put captions on all the pictures so we know exactly what's missing.'

'I don't need to see them at the minute, Mark. Just tell me what the captions on the missing ones are.'

'OK. One seems to be the same photo you had from the newspaper. Alongside the ordinary names of each person is their nickname as well. Roberts, or someone, had a nickname for them all. The second was a photo of Professor Courtney and Daniel Anderson standing either side of Kellie Beale with their arms around her shoulders and the last was one of the girl again. This time just with Kevin Donnelly with a comment in brackets.'

'Which said what, Mark?'

'Young love.'

'Thanks, Mark. I'll see the album when I get back to headquarters.' She closed her phone and turned to Maxwell. 'If it was Beale in Roberts' house, he has photographic evidence that it was Donnelly his sister was involved with.'

'Right. That explains why he might go after Donnelly but not why he would be punishing the others. How did he know they were involved?'

'I don't know but more importantly we don't know where he is, or Donnelly or Anderson for that matter. He could be holding them somewhere. They could be in danger. In fact, I'm sure they are, Paul.'

Her phone rang again. She almost didn't take the call. When she looked and saw it was Father Stephen she was about to let him leave a message. She needed to focus on finding Beale. Whatever he had planned, she thought – no, she knew – it would happen tonight.

'Father, I'm sorry but I'm really busy just at the minute. Could I phone you back later?'

She expected to hear his soft calm voice agreeing to her request. Instead, when he spoke, she could hear worry.

'Connor Beale was here.'

'When?'

'About three hours ago.'

'And you waited all this time to tell me?' Her voice exploded with reproach.

'I wasn't here when he came. He spoke to one of my parishioners. She doesn't know anything about him or your case.'

'Pity you weren't there but I expect if he'd told you anything you'd have claimed the seal of the confessional and not told me anyway.' She knew she sounded bitter but time was running out for her and, more importantly, for Beale's victims.

'He left a note.'

'For you?'

'No. It was addressed to you but Mrs O'Connor didn't know who you were, so she gave it to me.'

'I'll get someone to collect it from you but could you read it to me now? People are in danger. I'm racing the clock on this.'

She heard an envelope being ripped open and immediately thought of Seb, who had an aversion to opening letters with anything other than a paper knife. She pressed the speaker icon on her phone so Maxwell could also hear the priest.

Father Stephen began reading.

> *Chief Inspector, you don't know me but I've been watching you. I believe you want the truth and that's*

*what I want too. I need to tell someone what I've done
because I don't know what may happen tonight.*

So, she was right. Beale planned to take his revenge
tonight. Time was running out.

I'll probably soon be dead, one way or another.

'Dear God, don't tell me he plans to commit suicide
like his sister,' Father Stephen added.

'Go on, Father,' Gawn urged.

*I want everyone to know about my beautiful sister
and how sorry I am for what I did to Marcus
Roberts. I didn't mean to kill him.*

'So, he was the one who did that to Marcus?' The priest
was shocked.

'Go on, Father, please,' she pleaded. She needed to
hear the rest.

'Sorry.' He read on,

*The day I found Angel in the bath changed my life
forever. She was my guardian angel. But I've made a
good life for myself. When my father died I only came
back to Belfast to clear out his house. Then I found
her diary. I don't think my parents ever even knew
she kept one. I did but I'd forgotten all about it.
She'd hidden it under the floorboards in her bedroom
and no one ever went into that room after she died.
I've left it for you and you can read it and you'll see
what happened.*

'Have you got the diary?' Gawn cut in.

'Yes. It's here too.'

'We'll pick it up as well. Is that all he says?'

'No. He says she wrote about her friends in the diary,
four of them and about how one of them had forced
himself on her and she was afraid she was pregnant.
Connor says he never knew she was pregnant when she
died. No one ever told him. Then another one of her

friends was blackmailing her, trying to get her to sleep with
him too and she knew she would have to give in to him if
she wanted to get to music college. He said he could
arrange for an abortion for her if she would sleep with
him. Dear God, the poor young girl. Only fifteen.'

The priest's distressed voice sounded almost as if he
was in tears.

'What else, Father?' Gawn didn't have time to
sympathise with Kellie Beale's situation, not if she was
going to prevent more people coming to harm.

Father Stephen coughed and began speaking again.

'She was so ashamed and she thought there was only
one way out for her. But Beale says here he couldn't work
out who all the people were. All the names in the diary
were in code or some sort of nicknames.'

He had been paraphrasing what he had been reading,
now he started reading directly from the letter again,

> *I needed to know who these people were. They were*
> *supposed to be her friends. The only way I could*
> *think to find out was to talk to Danny. He was her*
> *tutor, her friend. He should know.*

'Christ!' Gawn's outburst shocked everyone. 'Sorry,
Father. We didn't realise Beale even knew Daniel
Anderson. Go on. Go on, please.'

> *Danny told me about Veronica. I didn't really*
> *remember her. I don't think she took me under her*
> *notice. I was too young to be important. But he told*
> *me to leave a bin bag outside her shop. He said that*
> *it would help to soften her up and get her to talk and*
> *then he would deal with her. He put a note in it and*
> *a bible reference to scare her. And he told me Marcus*
> *would know everything I wanted to know. I*
> *remembered Marcus from rehearsals. He used to*
> *make me tea and give me biscuits and talk to me*
> *about football. He was always kind. And Angel*
> *used to say he was always around; always watching*

them so I thought if anyone would know who it was who had raped my sister and who was blackmailing her, it would be him. Danny told me where to find him. But when I asked Marcus, he wouldn't tell me anything. I got him drunk, but he still wouldn't tell me so I hit him and I tied him up and I threatened him. That was all it was meant to be. I'd had a bit to drink. For Dutch courage. I don't remember exactly how it happened. I'd been searching and I was using a knife and it was in my hand and suddenly I was cutting him. I didn't stab him. I didn't want him to die. I only wanted to frighten him but then he just crumpled up in the chair and his eyes went all glassy. When he was dead I realised I could leave a message on his body to scare them all, like Danny had put in the note he sent to Veronica Fisher. Woe to the Wicked. I thought they were the wicked.

Marcus hadn't told me anything, but I found pictures. The nicknames were on them. I knew then. I'd been set up. I trusted him just like my poor sister did. Just like my mother did. Danny Anderson, the kind, caring tutor who used to come round to our house after Angel died and sit and cry with my mother; the pervert who wanted to have his way with my beautiful sister; the bastard who was blackmailing her into sleeping with him to keep her secret. He was the wicked. She killed herself because of him. I've arranged to meet him. Tonight is the anniversary of Angel's death and tonight at Hopewell someone will die. It'll be me or him.

'Dear God, Chief Inspector.'

'Thank you, Father. I'll get the letter and diary picked up.' She didn't want to get into a whole discussion with him. She didn't have time.

'There is something else.'

'Yes?' She waited.

'He says here he saw you in Dublin and at St George's Market and he'd seen you at Marcus Roberts' house too. He says if anything happens to him he believes he can trust you to get Donnelly and Anderson; to get justice for Angel. He can, can't he, Chief Inspector?'

'Oh yes, Father. He can.' Her jaw was set. That, she could promise. 'And Father, this must remain confidential. You mustn't discuss any of this with anyone.' She smiled to herself. This was one time when she didn't think she needed to issue that warning. She hoped his training in keeping the secrets of the confessional would work for her.

'I think you can depend on that alright, Chief Inspector. I'll be praying for all of you.'

'Thank you, Father. I hope we don't need it.'

When she put the phone down, she turned to Maxwell.

'We've been stupid, Paul. How did we miss it? If Beale tortured Roberts to get the names of the others on Sunday night, how could he have got everything in place – especially Anderson's letter posted in Belfast on Friday? It needed to be the work of more than one person. Anderson knew Beale was looking to avenge his sister. Beale had contacted him and it was Anderson who put him on to Veronica and Roberts to try to keep himself out of it. Poor Marcus Roberts didn't know what it was all about. From the other photographs in the album I would guess Roberts had his own dirty wee secrets, and didn't want to tell Beale anything for fear he would be exposed as a voyeur or worse. If he had said anything about Anderson, Beale probably wouldn't have even realised its significance until he found the photograph album with all the nicknames. We know from the writing under it that one of the pictures Beale found was the same as the one we have from the newspaper. It showed Anderson with the others; Beale must have realised then that he was one of the Amigos, not just his sister's kind tutor. Anderson was the one who was harassing Angel, wanting to have sex with her, not just

228

Donnelly. But by that time Anderson had got the others spooked. Then he started his plan to frame Beale for it all.'

'So, it was Anderson who attacked Osmond?'

'Yes. We only checked his alibi for the time of Roberts' death, not for when Osmond was attacked. We couldn't. He'd gone missing by then.'

'And now he's after Donnelly and Beale?'

'Yes. Donnelly was his real target all along and Beale just became a very handy scapegoat to take the blame for everything.'

Hopewell House. Beale was on his way there. She suddenly remembered the tea caddy sitting beside the cup on the shelf in the old pantry. She had seen the bright yellow packaging reminiscent of the yellow shipyard cranes peeping out the top of the open container but hadn't realised its significance. That blend of tea was new. Eva Anderson had told her it was her husband's favourite and it wouldn't have been around years ago when Hopewell House was occupied. Anderson had been there.

'They're meeting up at Hopewell House. Where else would be the perfect place? Beale doesn't know what he's walking into. Anderson's devious and manipulative and dangerous and probably a bit mad. He's been pulling everyone's strings, including ours, and setting Beale up to take the blame for everything. We need to get there. Fast!'

Chapter 72

It was a dark night. The moon was hidden by a covering of clouds. To their left was the jagged rock face of the coast road rising into the sky, to their right, the sea, seemingly infinite in its blackness. The mood in the car was tense. No time for sightseeing tonight or appreciating the rugged beauty of the coastline. Gawn was driving, Maxwell by her side. Her eyes were focused only on the road ahead sparkling after an earlier shower of rain as if tiny precious stones had been scattered directing their way, like a modern-day Hansel and Gretel. Neither spoke. They knew or at least they hoped they knew that it would soon all be over but whether they would find more dead bodies or not, they couldn't be sure. The possibility was in their minds. Would they get there in time? Gawn thought of the pretty face of Donna Nixon. She hadn't told Maxwell about Donna's message. If Anderson had lured her to Hopewell House with some tip-off, would she still be as pretty by the time they reached her? She thought of Daniel Anderson and of his wife waiting for her timid teacher husband to return home. Of Kevin Donnelly facing the wrath of a demented avenger. Of Connor Beale caught in his trap and, if Anderson's plan worked out, destined to take the blame for it all.

They were following tightly behind Dee's unmarked car and being followed by two marked police cars. She had decided ARU was unnecessary. It was a judgement call on her part. There was no indication Anderson was armed. She thought it was unlikely but, anyway, they were all wearing stab vests and armed with batons and their personal protection weapons, herself included. Nor had they used blues and twos. She wanted their arrival to be as much of a surprise as they could manage. That was their best chance of bringing this to a good conclusion.

Unexpectedly, Dee jammed on the brakes and with a squeal of tyres, turned into an opening in the blackness to their left. Gawn felt her car slew sideways on the slippery surface as she made the turn behind him having been taken by surprise. She regained control and followed him up the sweeping driveway. There was no building in sight yet, only blackness. Tonight, she had no time to enjoy the lush grounds. Her only focus was getting into the house as quickly and quietly as possible and stopping whatever Anderson had planned for his victims.

The line of cars followed the curve in the roadway and then suddenly, almost out of nowhere, the house rose up before them, spectral in its sudden appearance out of the night and darkly threatening now in silhouette as the moon peeked out from behind its cloud cover to offer some helpful illumination. Gawn thought of the gothic houses of her teenage reading, werewolves, the undead, Dracula and, of course, her favourite Thornfield Hall which held dark secrets in its attic. What horrors awaited them here? In daylight it had merely looked sad and neglected. Now it looked menacing.

Two cars were already parked opposite the front door of the house. Gawn recognised the battered Punto belonging to Donna Nixon. The other she didn't recognise but assumed it must belong to Daniel Anderson.

'Nixon's here!' Gawn hissed at Maxwell, her voice low but insistent.

'What?'

'That's Donna Nixon's car. She said she'd had a tip-off to the paper. The other car must be Anderson's.'

Then Gawn spotted a motorbike sitting propped up against the side of the building, almost hidden in its shadow.

'No, it's not. That must be Beale's car. Anderson is on a motorbike,' she said.

'What?'

She pointed to the motorbike and they both remembered the tracks they had noticed on their previous visit. She thought of the photograph in the Andersons' living room, of the teacher with the group of Hell's Angel bikers.

Figures exited the police cars at a run, aware that every second of delay might cost a life. Gawn shot an angry glance at Grant when his car door closed with a bang behind him. Their feet crunched on the gravel pathway, the sound loud in the silence. They made their way to the front portico with its imposing stone pillars. Maxwell led. He was first to reach out and try the door. It did not give to his touch. If they were inside, Anderson had locked them in.

'Go! Go!' Gawn ordered in an urgent whisper to the two uniformed officers behind her, one carrying a Blackhawk ram. He swung it at the door and it gave, hanging off its hinges at a crazy angle but the noise of the bursting hinges and splintering wood had echoed through the stillness of the night, through the cavernous hallway and the empty corridors and rooms. Anyone inside, anyone still alive, would have heard it.

'You lot, downstairs. Don't forget the cellars. Go! We'll take the upstairs.' Maxwell was issuing the orders now, his voice sounding breathy with excitement. He took the stairs two at a time. Gawn, Grant and Dee followed behind. Each held a torch and the beams of light illuminated the still elegant carpet and heavy mahogany banisters and skipped about madly as they rushed upwards.

At the first landing Gawn signalled with a wave of her arm that the two DCs should continue to the second floor. She and Maxwell split up and began to search the rooms on the first, he to the left of the stairwell; she to the right. Once the inspector had moved off just a few feet he was quickly lost to her sight, only the light from his torch swinging from side to side marking his retreat down the corridor. The blackness was intense no matter how hard she looked. She could discern nothing outside the range of the torchlight. There were no external windows in the corridor. It lay before her a long black nothingness. She could imagine all sorts of horrors lurking, waiting for her. She even imagined she could hear soft breathing as if someone was standing nearby just by her side watching her almost within touching distance. She shivered at the thought. She swung the beam of comforting torchlight from side to side as she walked slowly along. Sometimes she swung around suddenly to check behind her. The carpet felt deep beneath her feet muffling the sound of her footsteps. At each door she stopped and paused, listening before trying the handle. Surprisingly, each opened to her touch. She had expected they might all be locked.

She heard a bang from somewhere below and wondered if the others had found something or someone. She would know soon enough if they had.

Another door. She thought she could hear something, a noise from within. It was faint and she couldn't recognise what it was. She turned off the torch hoping that her senses would be heightened by the lack of visual stimulus. It was then she noticed the merest sliver of light coming from under the door. It was so weak. Was someone inside? She held her breath and listened. Nothing. The only way to know would be to open the door, take a step inside, face the unknown. Should she turn the torch back on to see whatever lay within or would that only make her a target? Her mind strayed to the occasions in the past when she had cleared houses of insurgents in Afghanistan.

She reached out and felt the cold metal of the handle in her grasp. It was icy to the touch. She was aware her breathing was shallow and she felt her heart pounding. Standing off to the side, she swung the door gently open. Nothing happened and at first she saw nothing within the beam of her torch. Where had the light come from? Then she saw the last stuttering flame of a candle stub in a glass jar sitting on the floor off to her left and as her torch moved round the room she saw a body tied to a chair. She recognised her instantly. It was the journalist and it was her eyes that caught and held Gawn's gaze. They were huge with terror. Her body was absolutely still, frozen, her mind unable or unwilling to process what was happening to her. But her eyes were darting around the room frantically.

Gawn took two steps towards the terrified woman before a sudden hefty push in the centre of her back sent her plunging to the floor. She reached out and saved herself, managing to land on her hands and knees on the soft carpet, and sprang up again almost immediately. She spun round, the torch still in her hand, but was only in time to catch a glimpse of a man's back and to see the door close behind her. Then she heard a key turn in the lock.

Just as the carpet had muffled her footsteps so it had done the same for Anderson's. She hadn't realised he was behind her. She hurried over to Donna Nixon.

'This is going to hurt a bit.' She ripped the tape off the girl's mouth in one swift action. Immediately the frightened woman let out a piercing scream. It didn't matter now. Anderson knew they were here. There would be no taking him by surprise.

'Are you hurt anywhere? Did he hurt you?'

The woman's screams subsided as quickly as they had begun. Between sobs now, she managed only to shake her head from side to side and repeat, 'No. No. I'm alright. I'm alright,' over and over again. Almost as if she was trying to make herself believe it too.

Gawn took her radio from her pocket. Anderson had the advantage of them. If he had been staying in the house, he would know every recess and hiding place in the building. And perhaps he would know a way of escape too. Gawn was sure there would be more than just a front and back door. They had not been able to get any kind of plan of the house on a Saturday when offices were closed so they were working in the dark in every sense.

'This is Leader 1. Target on first floor. He's locked me and a hostage in one of the bedrooms. Number 24.'

'Leader 1, understood,' Maxwell replied.

Gawn undid the bindings which held the trembling woman to the chair. She helped her up to her feet. She was unsteady, her legs unable to support her. Gawn held her, an arm around her waist, as they walked slowly towards the still-locked door.

'We'll have you out of here in a minute.' She tried to make her voice sound as calm and encouraging as she could. She knew this was far from over but if they could get Nixon safely outside, they could concentrate on finding Anderson, Beale and Donnelly, if they were still alive.

Where the hell was Maxwell? It shouldn't have taken him this long to get here. Gawn left the journalist propped against the wall waiting to hear the key turn in the lock and see Maxwell's concerned face. She moved to the window and looked out. She could see more cars arriving and an ambulance.

Then she heard the key. She hurried across to Donna Nixon again and put her arm around her so they would be able to make a quick exit. Then a thought crossed her mind and she prepared herself just in case it was Anderson back – it wasn't. Instead she was glad to see a familiar face, but it was Grant's worried face illuminated in torchlight, not Maxwell's.

'Where's the inspector?'

'I don't know, ma'am. We've finished upstairs. It's all clear. I was on my way down when I heard your message.'

'Take Ms Nixon out to the ambulance.'

'Where are you going?'

'I'm going to find Inspector Maxwell. You can join me when our hostage is safe and send Jack back up here too.'

'Copy that, boss.'

Now to play hide and seek with a madman who, she guessed, must be holding Maxwell. She felt a flutter in her stomach. What if she really was pregnant as Rose O'Hare had suggested? This was just the kind of situation Seb had warned her not to get involved in and she had promised him she would avoid. Too late now.

Chapter 73

Shouts were coming from every side now; from upstairs and down. She could recognise some of the voices. But none of them was Maxwell's. She was being careful, taking her time moving up the corridor in the darkness, fearful of what might be lurking, who might be lurking in the shadows. She considered herself lucky he had pushed her from behind. What if he had punched her in the stomach?

Then suddenly the whole place was illuminated with harsh light. She had to blink several times to accustom her eyes to this new brightness. She assumed someone had managed to make a connection to the electricity supply. That would make searching easier and hiding more difficult for Anderson.

It was so bright. Most of the light shades were missing, just bare bulbs were hanging down like stalactites from the ceiling, throwing a harsh glare over everything and casting dark shadows into the corners and door recesses. She realised then how the heavy curtains could have hidden their quarry. She had probably walked past him within inches. Perhaps the breathing she had heard had not been just her imagination. She was about to discard the torch she was carrying when she decided it might prove a handy weapon if she needed to defend herself.

Grant and Dee had already checked upstairs so unless Anderson had managed to slip past them in the darkness he must still be on the first floor where Maxwell had been searching, and Maxwell must be on the first floor too. Somewhere.

Gawn had already opened several doors and glanced into the bedrooms beyond them. She was coming near the end of the corridor now. Her choices were running out. It must be one of these last three doors. She eschewed any finesse and flung the first door wide open letting it bang back against the wall with a thud. An empty space.

Second door. A fifty-fifty chance she would find Anderson and Maxwell and maybe Beale and Donnelly too behind it. An incongruous thought that it was like playing some existential TV game show 'Who's the body behind door number...?' came into her mind. She recognised it for what it was – her mind helping her cope with the fear and tension she was experiencing, akin to the irreverent humour which troops employed before a major op.

Bang! The wooden door flew open and almost bounced back into her face, she had pushed it so hard. But no Anderson and no Maxwell either. OK. This was it. There were no options left. She faced the last door and then she noticed the number on it. It was number eleven. Just like the Bible verse.

She was aware of how incredibly dry her mouth was, the effect of the adrenalin which was coursing through her body. She tried to lick her lips to moisten them but her tongue was dry too and it had little effect. She couldn't wait; couldn't just call it in and stand back to wait for some of the others to arrive. Maxwell could be facing death just inches away on the other side of this door.

Anderson was mad, crazy. He wouldn't care about the consequences of killing a policeman. He was facing ruin, the loss of his reputation and his wife, and a future of years in prison. God knew how many other women might come forward now to accuse him of complicity in Courtney's grooming activities. Anderson must have been besotted with the girl, she thought, lusted after her, probably even imagined he was in love with her and hated Donnelly because he got to her first. So he had attacked Dave Osmond and now he intended killing Donnelly for what he had done to Angel. That was his plan. She was sure. She was so angry with herself that she had taken so long to figure it out. She reached out now and felt the handle give to her touch. She opened the door slowly, carefully, her body tensed for action, her senses acute. She didn't want to be caught out again.

The room was in darkness but the light spilling in from the corridor showed her an empty bedroom. She felt to the side of the door until her hand connected with the light switch. She clicked it on. At first glance the room seemed empty. She had expected Anderson to be here. Where else could he be? She checked behind the door this time before she stepped inside in case he was hiding there waiting to hit her from behind. She was not going to fall for that one again. But no one was there. She took a step into the room and immediately saw a pair of feet on the floor poking out from the far side of the bed. She recognised Maxwell's brogues, the white stain from the river water still on them. She discarded the torch on the bed and rushed forward. It was Maxwell lying face down on the floor. He wasn't moving.

'Paul! Paul, can you hear me?' She knelt alongside his prone body and turned him gently over. There was no blood, no obvious wounds to be seen. She put her head down to his face and felt his breath lightly on her cheek, then felt for a pulse. He was alive but his pulse was erratic. Then she became aware of a second body, propped against the wall, hidden from casual view behind the bed. It was Beale. She recognised him from the photograph on the murder board and in a flash of recognition she saw again the white-faced clown at the market. He was unconscious too but blood was trickling down his face from a deep gash across his forehead. Where was Anderson?

'Leader 1. Room–' She got no further. The radio was kicked from her hand, the blow catching her just above her wrist and sending a stab of pain up her arm. She looked up and saw Anderson's face contorted into a grotesque mask of fury looming over her.

'You can't stop me. I won't let you stop me. He deserves to die.' He was screaming at her now. She lay on her side beside Paul, defenceless, clutching her arm. And all the time thinking of the baby she might be carrying. What if he kicked her again? This time in the stomach. She drew her legs up into a foetal position.

'Come in Leader 1. Come in Leader 1. Where...' Gawn recognised Dee's voice on the radio before Anderson's foot stamped down hard on it, smashing it into a flattened pulp and silencing the detective's voice. She knew they would be on their way. It might take them a minute or two to find the right room, but she only needed to keep Maxwell and Beale and herself safe for a few more minutes. Then she smelt it. The sickly-sweet smell of petrol. She hadn't noticed it before. Anderson had lifted a large can from the wardrobe. He was pouring the liquid over the bed, splashing it up the curtains, all over the carpeted floor. She felt some splash onto her face as he passed her and tried to wipe it away with her hand. If he set it alight he would die too but somehow she didn't think that would deter him. He didn't expect to live. He probably didn't want to live, so long as he had achieved his goal. He locked the door and threw the key away across the room. She heard the metallic clang as it bounced off the far wall and out of sight.

How had she missed him? Where had he been hiding? She watched as he walked across to the bed and bent down. He was dragging something heavy out from underneath it. It was Kevin Donnelly, bound hand and foot with tape over his mouth but still very much alive. His terror was clear to see in his eyes and the uncontrolled shaking of his body. He had not been slashed as Beale had slashed Roberts and, unlike their first victim, he had been stripped naked. The area around his genitals was bloodied and purple marks of a kicking were obvious on his stomach and chest. Anderson poured the final drops of petrol over the squirming man's head and body. Gawn was sure Anderson had been enjoying extracting his revenge, making the man suffer, playing with him and taunting him. Now he was going to kill him and if he had to kill two police officers and Beale and himself as well to get Donnelly, he would. Gawn had no doubt. She thought there was probably nothing she could say to convince him to give himself up, but she had to try. Revenge for Anderson was to inflict terror and pain and extinction on the man whom he blamed for taking Kellie Beale from him. And strangely enough that was what her brother had wanted too, but now they were all going to pay the price for it.

'Daniel,' she tried to keep her voice calm but authoritative as if she was the one in control and he the errant schoolboy who needed to explain himself. She was surprised at how normal her voice sounded. If she could get him talking, she could gain them some valuable time. Once he lit the fire she knew it would spread quickly and there would be no time for any of them to get out without the key. He had ignored her so far. She struggled to sit up. Her eyes went to her heavy torch on the bed but it was out of reach.

'Why? Why are you doing this, Daniel? Tell me.'

He turned and looked at her. She was at his mercy and he was enjoying that feeling of power. She knew many murderers and stalkers liked to explain themselves, sought to justify their actions. If he took the time to explain to her now, these could be precious seconds until the others would arrive.

'He had her. He took her.' He pointed at Donnelly lying trussed up on the floor, his eyes pleading with her to save him. 'He spoiled her for everyone. She wouldn't even look at me, but she'd let him touch her. Let him make love to her. Make love. It was just sex to him. *I* wanted to make love to her. *I* loved her.' He was almost screaming at her again, all sense of reason gone. He stood over her and brought his face, full of fury, close up to hers as he

240

shouted, 'The Professor promised me I could have her. It was my turn. My turn. She was mine.' Flecks of saliva were spurting from his lips. His eyes were blazing and she knew he was beyond reason.

His voice was almost unrecognisable as human. It was more like an animal's howl of pain and his hands were bunched into tight fists. She was afraid he would punch her again but instead he straightened up and kicked out in fury at the bed leg beside her. Gawn winced as she felt the reverberations in her own body.

Suddenly she could hear voices outside the door. Someone tried the handle. Then there was banging as they realised it was locked and tried to force it open. She heard thumps as their shoulders bounced ineffectually off the solid surface. Gawn knew they would send for the Blackhawk to batter the door down but they wouldn't be in time. Not if Anderson had his way. He had already taken a box of matches from his pocket and was trying to extract one. She saw his hands were shaking with nervous anticipation. He dropped the box and bent to lift it from the floor. At the same instant, Maxwell moaned and opened his eyes. Anderson was distracted for a second. Just a second. This was her chance – maybe the last chance for all of them. She flung herself at him and caught him around the knees making him lose his balance and fall heavily on top of her. She felt his hands gripping her throat, and tightening, and then in his fury he released his hold with one hand and struck out with his fist just missing her head as she jerked away from him and brought her knee sharply up into his groin. She rolled out from under him as he curled up in pain and groaned. She was on her knees now and ready for him. As Anderson struggled to straighten up ready to come at her again, she pulled out her baton. With a flick of her wrist she racked it open to its full extent and brought it down hard on his leg just at his kneecap. She heard the crack and knew she had probably broken it. He cried out in pain and crumpled into a heap on the floor in front of her, whimpering like a hurt animal. Keeping her eyes on him she stumbled across to the door and shouted, 'I don't know where the key is. Just break the bloody door down. Now!' Then she stood back and waited.

Chapter 74

Maxwell had regained consciousness and was sitting up before the ambulance pulled away from the old house. He had managed a weak smile. The paramedics suggested that he would be kept in hospital overnight as a precaution. Gawn volunteered to phone Kerri and let her know. She didn't particularly look forward to it. She knew Maxwell's wife would probably blame her for his injury. But the truth was, this time she felt no personal responsibility. He was just doing his job. They had all faced the same danger.

It was almost 4am before Gawn made it home. She'd had to stay until first Donna Nixon, then Beale, Donnelly and Anderson had been despatched to hospital, until the site was secured, the Fire Service had cleared it as safe and the forensics teams had been able to begin their work. Only then did she leave.

She was beyond tiredness but still with adrenaline coursing through her veins. She knew she would never be able to sleep. Her main concern was she had missed her call with Seb. He would be frantic, she knew. When she turned her mobile on, she saw how many missed calls she had from him. She was sure he wouldn't be happy until he had spoken to her and knew she was safe. She was tempted just to text him or to phone, for she was afraid, if he could see her, he would know something had happened. She made herself a strong cup of coffee and opened her laptop. He would know there was something wrong if she didn't appear on camera. She was just glad he wouldn't be able to smell the overpowering stench of petrol from her clothes. Nor see the purple welt already beginning to turn a vivid dark red on her forearm underneath her sleeve. The paramedics had looked at it and suggested she have it X-rayed but she had refused.

The internet connection was speedy and within seconds there he was, her Sebastian, a worried frown across his face.

'Where the hell were you? What happened? I've been trying to get you for hours.' He wasn't angry but he had been scared, she could tell from his voice. The waiting, the not knowing had made him acutely aware of the distance between them. He had felt so powerless.

'I'm so sorry, darling. We were closing a big case tonight. The body in the Lagan. Remember?'

She didn't want to lie to him but she didn't want him worrying all the time either, at least not any more than he already was. She felt she had to give him at least part of the story as an explanation.

'Paul was hurt.'

She saw his reaction.

'Is he alright?'

'He'll be fine. Just a bump on the head.'

'Thank goodness it wasn't you. Does that sound awful? I wouldn't want him hurt either. Give him my best wishes.'

Seb took a drink of his wine and Gawn took a sip of her coffee. Both were considering what they should say next. He could see how energised Gawn was. He could see it in her eyes. They were sparkling even though it was the middle of the night for her. He knew how she lived for nights like this. He hated them. He hated that she put herself in danger. He hated that she faced the prospect of being hurt. But he knew he had to tread carefully. This was who she was and he had sworn that he would accept her as she was and would love her, no matter what.

'You know I worry about you all the time, Gawn. I just can't help it. I know you. You can never just stay behind a desk. I know you. Remember.'

She was afraid he was going to start another attempt to get her to join him now so she decided to forestall him.

'The biggest danger I faced in this case was nearly getting arrested as a prostitute.'

Seb burst out laughing. 'What!'

'A rather embarrassed young sergeant thought Donna Nixon and I looked suspicious sitting in her car at night.'

'It would be a brave punter who would proposition you, my darling.'

She laughed too then, relieved that she had distracted him. 'We got our man tonight, Seb. Well, our men actually. Case closed. A timid teacher who finally cracked and a brother bent on revenge, Connor Beale or should I say, Walter Plinge.'

'Walter Plinge!' He spluttered over his mouthful of wine.

'Yes, Walter Plinge. Why? I know it's a funny name. You don't know someone called Walter Plinge, do you?'

She couldn't think how Seb would ever have come in contact with Plinge or Beale and the name was so unusual she thought it highly unlikely he had met someone with the name.

'Walter Plinge is the name used by actors when they're playing more than one character in a play so their name only appears once in the programme. I thought you would have known that, darling.'

She hadn't. She wondered if she had talked to Seb about the case and mentioned Plinge's name would it have helped her solve it more quickly, maybe prevented Donna Nixon going through her ordeal.

'I can be useful sometimes, you know,' he teased.

'Oh, you can be useful in all sorts of ways.' She responded suggestively.

Then she paused. She had realised when she'd been lying at Anderson's mercy and wondering what would happen if she was pregnant, that she needed to make a decision about their future. Did she want to be a mother? Could she give up her career? She had realised in that moment that she could never leave the police force. It was more than just what she did. It was who she was. But she had realised too that she loved Seb and she wanted to make him happy. And she wanted to have his child; their child. Somehow, they would make it work.

'I have some news for you, Seb.'

'What?' Then a thought seemed to strike him. 'You're not getting promoted or something, are you?'

'Would that be good news?'

'No. Yes, I suppose so if it meant you'd be safely behind a desk all the time. But I'd be happy for you whatever it meant, you know that, darling. I'm really proud of you. You deserve to be the Chief Constable as far as I'm concerned.'

She laughed at the idea.

'Nothing like that, Seb. Nothing to do with work at all.' She hesitated. What she was going to say could change her life, their life, their relationship for ever. 'I've decided to make an appointment to see a gynaecologist privately. I need to know what my chances are of having a baby, once and for all.'

He didn't respond immediately. He had known she was struggling with the idea of getting pregnant although she hadn't said anything directly to him about it. Before they met, it would never have been part of her plans to be a mother again. He knew that. The few times she had spoken to him about her daughter, Max, he knew she felt guilty about giving her up for adoption, even though she had been only seventeen and unmarried. She didn't think she deserved another chance to be a mother and when she'd thought she was pregnant she'd confessed she didn't believe she could ever be a good mother. He realised that it was a big thing that she was taking this step now.

'I wish I could be there to go with you.'

'I'll be fine. I'll probably have to wait ages for an appointment and it'll just be a few tests. Anyhow it won't be that long until I'll be joining you in sunny California and then you can show off your surfing skills,' she consoled him.

'Take care of yourself, Gawn. Don't be doing anything stupid, please.'

'Like what?'

'I don't know. Tackling murderers or rushing into burning buildings or something. I know you, remember.'

'I promise. I will take extra care.'

'Promise?'

'I promise,' she agreed.

If she felt guilty about not giving him all the details of the night's events, she wasn't going to let it spoil things between them. Even the fact that they were six thousand miles apart couldn't spoil it. She remembered her mother's saying, 'What you don't know can't hurt you.' And he would never know what had so nearly happened at Hopewell House.

If you enjoyed this book, please let others know by leaving a quick review on Amazon. Also, if you spot anything untoward in the paperback, get in touch. We strive for the best quality and appreciate reader feedback.

editor@thebookfolks.com

MORE IN THIS SERIES

THE PERFUME KILLER (Book 1)

Stumped in a multiple murder investigation, with the only clue being a perfume bottle top left at a crime scene, DCI Gawn Girvin must wait for a serial killer to make a wrong move. Unless she puts herself in the firing line…

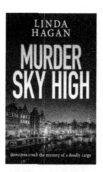

MURDER SKY HIGH (Book 2)

When a plane passenger fails to reach his destination alive, Belfast police detective Gawn Girvin is tasked with understanding how he died. But determining who killed him begs the bigger question of why, and answering this leads the police to a dangerous encounter with a deadly foe.

A FORCE TO BE RECKONED WITH (Book 3)

Investigating a cold case about a missing person, DCI Gawn Girvin stumbles upon another unsolved crime. A murder. But that is just the start of her problems. The clues point to powerful people who will stop at nothing to protect themselves, and some look like they're dangerously close to home.

THAT MUCH SHE KNEW (Book 5)

A woman is found murdered. The same night, state pathologist Jenny Norris goes missing. Worried that her colleague might be implicated, DCI Gawn Girvin in secret investigates the connection between the women. But Jenny has left few clues to go on, and before long Girvin's solo tactics risk muddling the murder investigation and putting her in danger.

MURDER ON THE TABLE (Book 6)

A charity dinner event should be a light-hearted affair, but two people dying as the result of one is certainly likely to put a damper on proceedings. DCI Gawn Girvin is actually an attendee, and ready at the scene to help establish if murder was on the table. But the bigger question is why, and if Gawn can catch a wily killer.

NOTHING BUT SMILES (Book 7)

A serial stalker is terrorising women on the streets of Belfast. The victims wake up with no recollection of the night before, but with a smiley-face calling card daubed on their bodies. DCI Gawn Girvin takes on the case although before long she herself is targeted. She must catch the sick creep before matters escalate.

OTHER TITLES OF INTEREST

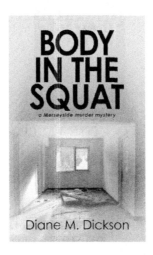

BODY IN THE SQUAT by Diane Dickson

After a bungled drugs raid, DI Jordan Carr suspects a mole in the force. Seconded to the Liverpool suburb of Kirkby, he encounters DS Stella May who is leading a murder inquiry. She has little to go on apart from the strange comments of an old woman who fancies herself as something of a clairvoyant. Can May convince Carr to support her line of investigation, no matter how odd it seems?

Available free with Kindle Unlimited and in paperback!

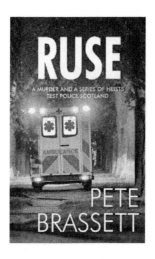

RUSE by Pete Brassett

When the barmaid of an ailing pub is found
murdered in the toilets, Scottish detectives struggle
to find a motive. And their workload gets heavier
when during a series of brazen heists, robbers get
away with luxury goods. Trouble is afoot. Will DI
Charlie West crack the case without relying on wise
retired cop DI James Munro?

Available free with Kindle Unlimited and in paperback!

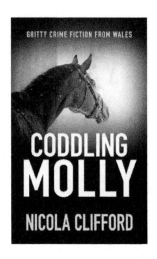

CODDLING MOLLY by Nicola Clifford

A teenager is found dead after a fall from a bridge on a winter night in Brecon. Nobody knows who she is and identifying her proves a challenge. DI Ben James and DS Erica Bevan manage to connect her to someone else with ties to a drugs gang. But when these crooks bother someone dear to ex-detective Heidi Holtz, she too will jump on their trail.

Available free with Kindle Unlimited and in paperback!

www.thebookfolks.com

Printed in Great Britain
by Amazon

41852207R00148